THE TALENTS OF BET

STEVEN HAMMOND

ROCKHOPPER BOOKS

THE TALENTS OF BET
Copyright © 2017 Steven Hammond
All rights reserved.
ISBN-10: 0-9986234-9-0

ISBN-13: 978-0-9986234-9-8
(RockhopperBooks)
1st Edition

Edited by Ella Medler
Cover art by Gabriel Barbabianca
Interior layout by Tanya Adams

Find out more at:
STEVENHAMMONDBOOKS.COM

Dedicated to

To Joy for believing more than I

ACKNOWLEDGMENTS

A special thank you to Dan Dunklee for all of his help and patient advice when I bug him during his lunch beseeching answers to questions I should probably know. Thank you to Tanya, for all of her patience and help. Thank you to Cathy Spieser for wading through early drafts and always giving me friendly, honest advice. Jon, for the read-through. Gabriel, for the amazing artwork. My Buster dog, who comes to me at two A.M. to let me know I've worked long enough. And thank you to my wife, Joy, without whom I'd still be dreaming about writing instead of doing it.

OTHER BOOKS
BY STEVEN HAMMOND

THE RISE OF THE PENGUINS SAGA

    RISE OF THE PENGUINS

    THE WARLORD, THE WARRIOR, THE WAR

    CROSSCURRENTS

    WHISPERS OF SHADOWS

    THE ROYAL CREED

    ORDER OF KINGS

    PREEMINENCE (coming soon)

THE TALENTS OF BET

One

"That wood won't gather itself, girl," an old round woman with a round head said through yellowed, barely attached teeth.

"Yes, ma'am," a girl of no more than fifteen years answered. Her shoulders dropped after speaking.

"Come here, Bethany, my darling," the round woman said. A glint of sadistic satisfaction sparkled in her recessed eyes.

"My name is Bet," the girl said stepping closer, jaw firm, eyes narrowed and defiant, knowing what was to come.

The woman's grimy hands grabbed Bet's chin. "I didn't ask for no sass."

Bet watched the woman's face crease into a mirthless smile. The smell of weeks-long unwashed hair and body burned her nostrils, staining her sinuses, causing her head to jerk back in revulsion. The meaty hand slapped her across the face, making her forget about the smell.

"You'll call me Mama, or you won't be calling me nothin'."

"I'm sorry, Mama. I just ain't no good at that spelling. I just got those silly little letters mixed up a bit." She took pleasure in watching Biscuit Head, as Bet had named her, try to puzzle out what she meant.

The second slap was no worse than the first, but no easier either. She had been slapped so many times since being purchased, her left cheek carried blotches of broken blood vessels in spider-webbed patterns across her fair skin.

Bet calmly walked out the front door, slamming it as she hurried from the wood panel house, and eliciting a loud complaint from Biscuit Head inside. She knew she had just earned another slap, but she'd get one regardless. She hopped over the bottom steps of the dilapidated wood porch, cinched up her moccasins, and dashed across the patchy damp yard, grabbing a hatchet from a post before vaulting the split rail fence.

She skirted the puddles in the rutty dirt road separating Malweather Farm and the forest edge until coming to the well-worn path leading to the creek. She looked to the sky. Still another two hours of daylight, but gray clouds obscuring the peaks of the Lorde's Mountains held the promise of rain. She'd have to hurry if she wanted to find any dry wood. But first she had to see Pooch-kin.

Bet walked a little farther along the road. Once she was sure she was out of Biscuit Head's sight, she hopped back over the fence and ran to the Chook-chook coop.

She pressed her back against the wood siding, rubbing away flecks of peeling white paint, and peered around the corner to make certain the old woman wasn't patrolling the south yard in search of some other problem to blame on her.

When she was sure it was clear, Bet fell to her knees and scurried through the flap door of the coop. Once inside, she delighted in the warmth radiating from the bodies of the fifty or more foot-tall flightless birds shuffling about with excitement, making quiet purring noises as Bet attempted to give each one a good scratch behind their floppy ears. A steady stream of hairy-feathered Chook-chooks patiently waited their turn for Bet's affection. The swarm of blue-gray, occasionally dotted with the dull orange plume of adolescent males, parted when a flaxen feathered mature male with rusty highlights hopped down from the uppermost roost, his bright red-orange crest and floppy ears bouncing on landing.

"Pooch-kin!" Bet said through a broadening smile. Her green eyes lit with joy. "How have you been, my friend?"

Pooch-kin rushed into her outstretched arms and waiting lap, nuzzling in her long red hair, and making whispered cooing noises, which the rest of the flock mimicked. He rubbed his broad brown beak against her nose, which always gave Bet a giggle. She had never seen Chook-chooks greet each other this way, and she was sure he only did it to make her happy. It always did.

Pooch-kin chirped, clicked and whirred a variety of noises, squinted, then widened his bright blue eyes, and hopped back the way he had come.

"Really? Already? Can I see?" Bet began crawling behind him.

The Chook-chook threw up his tiny clawed wings, acting surprised she even asked.

"Sorry," Bet said.

He began climbing the ramp to the third-level roost, but stopped and looked back at Bet. While whispering a grating noise, his bright eyes turned to a somber gray.

"I'll do what I can. I can't imagine what you must feel."

Pooch-kin looked at her, cocked his head, his crest falling sideways. The brightness returned to his eyes and he continued the climb. He reached the outside of his nesting box and barked a light yip.

"Ooh, I'm so excited." Bet's face ached from the constant grin. She leaned in close to the box, spotting the yellow eyes of a Chook-chook hen. Pooch-kin barked a double yap, and his mate stood, revealing a speckled sea-green egg. Bet reached in to give her a scratch behind the ear, and the hen screeched and quickly covered her egg.

"Oh no," Bet said, keeping her voice calm and quiet. "I'm not going to take your baby." She withdrew her hand and looked at Pooch-kin.

Pooch-kin whistled at his mate, and the hen settled in on the egg.

Bet looked at her friend with pity. "If there's anything I can do to keep Biscuit Head or the Old Man's hands off your egg or any of you, I'll do it again. You saw what they did to me the last time. I still have scars on my back."

She abhorred the idea of eating the animals of Malweather farm. She did her best to defend them, and each time she did, she was rewarded with several lashes by the Old Man. But whatever the consequences, she would do what she could to protect them.

Bet looked at the skylight. "I gotta go. It's getting late, and I have to see to my chores."

Pooch-kin gave her an inquisitive chirp.

"I'm going to the forest to gather wood." Her friend squawked. "Yes, I know. I'll be careful."

He chirped again.

"If you'd like to. I wouldn't mind the company. But it's dangerous out there for little Chook-chooks."

Pooch-kin barked indignantly.

Bet laughed. "I'm just watching out for you."

Pooch-kin marched to the door, pushed his head through and gave her the all-clear call.

Bet quickly followed. Once outside, she looked down at her diminutive companion, not wanting to miss what came next.

The Chook-chook trembled, ruffling his hairy feathers. Bet marveled, watching the bright plumage transform, beginning with his crest and cascading all the way to his downy feet, turning to various shades of gray, brown and black, which matched the muddy soil perfectly.

"That's some trick. I wish I could do that."

Pooch-kin clicked a laugh.

Being sure to keep the coop between them and the house, the two darted across the yard. Bet neatly vaulted the fence while Pooch-kin crawled under the lowest rung, and they made their way to the woods.

Two

The wind whispered through the pines, punctuated by the occasional snapping branch. The usual calls and chatter of birds and tiny leaf deer were silent. The woodland creatures, having better sense than human and Chook-chook, had taken shelter from the approaching storm.

Pooch-kin wobbled alongside Bet, snatching the sporadic grub exposed by the girl taking its cover for fuel.

Bet adjusted the bundle of twigs and small branches in the crook of her arm, complaining about the necessity of the task when there was an entire bin full of firewood and kindling back at the house. Even though she bemoaned the chore, there wasn't anywhere else she would've rather been than on an adventure with her best and only friend.

The pair crunched through the forest litter, talking back and forth about this or that, and teasing one another about seeing venomous Spit Adders or Howler Spiders. Both knew in truth that the shy creatures were only active during the spring and summer and had long made their way to their dens to hibernate through the harsh cold of the approaching winter. In fact, Bet had never even seen a Spit Adder unless it was in the talons of a wandering Day Owl.

They made their way to the top of a low rise. In the next gulley, the slow murky waters of Silt Creek meandered. "C'mon," Bet said, and the two shuffled down to the water's edge.

Bet planted her backside on a large flat rock and set down her load.

Pulling a strand of twine from her pocket, she tied the bunch together for easy carrying. "That's enough wood gathering for today."

The two sat in silence, staring at the thick stand of trees across the creek. Bet had never ventured to the other side of the creek. That was where the predators lived. She had only caught fleeting glimpses of them, never able to fully see what a Fangor or Moon Bear looked like in person. She had only seen them in picture books back at the orphanage. But as she had never crossed into their realm, neither would the predators cross over to her side. Fear of man's fire, snares, and guns kept them at bay.

A splash farther up the creek made them jump. After a moment, both laughed, realizing it was nothing more than a Crab-fish hopping back in the water, probably carrying its meal of an unfortunate Seed-mouse.

Another minute of silence passed when Pooch-kin began a series of chirps and whistles.

Bet looked at him, hesitating before speaking. "The orphanage?"

Pooch-kin made a gurgling noise.

"No. That's okay. The orphanage was... It was stark and sterile. Gray like the sky is now. I kept mostly to myself."

Pooch-kin clicked and tweeted.

"No, I didn't have any friends. Not really. There were a few passing rats I made acquaintance with, but no real friends."

Pooch-kin barked a rebuke.

Bet raised her brow. "Well, I guess from the point of view of a Chook-chook, they'd be evil. But they're not all bad. They just try to make their way in the world like the rest of us."

A low warble expressed Pooch-kin's doubts.

Bet laughed. "If you ever see one again, let me know, and I'll set it straight."

Pooch-kin whistled happily.

"I guess Baxter, the old guard dog, was my friend…sort of. But once the headmistress found me talking to him, she wouldn't allow me in the courtyard anymore. They thought I was weird or possessed or something for talking to animals. I never told anyone they talked back to me. I didn't realize I wasn't normal until then. When the other kids found out, they mostly stopped talking to me, or when they did, it was almost always a name-calling session, or they'd bark at me like idiots."

Bet stared at the water until Pooch-kin chirped again.

"Uh-uh. No, the city streets are far too dangerous for kids, full of criminals and thugs. I spent most of my time in the library, reading. I must've read every book two or three times. So, it wasn't all bad. I thought once I reached auction age things would be better. That's the way they made it sound, anyway. Little did I know…"

Pooch-kin let out a somber whistle.

"But I never would've found my best friend otherwise," Bet said with a smile. She reached down and gave him a scratch.

The two watched the tiny rodent-like Flit-hoppers leap from branch to branch, gliding effortlessly on outstretched legs with flaps of hairy skin between. They couldn't fly, but they fell gracefully. A Crab-fish crawled from the water. Seeing the bank otherwise occupied, it scurried back into the murk.

Bet watched it go. Beneath the eddy of disturbed silt, she caught a glint of something bright, almost shiny. With Pooch-kin watching curiously, she reached for the object, but it was just out of reach. Not wanting to get her feet any wetter than they already were, she took a stick from the bundle and pried it from the muck, dragging it back until she could grab it.

She gave the faceted object a quick rinse and held it up. The geometric stone almost seemed to glow. Bet rubbed it against her pant leg, removing a layer of mossy film, revealing its translucent gold, iridescent glimmer. "What do you suppose this is?"

Pooch-kin chirped a sarcastic reply.

"I know it's a shiny rock." She shook her head. "It's odd. Almost looks like quartz."

The two were staring at the shiny rock when Pooch-kin, without warning, hopped against the stone Bet sat on and hunkered down. His drab feathers transformed, giving him the appearance of nothing more than a clump of dead weeds. He whispered a warning.

Bet looked across the creek and spotted a pair of fluorescent green eyes. "Fangors," she said in a whisper. A light mist began to fall along with the night. "I think we should go now."

Pooch-kin agreed in earnest.

Bet stood, pocketed her treasure, and grabbed the bundle of sticks. "We're leaving now," she said, hoping the creatures understood what she meant. The Fangors' glowing eyes widened when she spoke, and Bet heard them disappear into the underbrush.

The pair made haste up the rise with Pooch-kin leading the way.

Three

"Remind me never to go out there this close to nighttime again," Bet said when they reached the road.

A series of grating squeaks let Bet know Pooch-kin's feelings on the matter.

Bet choked a laugh. "I didn't know Chook-chooks knew that kind of language." She looked down the road toward the house, spotting the warm glow of light coming from the kitchen window. She let out a long sigh. Such a sight should've been welcome when standing in the cold and rain. Instead, she felt like she'd swallowed a hot coal.

Pooch-kin nuzzled against her leg, cooing softly.

"I'll be fine," she said, reaching down and giving him a gentle reassuring squeeze on his wet ear.

He chirped and clicked.

"No, I don't know what makes people so cruel." She smiled at the Chook-chook. "Now let's get you out of this rain."

Before they took their first steps, they heard the sloshing clomp of hooves coming down the road. Bet squinted through the increasing rainfall and spotted the dim lights of a carriage. "It's the Old Man. I'll see if I can get us a ride."

An abrupt squeak expressed Pooch-kin's doubts.

"I know. Just hop on the bumper when I get in. It beats walking through the mud. If he even stops, that is."

When the carriage came around the bend, Bet stepped into the road, waving her arm. At first it seemed like the Old Man was going to pass by. But the horses came to a stop just far enough past her for the wide wheels to splash through a puddle, dousing her pants with an extra layer of mud. She looked back to make sure Pooch-kin hopped on the wooden bumper then climbed in. "Thank you, sir. The rain came quicker than I expected."

The Old Man said nothing, keeping his narrow face trained on the sloping windshield.

Bet pulled the bundle of sticks from beneath her coat, adjusted the hatchet hanging from her belt, and slammed the door. As expected, the Old Man said nothing. She had rarely heard him speak except when reciting the list of transgressions while doling out punishment at the behest of his biscuit-headed wife, or master, or whatever she was to him.

The Old Man pushed two levers forward, stomped on a pedal on the floorboard, causing wood blocks to clack together, and the carriage lurched into motion.

The short ride was spent in an odd, tense silence. The Old Man pulled back on the levers, causing the carriage to stop when they neared the front porch. Bet thanked him, hopped out, slammed the door and watched the carriage continue to the barn. She looked across the yard to see Pooch-kin's dark form making a dash for the coop. Satisfied he was safe, she made the slow climb up the porch.

She was met by a slap from Biscuit Head's grimy hand as she crossed the threshold.

"I told you not to slam doors," the perpetually foul woman said, droplets of spittle spraying across Bet's face.

"Yes, Ma... Yes, Mama." Bet pulled the hatchet and dropped it next to the door. Not in the mood for another slap, she handed the woman her bundle and hung her wet coat.

"Gone for all of that time and this is all you bring back? You're hardly worth the price I paid."

"It was all I could find. Everything else wasn't suited for a Mosquito Tern's nest." Bet unlaced her moccasins and placed them near the hearth, ignoring the parade of insults. "May I take a bath before dinner?"

"Please do. Your smell could make a pig retch. Be at the table before your papa gets in."

Bet bit back telling her she should talk. Instead, she dashed to the bathroom, happy for a few more moments of peace and solitude.

She peeled off her wet and mud-caked clothes and stepped into the stone floor bath, letting the warm water from the overhead faucet chase the chill away. It was the one luxury she'd never had at the orphanage. The showers there would only spout a slow trickle of lukewarm water, hardly enough for a proper bath. But she didn't have time to luxuriate in the bath, so she cut the flow.

She stepped from the basin, wiped the steam from the mirror and examined her red cheek. She had the notion to punch Biscuit Head square in her ugly round nose the next time she tried to slap her, but she'd probably get a solid beating from the much larger woman in return. Besides that, she didn't want to be sent to the correctional ward; she'd never see Pooch-kin again.

Bet draped her wet clothes over the hamper and wrapped herself in a shoddy robe. Remembering her shiny rock, she snagged the stone from the pocket, and ran to her room, stashing her treasure beneath a loose floor board in the closet. She dressed, threw on worn slippers, and ran to the kitchen, making it to the table just as the Old Man entered the door.

Bet watched him remove his long black coat and stupid pointy hat with a wide bill. The hats, once worn by aristocrats in the city, had gone out of fashion ten years earlier. Bet decided he was too far removed from style or too dumb to notice the change. He rinsed his hands in the basin, sat at the table, adjusted his long, rectangular black tie, and began spooning food from a platter.

Biscuit Head sat and offered Bet the platter of poached eggs, knowing full well she would refuse them.

Bet avoided looking at the woman's humorless smile while trying not to think of the Chook-chooks who had laid the eggs. She optioned for a bowl of root soup and dished herself a heap of plaque beans, which tasted exactly as one would expect from such a name.

"You gave the girl a ride home," Biscuit Head said to the Old Man. "Didn't you, Harrelle?"

The Old Man glanced at Bet, then at the woman. He dipped the corner of his fried bread in a runny yolk and gave a barely perceptible nod.

"If she doesn't have enough sense in that pea brain of hers to finish her chores before nightfall, that's her own fault. She should suffer the consequences of her laziness."

He dipped his bread again and chewed it with vigor while looking at Bet. "Can't afford for her to catch ill, Putrice," he said, and returned his attention to the bread.

It was as much as Bet had ever heard him speak at the table. She was even more surprised, as he sounded almost like he was defending her along with his actions. Though she knew better.

"It'd serve her right for being sloth," Putrice said.

No reply came from Harrelle, and the rest of the meal was spent in silence.

Bet sat staring at the juice lining her plate now devoid of any plaque beans, imagining the ecru sauce was a great sea and the bare spots were islands on a map. She fantasized that the islands were full of giants, dragons, and other fantastic creatures, that her and Pooch-kin would explore the new world searching for magic artifacts and treasures she had read about in the musky books of the orphanage.

"Clear the table and wash the dishes," Biscuit Head barked, snapping Bet from her daydream. "Then go to bed. The rain isn't supposed to let up for days, and there'll be sandbags that need filling in the morning."

Sand bags. Bet hated the words. The work was heavy and tiring, and her back would ache for days afterward. Worst of all, she wouldn't have time to spend with her friend or talking to the other denizens of the barnyard. "Yes, ma'am. I'm sorry, I'm sorry. Yes, Mama."

She excused herself to Harrelle, and got to work clearing the table, mindlessly stacking dirty dishes on the counter near the sink. She turned on the faucet and threw a handful of powdered soap in the sink. Taking a wet rag, she went to the table, squeezing her eyes in fatigue. She felt tired. More than tired, she was exhausted, wanting nothing more than to sleep. She took a breath and continued her chores.

First, she wiped down the table, which was relatively clean except for Biscuit Head's place, which was littered with crumbs and spills and bits of food she had spat out. It was as if the woman went out of her way to be as vile and disgusting as possible.

Next, Bet scrubbed the dishes, scraping the remnants in the trash pale. She reached for the bowl of broken egg shells and when she saw them, her bottom lip began to quiver. Amongst the shells were the remains of a speckled sea-green egg. "Pooch-kin," she said beneath a whisper. Her eyes welled up, remembering her promise to protect the egg. She closed her eyes, fighting against the tears, and took a sputtering breath. She couldn't let the old hag see her pain. If Putrice found out how much she truly cared, the woman would have Chook-chook eggs and meat for every meal.

She fought through the hurt. Whatever she may have felt about the egg, Pooch-kin was feeling it tenfold. Bet got on with her task, her gaze fixed on a rust bloom on the faucet. She was certain the tears would flow if she pulled her eyes away from that spot. She finished as quickly as possible, putting the last dish away with exaggerated carefulness, using all of her focus to keep her emotions hidden.

Bet walked through the front room to her bedroom, holding her head stiff, avoiding eye contact with either adult.

"No kiss goodnight?" Bet heard Putrice say from her chair near the fire. Bet didn't break stride. She would sooner cut off her own lips before showing that creature the slightest hint of affection.

She closed and locked the bedroom door behind her and fell onto the bed. Then the tears came.

Four

Take her when the time comes.

Bet woke with a jolt. Her body trembled with adrenaline. She looked around her room, wondering who had spoken. Only the pounding rain against the slatted roof made itself known. The hint of gray outside her tiny square window told her it was morning, but still early. The storm masked any possibility of sunrise. "It was just a dream," she said, still shaking from awakening with such suddenness.

She reached for the lamp on the bedside table. Nothing. The rain must've got into the generator again. That or another fox seeking shelter got too close to the transformer.

Her body ached. She sat on the edge wanting only to go back to sleep for the rest of the day. But she knew that wouldn't be possible. No sooner did she have the thought than Putrice's blobby fist began hammering on the door.

"Get up, girl. The bags need filled."

Sand bags… "I'm up," Bet yelled back, not caring about her tone. If she was always going to be accused of impudence, defiance, or back-talking, she decided she was going to play the part.

Bet stumbled into her clothes and searched the closet for her heavy boots. Her shoulders slumped when she remembered she had left them in the barn the previous week after cleaning the stalls. She would have to start the day with wet feet. Before she closed the door she stared at the loose board hiding the strange stone. The thought of the previous day's adventure brought on fresh pangs of pity for her friend's loss. She shook the thoughts away, continuing to stare at the board. She listened for Putrice's heavy footfalls coming to urge her along and heard the wretch barking something at the Old Man in the kitchen. She kneeled and pulled back the plank, half expecting the stone to be gone, and was relieved to find it still there. Holding the stone, she examined it in the gloom. The sides were smooth along the edge, but the ends were rough like it had been broken away from a larger crystal. She imagined a crystalline cavern high in the mountains made up entirely of the shimmering quartz and how a stalk of the stone broke loose, shattering on the cave floor and this one piece bounced free, finding the river and making its way down over the years all the way beneath the Crab-fish in Silt Creek and into her hands. She studied it a moment longer. "Nah. The tumbling in the river would've worn it smooth."

The stomping of Putrice's heavy feet in the hall pulled her back to reality. She stashed the stone and rushed to the door before the woman could start banging again. She yanked the door open to stare into Putrice's horrible face.

"It's about time. Any slower I would've brought in a mule to drag you out."

Bet doubted the statement was an exaggeration.

She squeezed past the woman without acknowledging her and went to the hearth to grab her moccasins. When she got there, she found her boots sitting beside them. Strange; she was certain she had left them in the barn. She dismissed her absentmindedness, put on the boots, pulling her pant cuffs over the top to keep out the rain.

"Quit dawdling," Putrice snapped. "Papa's already out there."

Bet snagged an apple from the counter, threw on her raincoat, and hurried out, making sure to slam the door behind her.

The cold wind and rain immediately washed away any remaining hints of sleepiness. She cinched her hood and dashed across the barnyard to a thatch-covered stall protecting a huge pile of sand. She avoided looking at the Chook-chook coop. There wasn't a way for her to console her friend at the moment and probably wouldn't be for days. The guilt she felt for not being able to protect them made it easier for her to avoid the coop.

The shovel, wheelbarrow, and stacks of burlap sacks were laid out awaiting her arrival. She let out a resigned breath, hung an open bag on the steel filling frame, and began shoveling. Five full scoops per bag. No more, no less. After filling the first one, she looked around, wondering where the Old Man had gone off to. He usually hung the empty sacks onto the frame to make sure she moved quickly.

Bet spotted him struggling to nail down a canvas tarp on the roof of the small shed covering the generator. The strong wind tore at the cover undoing each nail he drove in to secure it. She watched him for a minute, shook her head, grabbed the filled sandbag and went to his aid. For an old ranch hand, he wasn't as handy as one might expect.

Without a word, Bet hefted the bag on the corner of the low angled roof, pinning the canvas down. She then went to the next corner, pulled the canvas tight, holding it in place. The Old Man looked at her and began tacking the canvas along the edge, also without speaking. The covering was done in no time. "You'll probably want to put a bag on each corner to help keep it in place," she said.

The Old Man wiped the rain from his glasses, looking at her. He snatched his toolbox and crawled inside the small shed.

Bet heard the generator growl to life as she walked back to the sand pile.

She began filling the bags immediately. The longer she took, the longer she'd have to be in the rain. Her muscles protested and the rubber rain coat felt stifling even in the cold. She wondered if it would get cold enough to snow.

By the time the Old Man arrived, she had already filled one wheelbarrow load. He instructed her to make barriers around the generator shed, the cellar door, the coop, the front and back barn doors, the front and back porch, and to divert the flow from the driveway. So much for the hope of a short day.

It was midday by the time she started bagging around the coop. All the while, Putrice sat on the porch, stuffing her mouth with fried bread, sweets, and other morsels, watching her work.

Bet felt like her back was tied in knots. She dropped to her knees while placing the first bag near the flap door of the coop. Making sure no one could see her, she leaned in close to the door. "Pooch-kin, if you can hear me, I'm sorry. I'm so very sorry."

A moment or two passed before Pooch-kin replied with a series of mournful chirps telling her there was no need to apologize. There was nothing she could do.

"Still," Bet said. "I am sorry." When her friend didn't reply, she got back to her work, leaving him to mourn in peace.

Finished with the coop, there was only the barn and driveway left to do. Pushing the wheelbarrow back for another load, her head began to spin. Bet struggled to stay upright. She couldn't take it any longer and yanked her hood off. The icy rain felt like it evaporated as soon as it hit her head. The cold against her scalp felt like a tonic of relief.

"Put your hood back on," Harrelle said when she got back to her shovel.

Bet half obliged, leaving her forehead exposed to feel the cooling drops of rain. Her arms trembled with each bag she loaded. Having only eaten the apple, she tried to convince herself that it was the lack of food that was making her weak. She slipped and stumbled through load after load. The barn was nearly completed, but night would soon come and there was still the driveway to be done.

The final sandbags were placed around the barn, and Bet began to push the wheelbarrow back to the station. She heard the sound of a crashing tree somewhere in the distance, felled by the rain-soaked earth and strong wind. As she pushed the barrow she felt like the tree, sodden and dense. The world spun around her and her sight dimmed, her body feeling both weightless and heavy. She felt her face slap against the muddy ground. Bet didn't care; all she wanted to do was sleep.

Five

Putrice saw Bet fall. She muttered a curse, stood and pointed. "Harrelle! The girl."

The Old Man stepped from beneath the canopy, looking around the corner. He pulled up his collar and trotted over to Bet.

Putrice put on her galoshes, took an umbrella, and ambled her way toward them, grumbling the whole time. "Is she alive?" she asked, devoid of emotion.

Harrelle lifted Bet's head from the mud, looking at Putrice from the corner of his eyes. "Her skin's on fire." He took Bet in is arms. "Get the door."

"Pooch-kin," Bet mumbled. "Is he okay?"

"What'd she say?" Putrice asked.

Harrelle shook his head.

"You ate his baby. How could you? He said it wasn't my fault." Bet continued to mutter, through slurred words.

"She's delirious with fever," Harrelle said.

Putrice opened the door, glaring at Harrelle. "You're getting mud on the floor."

"I'll clean it later. Start the bath." He watched her leave then sat Bet on the floor and helped remove her jacket and boots. He leaned close to her ear. "Listen to me. You need to stop talking. Not another word. Understand?"

Bet nodded.

The Old Man stood when Putrice returned. "Is the bath ready? You'll have to take her from here."

They got Bet to her feet and Putrice guided her toward the bathroom.

"But that little Chook-chook is my friend. Nasty woman," Bet slurred, then looked at the Old Man. Harrelle shot her a warning look. "Oh yeah," she said, placing her finger to her mouth.

Putrice narrowed her eyes at Harrelle.

~ ~ ~ ~ ~

When Putrice returned, the Old Man was already mopping the floor in bare feet. "Did she at least finish her chores?"

He nodded. "Most of 'em," he said without looking at her.

"What was she talking about, Harrelle?" Putrice said, circling around him as he mopped, her voice cool and threatening.

The Old Man shrugged. "She's incoherent. Fever makes you say strange things, see things that aren't there."

"I know what a fever can do. She was very specific."

"How am I supposed to know?" He wrung out the mop and grabbed a handful of rags from the pantry to dry the floor.

"Talk to me that way again and I'll send you back to where I got you. They might even give me a refund."

Harrelle dropped the rags beneath his feet and began shuffling over the wet floor, not bothering to reply to her threats.

"Speaking of such, if she needs a doctor it'll cost me a lot of money."

The Old Man glanced at her. "I can drive her into town and save you the cost of a house call if it comes to that."

"But I might be able to recover the expense… and a lot more. If what she's saying is true. The Tribunal would pay handsomely for something like her. Wouldn't they? I might even make a good profit." Putrice laced her stubby fingers and bent them back, cracking her knuckles.

Harrelle picked up the rags. "I doubt she's one of them. She's just with fever."

Putrice walked to the window, staring out at the coop. "We'll see."

Six

Bet awoke three days later, her head groggy and her body feeling like she had wrestled a Gar Sloth and lost…badly. She had no idea how long she had been out. She remembered the Old Man telling her something about talking, the sand bags, and stumbling to the bathroom once or twice. She scooted up, resting her back against the headboard. She remembered pieces of her dreams and seeing a mountain-sized rock just off shore of an ocean, unfamiliar voices, and a woman with purple skin. She rolled her head and stretched, wiggling her toes against the sheets. Despite the lingering aches and stiffness, she felt almost refreshed.

She listened to the rain still pattering against the roof. Judging by her view of the window, it was either dusk or dawn. Her feelings of ease vanished when the door opened.

"You're awake." Putrice's grating voice blasted away her peace. "Harrelle, your patient's awake."

Harrelle squeezed between the woman and the door frame. He stood over the bed studying Bet's face.

Putrice croaked a foul noise and left. The Old Man closed the door behind her.

"Patient?" Bet asked through a scratchy voice. She reached for a glass of water beside the bed.

"You had a fever." He pulled a small glass vial from the pocket of his overcoat. "You've been asleep, mostly, for three days now."

Panic gripped Bet's chest. She didn't like the idea of being out for that long. "You took care of me?"

Harrelle looked at the door. "I did. Who else would?"

"Thank you."

"Quiet," he snapped, making Bet's half smile vanish. "Drink this." He handed her the vial.

"What is it?" She looked at it with skepticism.

"A mixture of swine's wort and carrot juice. Drink it quickly. It'll bring your strength back."

Bet wrinkled her nose. She didn't mind the carrot juice, but swine's wort was a weed that thrived on the manure around pig sties. Harrelle motioned for her to drink. She closed her eyes and swallowed the concoction in one gulp. She shivered. It tasted worse than it sounded.

"You'll feel like yourself, maybe even better, in about thirty minutes. But you'll need to eat soon." He went to the door. He looked back at her. "Don't drink anything 'til after you eat. Let it do its work," he said then left the room.

Bet shivered again at the aftertaste. "That's the most he's said…ever." She sat up, swinging her feet over the edge of the bed, her head feeling clearer already. Her feet felt unusually hot. She leaned over the bed and spotted a cast iron heating pan. "The old hag was probably trying to cook me." The thought made her laugh. The laughter made her think of her friend and then she remembered his egg. Sorrow threatened to well up. She lay back worrying about Pooch-kin.

An odd warm and vibrating feeling began coursing its way through her body. Pulsating waves of warmth passed through her, from the top of her head to the soles of her feet and up again. With each cycle, she felt the aches disappear and her strength return. The sensation lasted for several minutes. Before long she felt better. In fact, better than she ever had.

She sat up and stretched her hands out. They felt strong. Like the year of labor had made them powerful, but without the accompanying pain. "Wow," she said. "That stuff really works. Taste like sewer water, but it works."

Taking a deep breath, Bet stood, feeling light and rejuvenated. A smile crossed her face, but was quickly replaced with concern. "Ooh," she said. Her bladder suddenly felt like it was about to burst. She yanked open the door and shuffled as fast as she could to the bathroom.

Seven

As inviting as a bath sounded, a voracious appetite reminded her of the Old Man's words. She needed food immediately. Changing out of her sleeping gown into proper clothes, she was tempted to look at the shiny rock. But hunger wouldn't allow it, as well as the fear of it being gone. Putrice could've gone through any of her things while she had slept. She tied her hair back instead, firmed herself and went to the kitchen.

The couple were sitting at the table eating supper in silence. Putrice glanced up at her when she passed by, but said nothing. That's odd, Bet thought. Where were the insults? She went to the counter, cut a sizable piece of cornbread, and filled her plate with beans and rice from pans on the stove top. Usually the food was laid out on the table. Odd again. She ignored the pot of boiled meat, not wanting to know which animal had met its end, and sat at the table.

The meal was spent in silence. Putrice didn't lob a single insult or foul word. Bet thought of an adage about not saying anything, if you had nothing nice to say. If that were true, Putrice would've been rendered mute long ago. Still, the silence was disconcerting. Something was definitely amiss.

Putrice stood and took her dishes to the sink, dropping them in the basin with a loud clank. Bet looked at the Old Man who avoided eye contact. Bet scrunched her brow and continued eating. Several minutes of weird silence continued as Bet finished her meal. She scooted her chair back and Putrice finally broke the silence.

"You talk in your sleep, girl."

Alarms rang in Bet's head. Her eyes darted to Putrice, who met them with a disturbing smile. She looked to Harrelle who averted his eyes. What had she said? She remembered the Old Man telling her to stop talking or to be quiet, but everything else was too hazy to recall. She tried to act like she didn't care. She carried her dishes to the sink. "I hope I didn't say anything too insulting about you."

A flash of anger crossed Putrice's face, but was replaced by a greasy smile.

To Bet's surprise, no slap came. Instead, the woman sauntered past, went to the front room, and plopped down on the chair, its frame creaking in protest.

Bet spun back to the sink and wrinkled her nose at the filthy dishwater. There had to be two days' worth of dishes piled up. If the hag thought she was going to clean the mess, she had another thing coming. She hesitated to drop her plate in with the others. She would have to eat off the dishes in another day or two. Looking at the debris floating on the surface, something caught her eye. Something long and slender.

She reached in and pulled out a skinny gray Chook-chook feather. As bad as she felt about the Chook-chook, she was relieved it hadn't been Pooch-kin. Why had Putrice butchered the bird inside? She usually did it in the barn or the porch. Bet shook her head. She dragged the feather between her pinched fingers to wring out the water and the feather transformed from gray to a pale flaxen yellow. Her eyes widened and she struggled to breathe. Her mouth opened, but no words came.

Bet fought to make sense of what she held. Pooch-kin, her best and only friend, a meal for that horrible old hag. Tears welled up but were stymied by white hot hatred. She spun and saw Putrice staring at her with a sneering grin.

"What's wrong, girl? Was that one of your friends in the pot?"

Bet walked toward the woman, fist clenched, violence coursing through her body, trembling with rage.

Putrice stood, ready to meet Bet's wrath. "You really should've kept your mouth shut like you were told."

Bet froze. The sudden weight of what was said was more than she could bear. It was her fault. She remembered. Harrelle had tried to warn her. She looked at the Old Man, who sat at the table impassively staring at his plate, chewing on a piece of fried bread. Her mind swam and the walls felt like they were collapsing on her. She had to go. Bet shot Putrice an icy glare and ran to her room.

She grabbed her shoulder bag and began stuffing it with her few belongings. She yanked open the closet door, took out her coat, hat and gloves. Her hand stretched for her moccasins but she pulled back, looking at the plank that hid her shiny rock, the last reminder of Pooch-kin. If it was gone... Bet tore up the board, tossing it across the room. It was still there. Pocketing the stone, she scanned the room for anything else she might need. Nothing. She laced up her shoes with haste and stormed out of the bedroom, heading straight for the front door.

"Where do you think you're going?" Putrice demanded when Bet pushed past her, packed to go.

"Wherever you're not," Bet spat. She looked at the Old Man, who met her gaze then returned his attention back to his bread. When he made no attempt to stop her, Bet pulled open the door.

"You're not going anywhere. You're my property. I own you, girl," Putrice yelled, rushing toward Bet and grabbing her arm.

Bet twisted from her grip, turned and pushed the woman. Putrice stumbled back, lost her footing and hit the floor with a wood-creaking thud. Bet stepped outside, staring at the darkness and her escape.

"Stop right there!" Putrice screamed, struggling to stand.

Bet looked back. "Rot in hell." She slammed the door with all of her strength, breaking off the knob in her hand. Surprised, she looked at the handle and the splintered wood. No matter. She tossed the knob aside and ran.

Eight

Putrice sat on the floor, staring at the Old Man, who was still chomping his bread, indifferent to the fiasco. "Don't just sit there. Go and get her."

Harrelle looked at the woman, sighed, took another bite of bread, and scooted the chair back.

"Hurry," Putrice barked. "Catch her and lock her in the shed. They'll be here in the morning and I'll have my reward."

Harrelle walked to the hearth, took his boots, and slipped them on. He moseyed to the coat rack, shook out his jacket before putting it on, and grabbed his pointy hat with the wide bill.

Putrice managed to get to her feet. "Make certain you catch her. She'll bring enough money to move to the city. That's what you want, isn't it?"

Harrelle slung his satchel on, dropping in a lantern. Standing at the door, he looked back at her. "What I want is my freedom."

~ ~ ~ ~

Bet dashed across the barnyard, hesitating only slightly as she passed the Chook-chook coop. She desperately wanted to check on the other Chook-chooks, but didn't dare stop. She had to get as far away as she could and leave it all behind. She splashed across the muddy ground, turning up her collar to the wind, pulling her wool hat over her ears, and hopped the fence.

She stood in the road, looking both ways. South would take her farther into the country toward a few small communities, but some people knew her there. North led to the city of Hammerton where no one would know who she was. The city was dangerous, but at least she could get lost in the crowd. The city it was.

She saw the Old Man come out the front door and Bet ran as fast as the slick road would allow. After putting distance between her and the man, she jumped off the road to hide in the woods. She watched the Old Man shine his light either direction and head her way. She ducked deeper into the woods, hunkering down behind a stand of saplings to wait him out.

As the light drew nearer, she could hear him calling her name. Every so often he would shine the light on the ground. Bet hoped the rain would wash her tracks away before he got any closer. When he came even with where she had ditched the road, Harrelle stopped, shined the light ahead, and back to the ground. Bet's heart pounded. She wanted to make a break for the creek, but was certain he would hear. She let out a relieved breath when the Old Man pressed northward.

Her relief was short-lived when Harrelle doubled back to where she had left the road. "Now what do I do?" she whispered. She was sure she could ditch the older man in the woods. It was time to make a run for it.

"Bet," Harrelle called, shining his light into the overgrowth. "I'm not going to stop you. But I have a few things for your journey and something to tell you that you need to know."

"Yeah right," Bet said through a quiet breath. She was sure as soon as she exposed herself, he would snatch her up a take her back to the house. She stooped lower.

"Please, Bet. Trust me on this. I didn't try to stop you in the house and I won't now. You really need to know what I have to say." He stepped into the brush, waving the light, trying to spot her.

Bet kept her head down and her eyes fixed on the man.

He came closer, until he was almost right on her. "I know who your parents were."

Bet's heart skipped a beat. She had never known anything about her parents, and all her inquiries at the orphanage had come up empty. As far as she knew, she had been abandoned and her mother was one of the city's many smoke addicts. How would this old man know? He had to be lying.

"I know you're thinking this is a trick. It's not. I promise." He stood directly in front of her.

Bet slowed her breathing and hid her mouth beneath her coat, afraid that he would see her breath in the cold air.

"The medicine I gave you. The potion. There was a reason I gave it to you and why I knew it would work." He shined the light directly on her head. "There you are."

Bet got up to bolt.

"Stop!" Harrelle yelled. "I won't come any closer. Look." He put his hands in the air and took a step back.

Bet turned to flee, but stopped. Her mind told her to run, but her gut told her otherwise. She kept her distance, ready to go in a heartbeat. "Okay, what do you know of my parents?"

Harrelle put his hands down and pocketed the light. "We haven't much time, so I'll try to make this quick. Your parents were Saul and Edna Clarenhart. They... they died when you were an infant."

Bet's shoulders slumped. She had never harbored any illusions that they were still alive, but it didn't make it any easier. At least she hadn't been abandoned. "How do I know you're telling me the truth and this isn't some ruse to lure me back or catch me off guard?"

"You can't and you don't," he said plainly. "I don't want you to come back. You need to go."

Bet wasn't sure how to take that. "Anything else to tell me?"

"Yes. You were listed as deceased when your home was burned after your parents' trial."

"Trial? My parents were criminals?" She almost preferred thinking they had abandoned her.

"Just because someone is convicted doesn't mean they were a criminal. Your parents were like you. Users, people here call them. They call them other things in other places. They were tried and executed for sorcery and treason at the end of the war."

Bet had known she was different, but she thought it was nothing more than an anomaly or freakish brain mutation. She had read a snippet of a story about inquisitors and a great conflict, but it was considered fiction in the library. Maybe it wasn't.

"Someone took you before the house was burned. I don't know who, and the records at the orphanage listed you as surrendered and awarded to the state."

Bet heard what he said, but her mind was fixed on the stories being real. "The inquisitors, the tribunal, the war, all of that was real?"

Harrelle paused before answering. "There are those who don't want people to know it was real. There're laws against talking about it. But, yes, it was very real. I had my suspicions about you so I checked your records on my last trip to the city. You were received the day of your parents' execution. You confirmed it when you talked during the fever."

"Is that why Putrice is so cruel to me?"

"No…no. She's just mean, greedy, selfish, and maybe psychotic, and definitely ugly. She never suspected. But now she knows and the inquisitors are on their way. You have to go." He unslung his satchel.

"Why are you helping me?" Bet could tell by his body language that he was hiding something.

Harrelle scratched under his hat, then wiped the rain from his glasses. "You're not the only one she bought. And I'm… Let's just say I'm trying to make things right, best I can."

The sound of Putrice's screeching voice cut through the night.

Harrelle snapped his head toward the noise. "Take this." He handed her the satchel. "There's some food, and other things that'll be useful in there.

Do not go to the city. Head toward Raisin Town. Stay in the woods and off the road. Silt Creek meets up with Flourish River just before town. There's a crossing south of town. You'll be safe once you cross the river. The spot will be marked. I think. I hope."

Why would she be safe once she crossed the river? Wouldn't they just follow? There were a hundred questions running through her mind and no time to ask them. "Come with me. I don't know if I can do this alone. Get away from Biscuit Head—I mean Putrice."

"Biscuit Head?" he laughed. "It fits. No, I can't go. I'm too old. I'll stall them the best I can. I'll send them north. I'll try anyway." He handed Bet the light. His eyes looked hard and dark. "Go now."

Bet watched him for a moment, his expression changed to that of the man who doled out Putrice's punishments. "Thank you," she said, patting the bag. "Thank you for telling me about my parents."

Harrelle's face hardened. "Don't thank me. I was on the tribunal that convicted your parents." He turned and rushed to the road.

Bet watched him for a second, then ran toward the edge of the swollen Silt Creek, leaving Malweather behind.

Nine

The once sleepy Silt Creek had turned into a raging torrent, rising more than ten feet since Bet's last visit. Three days of unrelenting rainfall had transformed the forest floor into a sloshy mess. Broken branches and fallen trees made the start of her journey an arduous struggle. Not wanting to attract unwanted attention, she used her light sparingly. But there were times when it would've been impossible moving forward without it. Deep puddles and heavy runoff made some areas nearly impassable. She doubted she could make the five-mile trek to Raisin Town by daybreak.

Climbing over debris, slipping in mud, and falling over unseen obstacles couldn't distract Bet from her thoughts. Her mind raced with questions. Her parents had been Users, like her. But what did it mean? Did they also talk to animals or something else entirely? What little she knew of Users suggested that they were considered sorcerers or some other archaic sect. She had also read that they were evil. Bet didn't consider herself anything of the sort. She just talked to animals and had an occasional sense of foreboding that proved correct. Intuition wasn't sorcery. She didn't conjure or use magic or any other nonsense the name implied. Communicating with animals wasn't anything she had learned or sought to accomplish, it simply was. And the Old Man; if he used to work with the inquisitors, why would he help her? There had to be more to the story.

She stumbled over an exposed root, falling to her knees. Cursing her luck, she stood and flicked on the light. She recanted her curse at seeing a six-foot wide washout in front of her. Had she fallen in, she was sure she would've been washed into the creek turned river and likely drowned. So much for sensing danger.

Bet considered her options. Her only choice was to find the road and cross there. When she finally sloshed her way back to the road, any hopes of finding an easier way across were dashed. The washout was twice as wide here.

She thought on the problem for a minute. She could try to find a log long enough to bridge the gap, but she doubted she had the strength to drag a rain-soaked log far enough to accomplish the task. She thought about making a jump for it. Though her moccasins were great for light travel, they lacked the traction to get a good enough run going to make the leap. Feeling increasingly exposed standing on the open road, her mind fell on an idea. The Old Man had said she was a User. Why not try to conjure something up?

With her eyes closed, Bet concentrated, picturing a simple wood plank to walk across. She strained and thought of every magic word she had ever read; there had to be some truth in the legends. Her mind came to rest on one word. "Abracadabra," she said, and opened her eyes. Nothing. "Okay, that was stupid." She tried again, making up words and noises, going through wild gesticulations, all with the same results.

"I guess that's not how it works," she said, feeling defeated. "This would be much easier if I could fly."

She surveyed the ground. Only the faintest of moonlight hidden behind the thick layers of storm clouds illuminated the ground. "At least nobody can follow me on this road for a while. She stood with hands on hips, wriggling her feet in the squishy mud. "Now how do I get across without wings?"

The sound of a breaking branch in the forest pulled her from her considerations. She wondered where all of the forest dwellers took shelter in storms like this. Especially the little ones who were most vulnerable, like the Day Owls and hyperactive Flit-hoppers. She stood motionless, staring into the black of the forest. "Flit-hoppers!" she said and ran to the nearest tree, shining her light, looking for low-lying branches. Finding a good tree for climbing, she shined her light across the chasm. "This will do. Flit-hoppers can't fly and neither can I."

Bet climbed up the first branch, shining her light across the washout where she hoped she would land. No rocks or branches that she could see. She climbed higher, hoping her weight wouldn't push the rain soaked branches to the breaking point. Finding a solid branch about ten feet up, she secured her bags and began inching her way from the trunk. When the thick branch started to sag, she stopped. She took her light, shining it down. She was almost directly over the washout. If the branch gave way, she'd be in real trouble.

She took a deep breath and tossed her light across to her potential landing spot, giving herself a target in the darkness. Now to see if she could do the same. All she had to do was be like the Flit-hoppers and fall gracefully, and hope her trajectory would take her across the span. She let out a long breath, wishing she had the little critters' agility, and hoped she wouldn't break a leg or her neck, or anything else for that matter, on landing.

"Just go for it," she told herself. Letting out another breath, she nodded to convince herself that she could do it, took a single step and leapt.

Bet felt exhilaration and fear course through her weightlessness as she kept an eye on her landing spot. Her head struck a branch she hadn't seen, and her exhilaration disappeared leaving only fear. Oh no, was all she could think as she tumbled, helpless, through the air. The ground came suddenly, and she landed on her back with a sloppy thud. The impact stole her wind. She lay there gasping for air. She had made it, lacking the Flit-hopper's grace, but she had made it nonetheless.

The ground sagged beneath her. She rolled to her stomach and only then did she notice she had just cleared the washout. The soft earth moved again and the bank began to collapse into the ever-widening rent. Bet scurried to her feet, snagging her light, and stumbled away. Her foot caught an exposed root and she found herself back on the ground, but far enough away from the mini-landslide to be free of danger. "I'm definitely not a Flit-hopper."

Carrying bruises to her pride and various parts of her body, Bet pushed on through the woods, feeling a small amount of ease knowing she had put at least one obstacle between her and whoever might be coming for her.

Ten

The poor conditions slowed Bet's progress to a crawl, at times literally, and the unceasing rain and biting cold pushed her to the edge of exhaustion. Regardless of the effects of the so-called potion, fatigue gnawed at her. To make matters worse, the dark of night was beginning to give way to the first hints of a gray morning. She had to get to the crossing Harrelle had spoken of. He had said it was just south of Raisin Town, but she had no idea how far 'just south' was.

Bet tripped, fell, and stumbled her way to the forest edge where the heavy woods gave way to vast vineyards. She studied the vines, barren of fruit and leaves, wondering what to do next. She had lost the race against daylight.

She kicked at the ground in frustration. The swollen Silt Creek curved away to her right, joining the engorged Flourish River just as Harrelle had said it would. The road rested to her left, but that was out of the question. On the other side of the vineyard, hidden by a low hill, lay Raisin Town. Her only option appeared to be going through the field, but the prospect of trudging through ankle-deep mud curbed her enthusiasm. At least the gnarled vines would provide some cover from any travelers on the road.

Bet took her first step into the clearing and heard a man's voice urging his galloping horse along. She ducked back, watching the rider head toward Raisin Town. Worry crossed her face. The traveler had come the way she had. Had the road been repaired already? If that was the case, the inquisitors could already be on their way. Maybe there had been another way around she hadn't seen in the darkness. She hoped the rider had come from one of the farms between Malweather and Raisin Town. Bet squinted against the rain, watching the rider until he disappeared over the hill. Once certain he wasn't coming back, she began the slow march across the vineyard.

By the time Bet reached the hill, it was already well into midmorning. The rain had eased, but still came down steadily. Sporadic patches of grass gave her a little better footing, but even with the marginally improved conditions, fatigue wore at her. The vineyard continued over the hill, keeping her hidden from any stray eyes, though she doubted anyone in their right mind would be out in weather like this, the lone rider being the exception. Almost as if answering her doubt, Bet heard the sound of heavy wagons and shouts of men traveling from town. "Now what?" She peered between the vines for a look.

Two large carts pulled by teams of oxen, followed by a covered wagon, made their way along the muddy road. It didn't take a scholar to guess where they were going. The carts were laden with loads of gravel and sand, and the wagon likely carried men and supplies. "They're going to repair the road," Bet growled.

After waiting for the caravan to pass, she made her way to the top of the hill and chanced standing tall to get a lay of the land. Raisin Town was in sight, and her gaze followed the river to the west where it ran along the edge of town, driving several mills. She couldn't see where it narrowed enough for her to cross. Chances were the floodwater rendered any such crossing impossible.

Discouraged, uncertain, cold, tired and hungry, Bet pressed forward. Despite all these things, she felt determined. "There's no going back now. No place to go back to anyway," she said in a whisper.

She ran and slid her way down the hill until coming to the edge of town. Avoiding Raisin Town's one main road, she guessed her safest path would be one of its side roads or alleys. She pressed against the wood slat wall of the first building she came to and peered around the corner, down the main road. She spotted a solitary man hopping across puddles and into one of the few shops. Brick and stone buildings stood beside wood structures, some with tin facades, and others with louvered siding. All of the businesses along Main Street seemed to adhere to the idea of having large plate glass windows with etched or painted titles announcing their wares.

She darted across the road, jogged down an alley, passing the livery until coming to a row of houses. The homes, made mostly of stone and mortar, varying in size from shanty to two-story estates, looked warm and inviting, with every chimney billowing plumes of gray smoke. Wanting nothing more than to knock on a door and ask the residents if she could warm herself by a fire, she turned away, resisting the urge. She dashed down the lane trying to stay hidden behind fence lines and shrubbery.

It didn't take long to reach the other end of the small town. She ducked beneath the awning of the last building, getting a brief reprieve from the rain. Looking out at the empty terrain south of town, Bet didn't feel eager to continue her journey. She looked at the last house on the row, eyeing the barn behind the home. She rubbed her eyes, pinching the bridge of her nose. What should she do? Bet looked at the barn once more and made her decision. She needed the shelter to rest and wait out the storm until nightfall.

Bet ran across the way, hopped over the split-rail fence, and sprinted to the barn, keeping a watchful eye on the back porch. She pulled open the door and stepped inside, relieved to be free of the rain. Her relief was short-lived.

"Who are you? What're you doing in here?" a large man said, scaring the breath out of her.

"I…uh," Bet stammered, feeling for the door, ready to make a break.

The man stepped closer with a limp, hanging a bridle on a hook. "What are you doing in my barn?" the large man, intimidating in stature, wearing overalls, a long riding coat, and a wide brimmed hat, asked. His voice carried more curiosity than threat.

Bet composed herself beneath her shivering. "I…I'm just a traveler seeking shelter from the storm."

"A traveler? You picked a fine time to be on the road. Where's your horse?" He looked at her with narrowed eyes.

"My pony threw me about two miles back. Guess she had enough of the rain. Damn thing went back the way we came."

The man crossed his arms and cocked his head. "Where're you traveling from?"

Where was she from? Her mind raced until she remembered the only town she knew of near Raisin Town. "Glarehaven."

"Glarehaven, huh?" You've been traveling for a while then."

"Yes, sir," she said, trying to be polite.

"Where're you headed?" he asked, turning his attention back to the bridle and straightening it on the hook.

"Just outside Hammerton. I'm bringing medicine to my aunt." She patted the satchel.

He eyed the bag. "Who's your aunt?"

Bet cleared her throat. "Maybil. Maybil Rustfeather."

"Maybil Rustfeather? Never heard of her. Why doesn't she just get her medicine from the city?"

"She's old. She's suspicious of the pharmacies."

The man laughed. "Can't fault her there. Why didn't you come to the house?"

"I didn't want to trouble anyone. Figured I'd just rest in the hay loft until I dried out a bit. I apologize for the intrusion. I can be on my way." She reached for the door.

"No. No harm done." He rubbed his shaggy beard. "A girl your age shouldn't be traveling alone. C'mon in the house and get warmed up by the fire. I'll see if my sister can fix you up something hot."

"I really appreciate it, sir. But I don't want to cause you any bother." As inviting as it sounded, she had no desire to be trapped inside a stranger's house if the inquisitors came. She was sure they had already reached and left Malweather.

"It's no bother. You won't make it far anyhow. The roads washed out north of here. Dalin."

"Dalin?" Bet asked.

"Name's Dalin. I don't like being called sir. Yours?"

Bet hesitated, unsure if she should give her real name. "Bethany. Pleased to meet you." She offered her hand.

"Bethany? Why not Beth?" He shook her hand.

"Sounds like you have a lisp."

Dalin laughed. "Okay, Bethany." He grabbed his walking stick. "Let's get you dried off and fed."

Bet followed the man across the yard, looking at an assortment of cows and other animals in sheltered pens. As they climbed the back-porch steps, she couldn't help but notice his stiff-legged limp.

Dalin turned to say something and caught Bet staring at his leg. He tapped his stick against the wooden prosthetic. "Lost it in the war."

Bet's face reddened more than it already was from the cold. "I'm sorry."

"Nothing for you to be sorry 'bout. I's the one who was fool enough to volunteer for that mess." He looked at her feet. "Moccasins?"

Bet looked at her footwear. "Can't run as fast in boots."

Dalin eyed her for a second. "Best take 'em off out here and beat off the mud. They'll dry quicker and you won't make such a mess."

Bet did as instructed and followed him inside.

"Put your shoes by the fire. Yourself, too. Sister! We've got company." Dalin hobbled off to the kitchen.

Bet shuffled to the fire. She couldn't recall anything feeling this good. Her skin began to itch with pins and needles from the heat thawing her icy flesh, but she didn't care. The fire was delightful.

As Bet warmed her hands against the fire, a tall woman with jet black hair and striking emerald green eyes came in from the hall. She appeared to be half Dalin's age, who she guessed to be in his fifties, and she carried an aura of kindness Bet hadn't been around since…never, really.

"That's my sister, Anna," Dalin said from the edge of the living room. "Sister, this is Bethany. She lost her pony down the road. Figured she could thaw out here for a bit." He looked at Bet and stepped back into the kitchen.

Bet looked back at Dalin. He seemed to know she wasn't telling the truth, but if he did, he wasn't saying anything.

Anna walked to Bet and took her hands. Her brow wrinkled slightly as she stared into Bet's eyes. Her expression changed into a pleasant smile. "Sweetheart, you're chilled to the bone. Let me get you a robe and then I'll heat you a bowl of vegetable soup."

"Thank you, ma'am," Bet said. "I appreciate your kindness." She felt a warm easiness fill her body, like nothing she had ever known.

"Call me Anna. And it's my pleasure." Anna hurried into the hall.

Dalin stepped in, handing Bet a cup of hot tea.

"Thank you," she said, taking the cup. "I surely don't mean to impose."

"No imposition," Dalin said, flopping into a stuffed chair by the fire. "Sister likes caring for strays. Look at me. She took me in when no one wanted to give work to an old gimp like me."

"You're not that old," Anna said, returning with a plush blue robe. "Besides, you earn your keep."

Dalin waved his hand at her. "Long as you keep believing that."

Anna took Bet's coat, handing her the robe. "He's more help than he wants to admit. He helps me with the animals," she said with a smile, her eyes meeting Bet's.

Bet perked up. "You take care of animals?"

"Yes. I'm sort of the official town veterinarian. At least that's what they call me," said Anna.

"And I'm a vet helping a vet, or she's helping me. Either way..." Dalin leaned over to stoke the fire.

Anna shook her head. "Go get cleaned up and I'll get the soup ready. You're welcome to a hot bath if you'd like one." She looked Bet and her bags over. "Do you have a change of clothes in there?"

"Yes, ma'am. I mean Anna. Yes, I do."

"Good. Throw your dirty clothes outside the bathroom door before you get in, on the floor is fine, and I'll have them cleaned and dry in no time."

"Thank you. You're too kind." Bet relished the sense of ease she felt. Just twenty minutes in the company of strangers and she already felt more at home than she had in a year at Malweather.

"A person can be too much of many things, but never too kind. Now go get washed up," Anna said, taking the empty teacup.

Bet happily rushed off to the bath.

~ ~ ~ ~ ~

Anna returned with Bet's soaked clothing in hand and began hanging them on the clothes horse near the fire.

"What do ya think?" Dalin said, sitting up a little in his seat. "Story seems a little sketchy."

Anna said nothing, instead turning her attention to pinning Bet's clothing on a steel rod. She shook out Bet's pants and the fragment of quartz fell out. Picking up the stone, she examined the iridescent colors with a mix of curiosity and concern. She looked toward the bathroom.

"Well? What're you thinking?" Dalin asked again.

Anna looked at her brother and closed her eyes. "I think she might be in trouble," she said and pocketed the stone.

Eleven

Staring at her face in the mirror, Bet noticed a few scrapes and scratches along her forehead and face. She touched the web of broken vessels on her cheek wondering if they'd ever go away. She felt a wellspring of anger rise up at the thought of how many times Putrice had slapped her and all of the horrible things she had done.

Bet closed her eyes and forced calm over herself. She was gone now, and whether she got captured by the inquisitors, kept on the lamb, or even stayed here, she was sure she'd never have to see that awful biscuit-headed woman again.

She finished dressing, throwing the plush robe over her, relishing its warmth that almost seemed to quiet her aching muscles, and grabbed her bags. Remembering the shiny rock, she patted her pockets then searched the floor. Realizing she had left it in her other pants' pocket, she let out a sigh of relief. She trusted Anna wouldn't have any interest in an old rock.

Bet opened the door to find Anna's kind face, her hand ready to knock.

"Soup's ready when you are," the woman said with a smile.

"I'm more than ready, thank you," Bet said with an eager smile. She followed Anna to the kitchen, eyeing her drying clothes as she passed. Anna guided her to a small round table with two settings waiting. She sat down at the offered chair, feeling a little awkward at not serving herself. The rhythmic clomp of Dalin's steps came up behind her, and he took a seat beside her.

"Dalin never misses a chance at a meal," Anna said, raising an eyebrow at the man.

"You got that right," he said, nudging Bet with his elbow. "You never know when you'll get your next one, so eat while you can. That goes for sleep, too. That's about the only thing worthwhile I got out of the military and not much else."

"I've never met anybody who was in the war," Bet said, watching Anna spoon a healthy serving into each of their bowls. "Thank you," she said, as Anna sat with them.

"No? Well if ya did, you wouldn't know it. Most don't talk about it."

"Why is that? I can't find much to read about it either. You'd think for such a huge event there'd be more written. It almost seems like legend more than history. For someone my age, that is."

Dalin stole a glance at Anna, while crumbling a handful of crackers into his bowl. "History is a point of view written by the victors, and the winning side isn't always the right side," he said, returning his attention to his bowl.

Bet wondered if her parents had been involved in the war in some way. Whatever the case, all she could glean from the few books mentioning the war was that invaders came from the western seas and fought against the homeland of Persk for maybe four years before finally being turned away. But the stories were mostly allegory, with few facts. All she knew for certain was her homeland of Persk and neighboring Valdivia had been involved. "Maybe you can tell me about it?" She raised her eyebrows expectantly.

Dalin raised his head to speak, looking at Anna.

Anna put her hand on Bet's arm. "Brunch isn't a good time for such stories."

Bet hoped she hadn't offended her hosts in any way and dropped the notion. She nodded and mimicked Dalin by crumbling crackers into her bowl.

"If we have time, maybe I'll tell you a little bit about it later," Dalin said, spreading butter on a thick chunk of bread.

"I'd like that," Bet said with a smile.

The remainder of the meal was spent talking mostly of the animals Anna cared for and how Dalin would invoke his missing leg when there was a chore he wasn't fond of doing. He insisted that Anna had a heart of stone when she wouldn't excuse him of his duties. Bet truly liked the pair. They were so different from anyone she had known. There was genuine laughter and caring for one another. She felt a special affinity for Anna, who, like herself, seemed to really care for the animals.

Finished with her meal, Bet sat back, feeling full and relaxed. Her eyes felt heavy, like she could fall asleep right there at the table.

Anna stood and rested her hand on Bet's shoulder. "We have a spare room upstairs, second door on the right. You should try to rest."

Bet looked at her through drooping lids. "I suppose I could use a nap," she said with a crooked smile.

"Go on, then. The bed is comfortable and the room is warm." She gave Bet's shoulder a soft squeeze.

Bet nodded, excused herself and thanked them through a scratchy voice. She climbed the stairs, her legs feeling like the dreaded sandbags she so loathed, found the room and flopped on the bed. The room was indeed warm and the bed was as described, only better. She kicked off her pants for comfort, wrapping herself in the robe, and crawled beneath the covers, listening to the clank of cast iron pans and stoneware from the kitchen below. Her head sunk into the pillow and she quickly fell into a contented slumber.

Twelve

The sound of the creaking door pulled Bet from her dreams. She sat up and immediately knew something was wrong by the look on Anna's face. She heard Dalin's gruff voice yelling at someone from the front porch. "What? What's going on?"

Anna nodded toward the window.

Bet gave her a worried look. She poked her head around the curtain. It was midday and the rain had slowed to a drizzle. Through the mist, she saw an iron carriage drawn by two large black steeds bigger than any she had ever seen before. Standing beside the wagon was a tall man dressed in black, wearing a long coat and wide circular brimmed hat. "Who are they?" she asked, though she feared she already knew the answer.

"Dalverians," Anna said, pulling her away from the window. "More commonly known as inquisitors. They served the tribunal during the war, and the Worshipful Dalverious. It's been many years since they've come around. I had hoped they were disbanded."

Bet grabbed her clothes and rushed to get dressed, not concerned with modesty.

"Slow down. You're safe for now," Anna said. Her voice was calm, but it belied a certain nervousness. "You know why they've come?" She handed Bet her dry clothes, and Bet stuffed them in her bag.

Bet glanced at Anna. "I have an idea, but not much of one. I was only told a little bit last night. My former owner called them on me."

"Owner?" Anna asked, handing Bet her moccasins.

"I was sold from the orphanage in Hammerton last year. It's a long story."

Anna nodded. "Disgusting what they do with people there." She took Bet by the shoulders. "Sit, just for a minute. Stay calm."

"I can't. As much as I'd like to stay, I have to go. I'm not like you. I'm different, and those men want me for that reason."

"You can't go anywhere right now with them out there." Anna's voice soothed Bet, making her breathe.

"What if they just come in?"

"They can't. Not legally. They'll have to beseech the sheriff for a warrant if they suspect anything. And I can tell you Sheriff Paulson doesn't care too much for city folk. He'll dawdle and delay for a good while before signing off."

Bet let out an exasperated breath, shaking her head. "Harrelle didn't make it sound like they cared about such things as law."

"Harrelle?" Anna's brow furrowed.

"The old man where I lived. He was on the tribunal… a long time ago."

Anna shook her head. "It doesn't matter if they care or not. Dalin served them during the war and he doesn't like them. He'd probably shoot them if they tried to enter without a proper warrant. And he'd be within his legal right. And he'd likely enjoy doing it."

Bet stopped at hearing Anna's words. "I…I wouldn't want that. I don't want anyone in trouble on my behalf."

Anna guided Bet to the corner of the bed. "He wouldn't do it solely on your behalf. He would do it to protect me as well." She waited for the words to sink in. When Bet's expression changed from worry to understanding she continued. "We're the same, you and I. I sensed it in you when I took your hands."

"You understand animals, too?" Bet felt a sense of excitement. All of her life she'd thought she was a freak, some kind of anomaly that no one would understand. In the span of less than a day she'd learned her parents had been like her, and now Anna, too. She suddenly didn't feel so alone in the world. "You're really like me?"

"I do, and I am. Though I suspect not exactly the same. All of us have, or had, different abilities. Do the animals understand you as well as you understand them?"

Sadness tugged at Bet's heart. "Yes. Pooch-kin and I would talk for hours."

"Who's Pooch-kin?"

Her body sagged. "A Chook-chook. He's my friend, or was until that horrid woman who bought me found out and cooked him for supper." Bet felt her anger rise, teetering on the cusp of hatred.

"I'm sorry. People can be very cruel when confronted with what they don't understand. Their fear controls them. But you mustn't give in to hatred. People like us must learn to temper negative emotions. If you give in to your passions, it can…affect you."

Bet nodded. There was so much she didn't know, but with the inquisitors outside, she wouldn't have time to learn again. She heard the front door slam, followed by the clomp of Dalin's steps coming up the stairs. "Is he like us, too?"

Anna shook her head. "No. Strange how it's given to one and not another, even within families." She fished a leather pouch from her apron pocket and handed it to Bet.

Bet took the pouch and was surprised to find the shiny quartz fragment inside.

"It fell out of your pocket when I hung your clothes to dry. Tell me, how did you come across this?"

Bet shrugged her shoulders. "I found it in the creek a few days ago while

Pooch-kin and I were gathering wood in the forest. It's just a shiny rock, isn't it? Or is it something else?" Bet got a tingle of excitement thinking it could be more.

Anna's mouth formed a thin smile. "It could be… though probably not. But put it away. Keep it safe and out of sight."

Bet masked her excitement. She had the feeling it wasn't just a shiny rock like Pooch-kin had said. She returned it to the pouch, cinching it tight, and stuffed it deep in her pocket.

"I really don't like those people," Dalin said, pushing through the door, a ball of annoyed energy. "Arrogant little goat turds, think they can just push anybody around. I was hoping they all got Stim flu and died after the war."

"They're gone?" Anna asked.

"For now. They'll be back after they harass Paulson enough." He looked at Bet. "Seems they're looking for a young woman, 'bout fifteen or sixteen years old."

Bet hung her head. "I'm sorry," she said in a small voice.

"Ah, don't be. Things have a habit of being what they are. That's the way life is." He looked at Anna. "What're we gonna do?"

Anna paced around the room, wringing her apron.

"If I can make it to the narrow spot in the river and get across, I should be okay," Bet said to ease her friend's worry.

"How do you know that? Who told you?" Anna asked, trading a glance with Dalin.

"The old man…Harrelle. That's where I was headed. I traveled all night from Malweather farm. I needed a rest and went to your barn. I don't understand why I couldn't cross somewhere upstream, closer to where I was. It would've saved me and you a lot of trouble."

Anna let out a tired breath. "There's a gateway in the fabric about a mile south of here. People like us, Users as some say, can pass through there."

"A gateway in the fabric?" Bet was confused. She had never seen a fence or wall anywhere near the river.

Anna sat while Dalin went to keep watch out the window. "You see, after the war, a barrier was put in place between realms to keep the two separated. It was those two realms who were at war. The Users and the Non. Gateways were put in place so those like us could escape persecution. You can't see it, but it's there. The trouble is, the river might have flooded the location, or it could be gone. Once you cross, through, you can't return, and the gateway reappears somewhere else. If this gateway Harrelle spoke of has been used, then it's gone."

"I don't understand. Won't they just follow me across if they see me?"

"They'll try, unless they're experienced. They can't pass through the gateway. People who aren't like us can't. They can cross the river, climb the tree, walk into a rock, however the gateway presents itself, but to them there's no change."

Bet looked completely baffled, and Anna tried to explain. "You see, it's like this. Where I'm sitting still exists in that realm, but it could be a forest or a large city, depending on where the realms line up, and as we're completely unaware of what's happening on that side so is it the same for whoever may be occupying this spot over there."

"Oh, so it's like you die and go to the afterlife except you're not dead?" Bet said. "I mean you said you can't come back. That sounds like death."

"I guess it does. Though I never thought of it in those terms. But it is true, you can't come back." Anna gave Bet a solemn smile.

Bet's face lost color when the realization of what she was about to do washed over her. She had often thought about running away, either from the orphanage or Malweather, but this would be different. Everything she had ever known would be gone forever and she'd be in a world where she knew no one. "What about you? Can't you come with me?"

"No, I can't. I have to be here to take care of the animals and him," she nodded at Dalin, who grumbled something offensive.

"But I really like it here with you...with both of you. I've only known you a short time, but you feel like family." Bet realized she sounded like a pleading child, but she didn't care. Why was every bit of happiness so brief? She looked at Anna, then to Dalin, who averted his eyes, finding something interesting to scratch off the wall.

Dalin walked across the room, stopping at the doorway. "The world wasn't always like this," he said and left the room. "I'll get some things ready."

Anna watched him leave then turned to Bet with seriousness in her eyes. "There'll be a post on the side of the road, taller than the rest in the fence line, near a triangular rock. If you don't see the post, you can't miss the rock. Walk fifty paces from the post toward the river. Since Harrelle didn't tell you any of this, I assume his information was limited. He must've thought you'd know it instinctively. At exactly fifty paces you'll see a flat round stone on the ground with runes etched upon it in the form of a C with a slash through it, a trapezoid, and an X. If you don't see the runes, that means the gateway has been used, and you'll have to come back here. We'll think of something else."

Anna continued. "When you find the runes, step on the stone and you'll pass through. There are very real dangers on the other side, so keep your wits about you. Seek out Bathezine. He helped us years ago, and I'm certain he'll help us now. He'll get you adjusted."

"And what if the river is covering the rock? It's already swollen at least three times its size," Bet asked.

Anna pursed her lips. "Let's hope it's not. You'll have to try regardless. As far as I know, the next gateway is on the other side of the Pith Mountains. That's a long way off in the territory of Valdivia." She looked out the window once more. "Come now, I have some things that will help you once you're there."

The two hurried downstairs to the kitchen. Anna wrapped some bread and fruit, stuffing it in Bet's bag. She grabbed a stool and reached into the uppermost cabinet, pulling out a pouch. She handed it to the girl. "You'll need money. It doesn't do me any good here."

Bet looked inside at the large amount of oddly shaped coins. "I'll pay it back one day." She did her best to smile.

Anna ran her fingers through Bet's hair, tying it back. "I really wish we had more time. There's so much you should know."

"I wish I could stay with you forever." She fell against Anna in a tight embrace. "I'll never forget you."

Dalin came to the back door. "Ready to go?"

Anna gave Bet a warm smile, smoothing the girl's hair back. "Ride fast."

"Ride?" Bet asked nervously. She had never ridden anything, not even a bike.

Anna guided her out the door.

"You ever been on a Saureped?" Dalin asked, walking with them to the barn.

"Nope. I've never even seen one."

They entered the barn and a wide smile crossed Bet's face. The Saureped stood with saddle and bridle, ready to go. The hairless creature stood five feet tall at the shoulders on two slender, but powerful looking legs. Bet thought it looked like a featherless ostrich with tiny clawed arms pinned against its olive-skinned body. Its neck stretched up another two feet, supporting a small head with large brown eyes and a wide, toothy beak. Bet rubbed her hand down the Saureped's neck, who whistled happily. "My name is Bet. I'm glad to meet you."

Anna stepped beside her. "He understands you, but he can't reply vocally. They mainly communicate chemically, with pheromones, kind of like a bee."

"He's beautiful," Bet said, looking at his long flat tail, taking in every bit of the magnificent beast.

"Bet, huh?" Dalin said. "Suits you better than Bethany, and definitely better than Beth," he added, saying the name with a lisp.

Bet grinned sheepishly.

Dalin patted her head. "Best get saddled up. Don't know how much time we've got. When you get to where you need to be, tell him to go home. He'll listen." He looked at Bet and cleared his throat. "Now he's fast. Sit tall and don't hold the reins too tight."

"Thank you," Bet said, giving Dalin a tight hug. "Thank you both."

Dalin nodded and mussed her hair, his eyes moist. "Up you go." He boosted her into the padded saddle, wiped his eyes, grabbed his stick, and opened the barn door.

"I hope to see you again, one day," Bet said, fighting back her tears.

"You never know where fate will take you," Anna said. "Remember all I've told you." She looked at the Saureped. "Okay, Spiff. You take good care of her and get her there safely."

Spiff scratched at the ground, then sped from the barn.

Thirteen

Bet looked back to see Dalin closing the barnyard gate. She hoped she really would see them again someday. "Okay, Spiff. Go a little slow at first, until I get the feel of this."

They turned down the road. Bet bounced in the saddle, her head on a swivel, looking for any sign of the Dalverians. Their path led them to the main road on the edge of town. She looked down Main Street and spotted the iron carriage of the inquisitors parked in front of the sheriff's office. "Better pick up the pace a little, Spiff."

Trying to put her mind at ease, Bet focused on staying loose in the saddle. She remembered reading something like that somewhere about horseback riding and hoped it applied to Saurepeds as well. She heard the shouts of men and the slamming of metal doors in the distance behind her. Looking back, she saw the dark form of a man in black run from the sheriff's office and jump into the carriage. She didn't have to wonder what they were doing; she had been spotted. "Spiff, remember what I said about going slow? Forget it. Run! Run as fast as you can."

Spiff grunted in approval and bolted. Bet let out a startled yelp and held on for life. The Saureped moved with such speed, she swore his feet never touched the ground. She dug her feet in the stirrups and leaned into Spiff's neck, clinging tightly. It was all she could do to hang on.

The road began to curve, and despite the Saureped's powerful, clawed feet, he slipped in the mud, only just managing to stay upright. Bet wasn't so lucky. She flew from Spiff's back, tumbling in the tall yellow grass near the side of the road. She shook off the impact and called her ride back to her. Spiff quickly doubled back. He looked at her inquisitively with his big eyes, nudging her with his beak. "I'm okay," she said, scratching his cheek. She stole a glance down the road. Her pursuers were getting closer. "They won't be able to take the turns any faster…I hope."

Spiff squatted, Bet climbed back on, and they began again at a slightly slower pace. The road turned into a series of winding curves. Regardless of the slower speed, Spiff still had trouble keeping his footing in the mud. Bet could hear the rattle of iron and the heavy falls of hooves growing louder. "New plan. Get off the road. You should have better traction in the grass."

Without hesitation, Spiff shot into the field, and his speed doubled. Exhilaration coursed through Bet's body as the Saureped moved over moguls and low rocks with easy strides, cutting across the road where the curves brought it through their path. Had they not been chased, it would've been as good a time as she had ever had.

The broken fence line appeared and Bet studied the posts, hoping her marker was still there. The road began to straighten out once again, and she asked Spiff to slow his pace and get back on the road. Bouncing in the saddle, she spotted the taller post surrounded by tall grass near the large triangular rock just as Anna said it would be. "There it is!" She took a chance and pointed ahead.

"Don't stop. Slow down. I'm going to hop off and I want you to keep going to try to draw them away. Then go into the field and head back home."

Spiff lowered his head, which Bet took as him understanding. When they approached the post, he slowed to a trot and Bet slid off. Spiff looked back at her. "Go now! And thank you for your help." She watched him run off.

Bet touched the weather worn post and looked toward the river. The water crashed against rocks on the bank blocking its course. Fifty paces to a flat rock with runes, she remembered. She watched the angry water slamming against the natural barrier, surging around it for an easier path, and dearly hoped the stone wasn't in that spot.

Ten paces. She could hear the clank of the wagon drawing nearer.

Twenty five. Thirty. The inquisitors were just around the bend. Forty. She ducked down, hoping the tall grass would hide her. The carriage slowed and the team trotted past the post. Bet held her breath. Another three paces and she would be at the water's edge.

A man's voice called out, followed by the grating screech of the wheel brake. No point in hiding now; they had spotted her. She stood, trying to keep her paces steady. At forty-four paces she was ankle deep. She heard one of the men tell her to stop.

"Yeah right," she said, taking three more steps. She chanced a look back and saw one man, with long shocks of bright blond hair draping from beneath his black hat, and skin as white as cotton, standing with his hands on his hips, instructing another man who fished a long pole with a looped snare out of the back of the carriage.

Another step and the current tugged at her leg. Another quick peek over her shoulder and she noticed they seemed to be hesitating. She guessed they weren't sure what she was capable of. Another step and the water surged over her knees. She fought to stay standing. The ground was soft beneath her moccasins. She slid her right leg forward, not daring to lift it. Her toe felt the edge of a stone. This had to be it.

She started to drag her back leg forward and the rapids caught her. She felt the world spin as she desperately tried to maintain her footing. It was too late. The powerful current yanked her legs out from under her and she tumbled and twisted until she slammed into the rocks.

Bet fought and pushed, trying to edge her way to the bank. If she stopped, she was sure the inquisitors would have only a drowned bloated corpse as their prize, if they ever found her at all. With a great heave, she pushed away from the rocks and fell toward the shore. Her hand struck the bank and she crawled up, relieved to be free of one danger.

But the other danger remained. She saw the man holding the snare drop it and retrieve a net from the trunk of the carriage. The blond man kept his eyes trained on her as he and the darker skinned man unfurled the netting. The men began to walk toward her.

Bet scrambled to her feet, trying to get back to the path to the gateway. A loud squeal came from behind the men. She spun to look just in time to see Spiff, running at speed, barrel into the pair. "Spiff!" she yelled in excitement.

The blond inquisitor took the brunt of the blow and flew through the air, landing in a crumpled heap ten feet away. The other was brushed aside and spun into the side of the iron carriage, then dropped to one knee. The man stood, shaking his head clear, leaning against the wagon. He threw open the door and pulled out a long rifle.

Panic set in. They were no longer taking prisoners. Keeping a careful eye on the armed man, Bet tried to formulate a plan. Nothing came to mind. This was the end of her journey.

The man brought the weapon up to his shoulder, but to Bet's surprise he didn't aim it at her. Instead, he leveled the weapon toward Spiff, who was coming back for another pass. Fire burned in Bet's veins. No. No one else would die because of her. She had to protect him. She wouldn't let Spiff die like Pooch-kin.

She searched the ground, trying to find something to stop the man from killing Spiff. Her eyes fell on a small rock protruding from the mud. She snatched it up, drawing her arm back as the man pulled back the hammer. Without further thought and through a blinding fury, she threw the stone. The rock flew from her at an unnatural speed and hit the man's face in an explosion of blood. Bet watched in horror as the man's lower jaw hung from a strand of flesh until falling to the ground. The man brought his hands to where his jaw had been, and collapsed to the muddy road.

Spiff came to stop over the fallen man, lowered his head to inspect, then lifted his head toward Bet.

Bet stood trembling, eyes wide, stricken with shock at what she had done. "Go, Spiff," she stammered. "Go!"

The Saureped looked at her once more, then sprinted away.

Bet stood, unmoving, her mouth dry, craving for moisture that wouldn't come. "What did I do? I, I… How?" She took a step toward the downed man. Had she killed him? She had to know. Her mind swam in circles of confusion, trying to make sense of what had happened. "How did I…"

The door of the carriage swung open with a bang, and a very large man stepped out. The vehicle rose, free of its burden.

Bet froze. The man, dressed in black like the others, stood at least seven feet tall. His torso looked like two halves of a barrel side by side. Black eyes, shadowed by a single bushy brow, stared at her, burning with menace. A long black beard rested against his massive chest, tapering into a knot tied with a red ribbon. He reached inside his long coat with both hands, pulling two wide and very deadly looking blades from beneath.

Bet stood for only a second longer. She had to get to the gateway. She didn't care if the river took her—drowning would be better than what the beast of a man had in store for her. She ran back to the rapids, not looking back. She didn't want to know. The river pulled at her. She didn't care.

Her foot found the slab of rock. She looked around. Nothing had changed, and the hulk was still coming toward her. She rubbed her foot on the stone, feeling the grooves of the etched runes beneath her, but still nothing happened. Her heart raced. The man was getting closer, moving faster, with arms wide, blades ready to slice.

A distant roar came from somewhere upstream. At first, Bet wasn't sure if it was real or imagined by her fear-stricken mind. A moment later she saw that it was very real. An enormous wall of water rushed toward her. The water transformed and began to spin, looking like a tornado resting on its side. She stole a glance at the man who looked at the approaching phenomenon. He sheathed his blades, then turned back toward the carriage, walking without any sense of urgency.

Bet watched the water. Its narrow tip widened, turning into a dark vortex. A small noise escaped her mouth. Anna hadn't mentioned anything like this. She clutched her bags, and the spinning wall of water struck her, and all she knew turned black.

Fourteen

Weightlessness. The sensation filled Bet's being. She tried to open her eyes, but her lids wouldn't budge. Something tight and uncomfortable wrapped around her waist and chest. She reached to loosen whatever bound her, but her arm dangled uselessly at her side. Cool, almost soothing wind caressed her face and tussled her hair. *I'm dreaming.* She remembered reading about lucid dreams where you could control what took place. Then she recalled telling Anna crossing the gateway was like dying. *Maybe I'm dead.* Her mind relaxed, and she fell back into unconsciousness.

Did she survive? It was the same discarnate woman's voice Bet had heard in her dream back at Malweather.

"Not dead."

"Not dead."

"Doesn't smell dead."

Bet heard the three voices and realized she was awake. The sensation of weightlessness was gone, and she was lying on something soft, yet firm. She stretched out her hand and felt a clump of plush grass. Her eyes fluttered open, but the brightness made her squeeze them back shut. Her head throbbed. She brought her hand over her eyes and opened them again. When she pulled her hand away, she saw three heads silhouetted against a bright blue sky.

Bet sat up quickly, making her head pound harder. Through her blurry vision, she saw that the three heads were attached to one body—a crow's body. But it was bigger than any Courser Eagle or Condor she had ever seen.

"Eyes are open," one head said.

"Sitting up," said the middle one.

"Time to go," the last said, and the crow began to hop away.

"Wait," Bet said, trying to stand but failing. "Who are you? Where am I?"

"You're there," the left head said.

"There," the two others repeated.

Bet shook her head. "I know I'm here," she said, patting the ground. "But where is here?"

The crow clucked. "The woods."

"The forest."

"The hinterland," they said, from left to right.

"I'm Her."

"I'm Gad."

"I'm Ishu," they said in the same order.

"My name's Bet," she said, getting to her knees.

"We know," the heads said in unison.

"You do?" Bet said, surprised by the answer. She was in an unknown land and this bird knew her. "Who else is here? I heard another voice."

"You did?" they said, and their heads swiveled around, looking about and at each other.

"Just you there."

"And me."

"Them and me and you."

Bet finally got to her feet.

"She's up," Her said.

"Gotta go," said Gad.

"Time to fly," Ishu said.

"Bye," they said together and took flight.

"No, wait!" Bet called. "Come back. Where—"

Her-Gad-Ishu ignored her, and Bet watched the huge crow disappear over the trees. She allowed herself a small curse and kicked at the ground.

Standing in a clearing surrounded by tall pines, Bet saw tall snowy peaks above the tree line of redwoods, firs, and strange shrubs resembling junipers with magenta foliage she had no name for. She could hear the calls of animals bustling through the forest she recognized as chipmunks and Flit-hoppers, while others were unfamiliar.

Bet was sure she had crossed the gateway, but she had no idea where she was. How was she supposed to find this Bathezine person if she was lost? Did he live in the mountains? And why had she been dumped in the forest? She guessed her weightlessness meant the crow had carried her here. Where had the crow found her?

She pushed the questions away. "Well I can't stay here," she said. She stretched, her throbbing headache beginning to ease, and started walking—to where, she had no idea.

Fifteen

Bet traveled down the mountainside for nearly an hour, passing through thick stands of trees and shrubs, when she finally caught sight of the horizon. Mountains as far as she could see, and a smoky haze hung over what appeared to be a valley. She hoped the haze came from an unseen mountain hamlet. She couldn't guess how far away it was. Fifty miles? More? She didn't have a clue.

A rumbling in her stomach persuaded Bet to check her bag for the food Anna had packed. She found a good sized rock to sit on, swung the bag to her lap, and hoped her encounter with river tornado thing hadn't soaked her bread to mush. She was happy to find it hadn't. Wrapped in what looked like a cheese cloth, the bread had stayed fresh and dry.

Bet sat, enjoying her meal, taking a few conservative sips of water from a flask that Anna had packed for her. She basked in the warm sunlight. It was a welcome change from the dreary cold and rain back home. As she sat, recounting the day's events, tiny movement near her, on the rock, caught her eye. She looked to find a lizard taking in the sun's energy, as well. "Hello there," she said. "Can you speak?"

The lizard opened its eyes and cocked its head at her. It did several quick pushups then sprinted back into cover.

"Guess not," Bet said. She packed her bag, and patted her pocket to reassure herself she still had the stone, unsure why Anna had thought it important enough to keep in a pouch. To her, it was a reminder of Pooch-kin and nothing more. She fought back the feelings of sadness at thinking of her friend as she headed across the glen to who knew where.

Pushing through thick undergrowth, up steep inclines and over ravines, and tripping over unseen obstacles buried in the forest litter started to take a toll on Bet's stamina. To make matters worse, the sky was turning from blue to orange and violet, ushering in impending nightfall, and she was nowhere nearer to any signs of civilization.

The warm air began to cool in anticipation of a cold night on the mountain. Bet had to stop for the night and find a way to build a fire. Finding a clearing between two redwoods, she began kicking and dragging away debris, exposing the soil beneath. Fine dust, kicked up by her work, elicited a sneeze, which startled a nearby Flit-hopper.

"Wish they'd come closer so I can ask where to go," she grumbled, gathering sticks and needles for fuel. Scouring the area, Bet found several chunks of granite to contain the fire.

With daylight fading fast, she rummaged through her bag, hoping to find something to aid her in her quest for fire. Finding nothing in the first bag, she looked through the satchel Harrelle had given her and immediately found a flint. The old man wasn't much of a farm hand, but he seemed to know how to be prepared. She put a small pile of pine needles on a rock in the center of her pit and started striking the flint. She struck at it repeatedly with no success. "Come on, it can't be this hard. Cave men started fires with less."

Determined to succeed, she struck again and a tiny spark jumped off, landing in the needles. It began to glow. "Yes," Bet shouted, celebrating her victory. The glow faded away. Bet groaned and tried again.

Several tries later, the needles caught, and she cupped her hands around the tiny ember and blew softly. The needles ignited. Adding small sticks, Bet nursed the fragile flame, putting ever larger sticks on until she had a full-fledged fire. Feeling accomplished, she leaned back and stretched her aching legs.

Staring at the fire, she longed to be back with Anna and Dalin, enjoying a good meal with good people. She retraced the events of the day until coming to rest on the inquisitor she'd struck with a rock. She tried to shake the image from her mind, but it hung before her, refusing to leave her sight. She had only wanted to protect Spiff, not kill the man. Bet tried to tell herself she hadn't killed him, but she couldn't see how he could've survived such a grievous injury. She closed her eyes, trying to free her thoughts by remembering the good times she had shared with Pooch-kin. Her heart began to ache again.

"Quit it," she said. "Focus on right now." Right now, she was alone and tired. She threw another round of wood on the fire and warmed her hands.

A muted snap of a twig pulled her eyes from the flame. A second snap forced her to pull her light from the bag. She hoped whatever had broken the silence was nothing more than a curious fox, or something as equally nonthreatening, but she didn't know what sort of creatures made this place home. She waved the light across the darkness. "Hello. Who's there?" she said, hoping for a friendly answer. No reply came.

She moved to a squat, squinting her eyes, hoping to catch sight of what lurked in the darkness. "Hello," she called again.

A pass of the light caught a glint of something. Her heart raced. She swung the beam back and saw the glowing green eyes of a Fangor.

Bet jumped to her feet.

The Fangor didn't move, its gaze resting steadily on Bet, who stood equally still. She swallowed hard. "Hello. I don't mean you any harm," she said in the calmest voice she could muster, remembering how the creatures were persecuted back home.

"Like you could do me harm," the Fangor growled, stepping into the light of the fire.

Bet gasped. She had never seen one up close, only their glowing eyes watching from the other side of the creek. The Fangor stepped closer, looking everything like a wolf, but with a hairless face and a tuft of wiry hair perched atop its head. Two long canine teeth hung over the bottom jaw, accounting for the creature's name. "I suppose you're right. I doubt I could do you much harm."

The Fangor pulled its head back, pointy dog ears standing erect. "You're one of them," it said, and began to slowly pace beyond the flame.

"One of what?" Bet asked.

"An Oragoth. You understand my speak."

"An Oragoth? I guess, but I'm new here and don't really know what that is."

The Fangor stepped closer, sniffing the air for a trap.

"It's okay. I don't have a gun or anything like that." She hoped her words would ease the creature's fear.

The Fangor lowered its head. "Only a fool announces she's defenseless while alone in the woods."

"I guess I'm a fool then. Though I never said I was defenseless," she said, eyeing a rock near the fire.

The Fangor stopped its pacing. "I suspect not. Why are you here, alone and so far away from your den?"

Bet's tension eased slightly. "I came through a gateway and was caught up in a flood. A big, three-headed crow, Her-Gad-Ishu, must've fished me out and dropped me farther up the mountain."

"Her-Gad-Ishu? The idiot probably meant to drop you in a den-town, but got lost or confused."

"I don't know. He didn't stick around long enough for me to judge him an idiot. But it seemed intentional." Bet sat down after determining the Fangor wasn't going to eat her. She hoped her assessment wasn't wrong. "My name is Bet. Do you have a name?"

The Fangor tilted her head. "You're different from the others. Most don't bother asking. They just run away."

"Well, you do have me at a disadvantage. But we all share the same world; might as well try to get along."

The Fangor let out a growl Bet took as amusement. "If you say so."

"I do," she said with a smile. She hoped to make a friend, or at least make well certain the Fangor wasn't going to make a meal of her. "So, do you have a name?"

"I'm called—" The Fangor let out a series of quick growls punctuated by a yip.

"I couldn't possibly pronounce that," Bet laughed. "How 'bout I call you…Tooth?"

The Fangor reared her head back. "That's stupid."

"Stupid? Why? It fits."

"How 'bout I call you Face, or Nose? That fits, too."

"You have a point. Toothy?"

"Worse," she growled.

Bet studied the Fangor, her eyes resting on the auburn shock of fur on its head. "Okay…Tuft. I like Tuft."

The Fangor seemed to consider the name. "If you must. Better than Toothy."

Bet laughed. "True. She leaned back against the trunk of the redwood. As she warmed her hands against the fire, she noticed Tuft become fidgety. "You don't like the fire?"

"That stuff will kill you."

"Nah, it's safe. If you're mindful." Bet put her hands closer.

"You don't live in the forest. Trust me, it can kill."

"I'll make sure it stays where it is."

"Be sure that you do," Tuft said, returning to sniffing the air.

"Do you think you can help me? I don't know where a town is, and I could really use a guide, someone who knows the terrain."

"No. We don't go anywhere near there. If you travel to the river, it will lead you there…eventually."

"Okay. Where's the river?" she asked, disappointed that Tuft wouldn't be her guide. She could really use the help and a traveling companion.

"Through the trees to the east, about a half a day's run. A full day for you. Be cautious. The woods are deep, and there are many dangerous things there. Stay near the water and you should survive."

The thought of a Fangor fearing to go there made Bet shiver. What could such a formidable creature have to fear? "Are you sure you don't want to lead the way?"

"No. There's an injured deer nearby, and I have a litter to feed. I must be going now."

Bet didn't like knowing the Fangor was going to make a meal of the hapless deer. "I wish you didn't have to eat the poor thing."

Tuft looked back at her. "If the plants were gone, the deer would starve. If the deer were gone, we would starve." She started to walk away.

"You don't want to stay a little longer?" Bet asked, looking around the surrounding darkness.

"Rest. Sleep. There's nothing nearby that will want to eat you," Tuft said, then ran off into the night.

"Thank you," Bet called out after Tuft had gone. She added more wood to the fire and hoped Tuft was right.

Sixteen

Something cool and wet pressed against Bet's cheek. She shifted in her sleep. Warm air tickled her ear and neck. She half-heartedly tried to brush the sensation away. Her hand touched something large and furry. Her eyes fluttered open to find an enormous head with big blue eyes staring at her. She let out a startled scream, sat up, and scooted away on her backside.

The huge lumbering creature stepped toward her.

Bet scanned her surroundings. The first rays of dawn cascaded over the eastern mountains, pushing a cold morning breeze through the trees. She looked at the Moon Bear. Its puffy white and yellow fur, and almost comically round head with equally round ears and stubby snout made it look like a cuddly stuffed toy, but she knew the creatures were very capable predators.

The Moon Bear got close enough for another sniff. "Quit it," Bet said. "I'm not food."

The bear's head tilted. "Smell like food," it said.

"Well, I'm not. Go find some berries or something." She scooted farther away, stood, and brushed the dust from her clothing.

The Moon Bear sat. "Where are the berries and something? I've never eaten a something."

"I'm sure you've eaten plenty of somethings," Bet said through a laugh.

"There's food in here," the bear said, sniffing at her bags.

Bet pulled the bags away. "That's my food. Go get your own." She decided that if the bear was going to eat her, it would've already done so.

"Smells good." The Moon Bear raised its padded paw toward the bag.

Bet jerked the bag back. Her shoulders slumped. "I'll tell you what. If I give you an apple, would you go find somebody else to beg from? I have a long journey ahead of me, and unless you're here to help me, you need to go." She pulled out an apple and tossed it to him.

The Moon Bear let the apple bounce off his face, then sniffed it and gobbled it up, crunching noisily. "Where are you going to journey?"

Bet pointed east. "That way. I'm headed toward the river and then I'm going to make my way toward town. Wherever that is. Do you want to show me the way?"

"I don't like that way. Not fun," the Moon Bear said, backing away as if it was a threat.

"I'm not here for fun. That's the way I was told to go, so that's the way I'm going."

"Who told you that way?"

"Tuft."

"Who's Tuft?" The bear sniffed Bet's bag again.

"He's a Fangor," she answered, swinging the bag behind her back.

"What's a Fangor?"

Bet let out a heavy breath. "You know, four legs, pointy ears, bushy tail, and long teeth." She put her fingers to her mouth, mimicking the Fangor's long canines.

"Oh! A toothy!" the Moon Bear said with excitement.

Bet closed her eyes and grunted while nodding. "Yes, a toothy."

"Watch out for the mushrooms," the bear said. He shook from head to stubby tail and walked away. "Gotta find a something."

Bet raised her eyebrows. "Good luck with that." She kicked at the ashes in the pit and buried them in dirt to suffocate any hidden embers. After double-checking for anything she might have left behind, she headed off in the opposite direction of the Moon Bear.

Seventeen

Bet traveled down the gradual mountain slope with as much speed as she dared. Before long, her path turned into a sharp descent. Clinging to trees and saplings, and the gnarled roots of gray-leafed pumice oak, she struggled to keep her footing. Hours passed in the difficult terrain, and still she neither heard nor saw any sign of the river. She had to wonder if Tuft had sent her this way so she could make an easier meal of her later. But she hadn't sensed any malice from the Fangor, and besides, it could've easily taken her while she slept.

She slid from tree to tree, with the thick forest the only barrier keeping her from a long tumble. Scooting to the next tree in line brought her to the edge of a steep drop-off. Bet peered over, spotting the exposed roots of the tree she clung to where the soil had eroded. She could see the tops of juvenile trees struggling toward the sunlight they would never reach, destined to languish beneath the canopy of the old growth forest. "Can't go that way," Bet said, skirting the edge, hoping an easier path would present itself.

Bet listened to the distant chatter of Flit-hoppers as they swung between the branches, gliding effortlessly as if mocking her difficulties. Every so often they would stop and watch her, never getting too close to the stranger in their woods. She tried talking to them, hoping that since the Moon Bear and Tuft had spoken to her in her language she would finally be able to communicate with one. But every time she tried, they flitted away out of sight.

Watching them, still jealous of their ability, she continued on until her foot met softer ground. She looked down, realizing her peril. It was too late. The loose ground gave way, taking Bet with it.

She fell ten feet, landing on a slope. Scrambling for a grip, Bet groped at a root to keep from falling farther. The root tore away, and she continued to tumble and roll down the steep incline, wildly grasping at small trees and dirt, anything her whirling vison caught sight of, to slow her momentum. Her unwanted acrobatics kept on until she finally crashed against an upturned tree stump. An angry swarm of Dart-birds flew from inside the dead tree, disturbed by the impact. They encircled Bet's head, chittering loudly, then flew away in search of a more peaceful abode.

"Sorry," Bet said, waving her apology. She stood, tried to shake the dizziness away, taking inventory of any injuries. Finding none, she took a step. The ground gave way again, and the tumbling resumed.

The rolling fall didn't last for nearly as long as the first bout, and didn't carry the same dramatic flair either, but the discomfort and injury to pride was no less impactful. Bet slid to a stop in the sitting position and moaned in disgust at herself. She looked back the way she had come, making certain she hadn't dislodged a boulder intent on braining her as a final insult. Seeing none, she stood, paying special attention to her footing.

Bet stood on the edge of a much deeper and darker part of the woods. The forest seemed louder. At first, she thought it was the humming of her dizzy head, until she realized the noise came from farther in the forest, sounding like rushing water. "Finally," she said, happy with the results of her unsolicited shortcut. She entered the dark copse without hesitation.

The pines and oak gave way to heavy clumps of bright green bamboo with their hollow stalks reaching high into the canopy. Bet tried to push her way through the unyielding clusters, but a few feet in she realized the futility of her efforts and retreated.

She circumnavigated the bamboo, eventually finding rocky ground where the plant couldn't grow. Happy to have solid ground under her feet, she hopped from rock to rock until at last she stood over the river twenty feet below. Before getting closer, Bet looked upstream, cautious of another flying eddy of water. With the day she was having, she wouldn't have been surprised.

"At least I found the river. Now to follow it for who knows how long," Bet mumbled to herself. She lightly climbed and hopped across the rocks, making a game of her task.

Her game grew tiresome after no more than twenty minutes, and the hopping turned to sluggish stepping. Coming to a sharp bend in the river, Bet ended her game altogether. She had walked to the edge of a ravine.

Peering into the ravine, watching the whitewater crash into the course-altering stone-faced gorge, she sat to ease her tired legs and take a bite or two of bread. While rummaging through the satchel, Bet pulled out the various vials Harrelle had given her. Each was marked with a symbol the old man hadn't bothered to explain. Bet wondered how he had got them, and how he had kept them hidden from Putrice.

Bet would have liked to take the potion that gave her strength and stamina again, but didn't know which was which. She was sure she could smell the carrot juice, but as the cork stoppers were sealed with wax, there was no smell. She didn't want to unseal them as she didn't want liquid leaking into her bag. Besides, for all she knew, they all had a carrot juice base.

She considered drinking one at random, but didn't know what its effects would be. It could be a sleeping potion—or worse, a love potion. Bet didn't want an amorous Moon Bear chasing her through the woods to add to her troubles.

Bet laughed at the thought and dropped the sturdy vials in the bag with a clink. She stood, stretching her soreness away, and resumed her rock hopping.

Eighteen

Bet walked as far as the rocks would allow before they became too narrow and steep to negotiate. Her only option now was to travel through the forest once again, a thought she didn't want to entertain, but she didn't have a choice.

It was past midday, there was still plenty of daylight left, but the woods seemed somehow darker. The branches of old growth pines hung low and listless, as if the years of standing firm and strong had taken their toll and gravity had won the battle. There was no bamboo, no colorful junipers, there were no colors at all, only dark, charcoal green fir and deep brown, almost black soil. A nervous chill crept through Bet's body.

The woods were filled with an eerie hush, an oppressive silence devoid of the slightest chatter of Flit-hoppers, squirrels, or birds. Even the sound of the river became muted. Only the crunching of Bet's careful footfalls and the occasional buzz of an insect disrupted the stillness. The silence was impossibly complete.

Bet kept Tuft's warning and the Moon Bear's refusal in her mind, and her eyes wide and unblinking, alert for any danger.

Each step seemed amplified in the gloom. If there were predators or unknown beasts lurking, she was sure they knew she was there. Bet moved as fast as she dared, prudence guiding her every stride. It wouldn't do for her to have another incident as before, not here. Regardless of her caution, she picked up the pace and knew at once it had been a mistake.

Somewhere, hidden from sight, she heard the rustling of forest litter. She stopped, and so did the noise. Bet stood, her legs feeling like iron posts stuck in the ground, cemented by fear, waiting for whatever hid in the shadows to show itself. Movement from somewhere behind her encouraged her legs to move again. She decided to head back to the river. She didn't care about the steep rocks. If she fell in, she would let the current take her the rest of the way and be done with this loathsome journey.

She made it no more than a few yards before movement ahead stopped her. The soft earth began to rise. A dome shaped object rose from the dirt, three feet in diameter, with red-orange, wrinkled nodes sporadically placed on the pale-yellow cap. As the thing grew taller, she saw blood red and brown gills beneath the domed head, resting on a large gray stem.

"A mushroom? I'm running from a mushroom?" Bet stood and watched as it continued to rise, standing at a full six feet tall. Long, milky white strands sprouted from the stem, reaching out and grabbing at the trees. The tendrils went taut and pulled the mushroom body closer to her. The Moon Bear's warning rang in Bet's head, and suddenly the bear's words made perfect sense. A shoot sprang from the ground in front of her, groping blindly toward her feet. The shock of what she saw nearly paralyzed her. "Run, you fool," she whispered.

More mushrooms rose from the earth, blocking her path to the river. She jumped over logs, zig-zagged through trees, dodging reaching tendrils, searching for an escape. Her only reprieve was the slow pace at which the mushrooms pulled themselves through the woods. But the sheer number of fungal filaments erupting at every turn made up for the difference in speed.

Bet tried once more for the river, but a webbing of strands blocked her path. A crosshatch of cilia grew to her left and right, and the pursuing mushrooms behind seemed to be trying to corral her forward. It was working. She had no choice but to continue that way.

She broke through a stand of sickly saplings and saw what awaited her. A mushroom, twice the size of the others, stood with tendrils outstretched. A thick ichor of umber ooze dripped from beneath the crown, as if salivating in anticipation of its meal. With nowhere to run, Bet stopped, fenced in, with no escape. The vine-like shoots blindly groped at the ground around her. "They must feel my footsteps. At least they can't see me…I hope."

The mushrooms behind her continued forward with a steady slide and drag. With no other recourse, Bet searched the ground for a rock, but none could be found. She spotted a broken branch as big as her forearm and snatched it up, and immediately began beating the nearest tendril, mashing it to a pulp. She eyed her nearest pursuer and drew back her arm. Letting fear and anger overcome her as it had at the river back home, she chucked the branch like a tomahawk at the beast. The branch lacked the velocity of the rock, but still had more force behind it than she thought possible.

Bet watched in satisfaction as the branch found its mark, splitting the mushroom cap in two. The thing exploded into a cloud of gray dust, then collapsed. A smile crossed Bet's face as the plume sprinkled down. "That's what you get," she said with a new-found confidence. But her confidence disappeared as quickly as it came. Everywhere the dust had landed, new, smaller mushrooms emerged from the earth. "Bad idea," she muttered, dancing away from more groping vines.

Bet tried to think. There was no escape through the webbing, but there had to be a way. "The trees!" she shouted a little too loudly at finding her salvation. Taking two long strides, Bet jumped, took a hold of the nearest low limb, and pulled up, hoping the branch would support her weight. The branch sagged, but held.

The fungus sprouts waved blindly in the air, unable to find their prey. The tendrils wrapped the trunk, spiraling upward, nearly as high as Bet's perch, but retreated when they came up empty. The probing arms disappeared into the soil, along with the mushrooms, leaving the webbing behind.

Bet suffered no illusions about the mushrooms giving up. She knew they were there, waiting just below the surface to snag her as soon as her feet touched the ground. She looked at the sky. Traces of orange highlighted against the blue and teal backdrop told her the day would soon be cast away.

"I can't sit in this tree for the rest of my life," she mumbled, frustrated at her predicament. She studied the next tree over. "But maybe…" Bet scooted farther along the branch, grabbed the closest limb of the next tree and pulled herself across. A light rain of pine needles fell to the earth. She waited to see if the mushrooms felt them. The ground roiled but nothing emerged. To test her theory that the creatures hunted by feeling vibrations, Bet plucked a pine cone and tossed it down. Several grabbers sprung up, felt around, then retreated. With her suspicions confirmed, she pressed on, moving from tree to tree through the dense forest.

With the sky transforming into a vivid sunset, Bet felt she had put enough distance between her and her pursuers. She cautiously climbed down. Placing her first tentative step on the ground, she waited to see if she had been noticed. Nothing came for her, and with daylight waning and having no idea how far she had ran from the river, she pulled out her light, threw caution aside, and started running at a solid pace.

The snapping of branches far behind her urged her on. Running while keeping a wary eye for any mushroom burst, Bet hammered forward, even as night began to fall. She finally came to a stop when confronted by an enormous fallen wall of a tree blocking her path. She pocketed her light and leapt on the side of the log to climb over. The decayed bark gave way beneath her feet and she fell back, landing flat on the ground. Retrieving her light, she looked either way down the length of the dead tree. Both ends disappeared into the darkness beyond her light's reach. Still sitting on the ground, she noticed a depression under the tree. She shined her light in the hole. It seemed to span the width of the twenty-foot-wide tree clear through to the other side. Not wanting to waste any more time, and with ever-creaking branches announcing the presence of advancing predatory mushrooms, Bet crawled in, scooting on her belly, hoping she hadn't made a fatal mistake.

Half way across, a whispered voice stopped her. "What are you doing in these woods, little monkey?"

Panic set in. Bet twisted back. "Who said that?"

"Me, of course. Who else?" The whisper came from above.

Bet rolled to her back, seeing only the rotted tree bark. "Where are you? Show yourself."

The bark parted lengthwise, revealing smooth wood beneath, opening and closing several times. "I am here. Where else could I be?"

Bet aimed her light directly in the parted bark, and it slammed shut. "Turn it away. I haven't seen such light in an age," the voice said.

Bet redirected her light. "My apologies," she said, baffled by what she was seeing. She examined the eye when it reopened. She had never seen such a thing, but then again, she had never seen killer mushrooms either. "I don't mean to sound rude, but I didn't know trees could talk. And to be honest, I didn't know you were alive."

"Thought I was dead because I've fallen, huh? Well, little monkey, that's what the beetles believe, too. You should know that a tree can live for a good while after falling."

Bet wasn't sure what to say to the old tree. "Well, now I know. Can other trees talk, as well? If so, they haven't said much."

The wood eye blinked. "Hah! Pines and firs don't talk. They are as mute as that nasty little bamboo weed. Tell me, little monkey, why are you here? These woods have become dark and dangerous."

"I'm actually not a monkey."

"So you say," the tree muttered.

"I didn't plan on being here, and I'd like not to be." The cracking of twigs brought her attention back to her task. "If you don't mind, I'd love to stay and chat, but those mushroom things have been after me most of the afternoon. I have to go."

"No!" the tree said. "It's too dangerous at night. You'll never see them coming. The Floragads are everywhere now."

"Floragads?"

"The mushroom things, as you call them. Aberrations, created for the war. Now they've gone feral in these parts."

"Well, I can't stay here." Bet looked the tree over, trying to determine where its mouth was.

"Crawl to the other side, go down a way. There's a hole where the beetles have eaten through. Climb in there. You'll be safe for the night. Go, go, their feelers are getting closer. And if you don't mind, smash a beetle or two hundred while you're in there."

Bet had no intention of killing anything unless it was a mushroom. She scurried out the other side and started searching for the safe haven.

"The other way," the tree said, sounding annoyed.

Bet threw up her hands. The talking tree hadn't been specific. She found a cavernous opening where rot and insects had eaten away at the tree. "Here?" she asked.

"Yes, yes. Hurry, little monkey. They're almost here."

Bet pulled herself up in a rush and fell into the hole, feeling the crunch of several insects beneath her. She shivered in disgust. "This is gross."

"I'd feel the same way if I crawled inside of your chest," the tree said, its voice sounding as near as it had when she was underneath the eye.

Bet shook and curled into a ball, trying to ignore the creeping interior.

"Don't go banging around like monkeys do. The Floragads can feel the vibrations."

"Yeah, I figured that out. Won't our voices attract them?"

"No, they feel your feetsteps."

Feetsteps? Bet ignored the grammar; she was talking to a tree, after all. "Speaking of, well…speaking. Where's your mouth?" The last thing she needed was to be tricked and eaten by a carnivorous tree.

"Mouth? Why would I need a mouth?"

"You know, to talk."

"Hmm," the old tree said. "I've never thought about mouths except for the beetles'. I don't need one. My voice is wherever I need it to be."

"Oh," Bet said, not really getting it. She guessed a tree wouldn't need one, as they got their nutrients from their roots and leaves. But then again, why would it need to see? "Then why do you need an eye?"

"Eyes are different," the tree said, not elaborating.

Bet didn't pursue the question. The next half hour was spent in silence, listening to the probing arms of the Floragads come and go, and nervously hoping the tree was right about her safety. She tried to relax as best she could, continuously brushing away investigating beetles. "Do you have a name?" she asked, trying to get her mind off the bugs and her predicament.

"A name? A name, a name, a name. Seems I did once, but the beetles have eaten away that part of my rings."

"Rings? You mean your tree rings?"

"Yes, yes, little monkey. Each ring within my body carries the memories of the year before. Soon, they'll eat my memory away, and all that I am will be no more."

"Then I guess I should smash a few more bugs for you."

"No, no. I was merely jesting, and would never truly ask you to do such a thing. The beetles and worms fed me from sapling and 'til I was felled. They nourished me with those who came before me. They are not to blame for the ravages of time. When they devour my rings, I will no longer care. We are all the sum of our memories."

Bet sat quietly, not sure how to respond. When the chitinous crawling became too much to bear, she continued the conversation. "Are there more trees like you?"

"I suppose there had to be, or else how could I exist? It seems there were, but just beyond this forest there is a great expanse of barren land, flattened by the war. I suppose if there were more like me, they may have died there."

The war again. For such a catastrophic event, there was very little she knew about it. "Who fought this war and why? And how did it start?" Bet hoped to finally get some answers. "Nobody talks about it where I'm from."

"The war? Who knows why men do such things. It is unique to their species, though others become involved. And it's a question I have no answers for. Makes little sense to me. The victors do nothing with those they kill. The Fangors, the Blue-hawks, they only kill what they will eat, as do the beetles. Indeed, it makes no sense. And I don't waste my time trying to understand why."

Bet shrugged. The nameless tree didn't seem to know any more than her, or if he did, he wasn't telling either. She moved on to more pressing matters. "Do you know how far it is to the nearest town?"

"That I couldn't tell you, curious little monkey. I measure distance in the passing of time, not distance traveled. But I suppose it would be many days, if you follow your course," the tree said, not disappointing Bet's lack of expectation. "There was once a town in the Waste. But I doubt that does you little good now."

"I'd like to get back to the river. I was told I could follow it to a town."

"Whatever path you choose, you should free yourself of these woods. But move quickly once you enter the Waste. The Floragads cannot enter the dead earth, but the region holds its own dangers for such a little monkey."

"Why doesn't that surprise me?" Bet wondered why Anna would send her to such a perilous land. But she was sure Anna hadn't counted on the stupid crow dropping her in the middle of nowhere. With a hundred more questions swimming in her head, but none she felt up to asking, Bet curled into a tighter ball and tried to rest until morning.

Nineteen

Bet popped her head out at the first gray light of dawn. Her sporadic sleep felt like no sleep at all. "Is it safe to go out now?" she asked, listening for any signs of the Floragads.

The old tree moaned and creaked as if waking from its own slumber. "Yes, yes, it is safe for the time."

"No killer mushrooms near, then?" She swung her cramped legs over the edge.

"Not near enough to cause you trouble," the tree said. "Though I can't say the same for the injured leaf deer who wandered in during the night."

Bet wondered if it was the same deer Tuft had been pursuing. She had rather the Fangor had taken it to feed her litter than the accursed Floragads. She extended a little more, letting herself drop softly to the ground. She stretched her aching body, surveying her surroundings. "The Floragads got the deer?"

"She will be digested and returned to the soil, as we all shall be one day."

Bet nodded. The thought made her think of Pooch-kin, and she felt anger well up inside, thinking of his fate.

"Your path is safe only for the moment," the old tree said, breaking Bet's thoughts. "Do not tarry any longer."

"Thank you for your help and company," Bet said and turned to leave.

She stopped and looked back at the tree. "I'll keep you in my memories."

The tree stayed silent for a moment. "Then I shall live many more days. Go now, and be safe, little monkey."

Bet laughed at the nickname and hurried off.

~~~~~

She reached the edge of the forest in no time, still brushing off the occasional beetle or two. Looking across what the old tree had called the Waste, she saw that the name fit, if not understated. The flat land stretched into the horizon, meeting what appeared to be low hills miles away. The gray, ashy landscape held nothing to fix her eyes upon. No trees, no ruined structures, nothing except the occasional spiral of dust devils broke the expanse. "What happened here?" she whispered, marveling at what could've caused the type of destruction presented to her.

The edge of the forest was exact, a perfect delineation between life and death. No scorched earth, the trees of the forest, whether fallen or still standing yet dead, cut as if perfectly sliced. Heeding the old tree's warning, Bet stayed close to the woods, not wanting to venture onto the powdery wasteland.

Not feeling up to running any longer, she strolled along, hoping to find the river soon. Her plan was that once she found the river, she would find a log and float the rest of the way. She wasn't in the mood for any more excitement. But it didn't take long for excitement to find her when a Floragad tendril reached out from the dark woods in a final attempt to snare a meal. Having no desire to contend with the mushrooms again, she ran farther into the Waste, safely out of reach. Bet found herself ankle deep in the powdery soil. She grunted in dismay. "If I ever see that crow again, I'll pluck its tail-feathers and make all three heads choke on them."

She trudged along, keeping a constant scowl on her face, no longer afraid of the Floragads; her fear had turned to annoyance at their persistence.

After a while, Bet pulled a piece of bread from her bag, tearing away mouthfuls angrily, stomping, and creating clouds of dust, warning any newcomers of her mood. She came to a stop when something ahead of her didn't get the hint.

The soft dirt roiled and squirmed. She knew it couldn't be the mushrooms; they would've taken her before now. "Now what?" She stuffed another bite in her mouth and prepared for whatever was to come.

Two yellow eyes, resting on long stalks, popped up from the dust, followed by another set to the side of the first. She reached into her bag, rummaging while keeping watch on the eyes ahead of her until she found the small knife Harrelle had packed. "If this thing tries to eat me too, I swear I'll cut off its eyes and be done with it."

The eyes retracted into the dust, and a flat head rose from the ground, supported by a gray and black spotted eel-like body. "Food!" the first one said.

The second rose beside it. "Food! It's mine."

"No!" said the first. "You got the last one."

"No, I didn't. You said the next was mine," said the second eel.

"No, I said the next was mine."

Bet watched the quarreling creatures, holding the knife between her and the two. "Neither of you are next," she shouted. "I'm not food!"

"Yes, you are," said the first.

"Yes, definitely food," echoed the second.

"No...I'm not," she said deliberately. "Go into the forest. There's a wounded deer in there for you to eat."

"Tricky thing," the first eel said. "We'll become food in there."

"I'll eat you first and then I'll see about the deer," the second eel said.

Bet waved her knife. "I'll cut your head off and feed what's left to that one," she said, motioning toward the other.

"Bleh!" exclaimed the first eel. "I'll not eat that."

"Then I'll cut off both of your heads and leave you to rot." She waved the knife at the pair.

"It wants a fight," the second eel said.

"It will cut off your head and then I'll eat it," said the first.

"No, it will cut off your head and then I'll eat it. My belly will be full for a month, and you'll have no head to eat with."

"No, you won't have a head and I'll eat it and everything else that comes in the Waste."

As the two eels argued over who got to eat her, Bet spotted a shadow. Looking up, she saw Her-Gad-Ishu swoop down.

Her took the second eel in its beak, tilted its head back, and swallowed the large eel whole.

"Hey!" the first eel cried. "That's my brother. You can't—"

Gad repeated Her's actions, swallowing the eel whole. Ishu watched silently.

Bet sheathed her knife and stuffed it back in the bag. "So, what? Have you come to put me back on the mountain?"

"Do you want to go back?" Her asked.

"You want to go back to the mountain?" asked Gad. Ishu stayed silent.

"No," Bet snapped. "I want to go to the nearest town and have a bath, and something to eat besides bread and apples, and use a proper toilet. I don't want to go back."

"All right," Her said.

"That's why we've come," said Gad. Ishu was still silent.

Bet looked at Ishu. Curiosity crossed her brow.

"You're not ready," Her said.

"Not ripe," said Gad.

"Not ready, not not ripe," Her said.

"Not ready, not ripe. Makes no difference," said Gad.

Bet looked at Ishu, who remained silent. "I don't know what you're talking about. Why is this one so quiet?"

Her and Gad looked at Ishu, who shook his head.

The two others raised their beaks at him.

Ishu lowered his head and spat a ball of feathers onto the dusty ground. "It followed you through the gateway. She said you would want it, but I wanted to eat it."

Bet looked at the wad of feathers covered with saliva and dust.

The small ball of feathers and muck shook, revealing floppy, hairy feathered ears and a wide stubby beak. "I thought that beast would be the end of me."

"Pooch-kin!" Bet screeched, falling to her knees. She snatched the Chook-chook up, hugging him as tight as she dared. "I thought you were dead. But you're not. You're here and you're not dead."

"I'm glad to see you, too," Pooch-kin said.

"I thought the old hag ate you. But you're really here, aren't you?" she said, setting him down.

"She nearly did, but I hid in the hay." Poock-kin shook, transforming his hairy feathers into the color of the dirt, though with so much dust already clinging to him, the effect was lost. "I can't say the rest of us fared as well."

Bet brought him to her lap, looking into his eyes. "I am so sorry. It was my fault. I fell ill with fever and I said things, and that horrible Putrice heard me. She—"

"Bet," Pooch-kin interrupted her. "My friend, it was inevitable. It would've happened eventually. That's why we were there. That's why most of the animals were there."

She wiped him down, removing most of the muck. "I know. But I was supposed to protect you. I failed."

"No. You did more than most would ever think of doing."

Bet nodded. She watched him, unable to erase her smile. "It's been a rough few days for me here. So much has happened. But I just can't tell you how happy I am to see you." A tear rolled down her dirty cheek, leaving a slightly lighter trail behind.

Pooch-kin warbled, nuzzling his beak against her hand.

"It's weird. Since I crossed over, every creature I've spoken to talks. Well, talks like me. Or at least that's how they sound. You too. I used to hear your chirps, and I understood you, but now you don't chirp."

Pooch-kin tilted his head. "You still sound the same to me."

Bet stared at her friend, stroking his ears. She looked around and stood, still holding the little Chook-chook, who didn't object. "We should get moving. It's not safe here." Standing nose to beak with Her-Gad-Ishu, she raised her eyebrows. "Well?"

"Well what?" Her said.

"Well, well," said Gad.

"What well?" Ishu followed up.

Bet looked away, shaking her head. "Where are you taking us? You said I wasn't ripe, whatever that means."

"Illguard," Her squawked.

"Napeville," Gad said.

"Fiverton," Ishu cawed.

Bet watched the heads argue for a minute. "They're really quite tiresome," she said to Pooch-kin.

"And their breath isn't so fresh, believe me," Pooch-kin said.

"I should have eaten you," Ishu said, taking a break from the squabble.

"I would have torn your stomach out had you tried," Pooch-kin said, glaring at the talking head.

"Are you taking me somewhere, or should we continue toward the river?" Bet interrupted.

"Illguard," Her said, shooting a warning glare at the others. "That's what she said."

"Who said?" Bet asked.

"The purple one," Her answered.

"Violet," said Gad.

"Lavender," followed Ishu.

"Stop!" Bet demanded before the trio started arguing again. "Who is she?"

"The one who watches you," the trio of heads said in unison.

Bet looked at Pooch-kin. "I'm really tired of vague answers."

"Lay down," Her said.

"On your stomach," said Gad.

"Put that in your bag," Ishu said, motioning toward Pooch-kin.

"Sorry, my friend," Bet said, opening her bag. "It's cramped, but I'm sure it's better than riding in his beak again."

"Anything is better than that stink," Pooch-kin said, drawing a glare from Ishu.

"Now go to sleep," the three said, followed by a low clucking noise.

"But I want to…see…the," Bet's eyes grew heavy and her head slumped. She felt the firm grip of the crow's feet, grunted softly, then fell into a deep slumber.

Twenty

Bet dreamed angrily. She was aware she was dreaming and fought to wake up, upset over being put to sleep by the stupid crow and its stupid crow noises. She dreamed of plucking a crow and tossing its naked pink featherless body into a river. But the dream held images of a woman's face with varying shades of violet skin and narrow eyes so bright and white, they glowed. Shimmering silver hair hugged the contours of her cheeks, and a simple blue sack of a hat sat on her head, contrasting with the woman's elegant appearance. The images had a calming effect, but the discomfort of the Her-Gad-Ishu's grip transcended reality to unconscious dreaming, and the images shifted back to plucking a crow.

Bet's dreams ended when she felt the hard ground beneath her, followed by the sound of a series of cackles from the crow. Her eyes fluttered open, and she tried to rub the bleariness away. Bet sat up, still feeling groggy, and also the beginning of another headache.

"She's awake," Her said.

"Awake," said Gad.

"Wakey, wakey," Ishu said lastly.

"Don't ever do that to me again. Whatever it was you did," Bet snapped.

"She's angry," Her said.

"Upset," said Gad.

"Livid," Ishu followed up.

"You bet I'm—"

"Time to go," Her-Gad-Ishu interrupted and took flight.

"Wait! Where are we?" Bet called out, but the bird flew too quickly to answer her questions.

Bet surveyed her surroundings. She sat beside a dirt road lined with oaks and pines. The sky held the last traces of daylight; it would be dark very soon.

She unfastened the flap on her bag, freeing Pooch-kin. "Did you sleep, too?"

"No," Pooch-kin said. "Though I wish I could have rather than listen to those three heads babble on. Consider yourself lucky."

Bet stood, rubbing her throbbing head. "I wonder where we are."

"Near Illguard, if the three of them combined for a coherent thought, that is. It's this way." Pooch-kin headed west up the road toward the final remnants of day.

"Did I... Did I kill that man back near Raisin Town?" she asked as they walked along the rutty road. The worry had been with her since it'd happened, and she feared the answer.

Pooch-kin looked up at her, not saying anything right away. "No," he finally said. "But he would've killed you and the Saureped. You did what needed to be done."

"Still doesn't make it right. How do you know he wasn't dead?"

"The other two helped him to the carriage, then they headed south at speed. After tearing down the posts, that is."

Bet felt a pang of guilt knowing the gateway was gone, and so making it harder for Anna to escape if she needed to.

The rest of the journey was spent with Bet recounting her adventures. Pooch-kin was impressed she had survived. A thought occurred to Bet.

"How did you get here?"

"I don't know. I arrived at the home of the Oragoth, and the next thing I remember I was at the river. I hid during your fight, then the Saureped carried me to the gateway, though I nearly drowned in the process."

"That water tornado-vortex thing is a little rough, huh?"

Pooch-kin looked at her, puzzled. "I don't know what you mean."

Bet stopped and squatted down. "You mean nothing swept you away?" Her brow wrinkled in her confusion.

Pooch-kin shook his head. "No. I stepped on the rock, and then I appeared on a large flat paver on the edge of a great city made of blue stone. That's when that stupid crow snatched me up and carried me to you."

"That's strange. I thought the gateway disappeared after somebody used it. Maybe it's different for everybody," Bet said, though she wasn't convinced by her reasoning.

Twenty-One

They came to the outskirts of Illguard, a small hamlet consisting of log and stone buildings, not unlike Raisin Town. Warm amber light shone through the windows of nearly every building on the row. Bet wondered which establishment to ask for directions and help first. A two-story structure in the center of town seemed to be the best choice. "We'll try to find a place to stay there," she said to Pooch-kin, pointing down the lane.

Horses, Riding Elk, and a muscular, armored Rhinodon were tied to the hitching post outside the building. She said hello to the animals, who returned the greeting with various noncommittal grunts.

Bet stepped on the wooden walkway, looking at the long wood sign with the words Handover's Dining Inn in bold, burned in lettering.

"Your Chook-chook should wait outside," a baritone voice said as she reached for the door.

Bet turned and looked at the speaker, a curly antlered Riding Elk. "Excuse me?"

"The Chook-chook. They might think he's dinner in there," the elk said.

Bet looked at her small friend. "Do you want to wait outside or…" she held up the bag.

Pooch-kin looked at the surroundings. "I'll take my chances in the sack, thank you."

Bet picked him up and gently placed him in the least crowded bag. She grabbed the brass handle of the finely polished door, and entered.

She was greeted by warm air and a bouquet of delicious aromas. Music played over the din of people enjoying conversation and meals. Bet looked around, noting the patrons varied from humans of a multitude of sizes and colors to species she had never seen or heard of. Some had rat-like heads, while others looked like bipedal sheep. One caught her eye in particular: a very large creature who looked like a cross between a man and a bear. The music, performed by a trio of bulbous-eyed creatures playing a zither, a banjo, and bongos, had an upbeat but smooth tempo.

"Can I help you?" a voice said from behind Bet, pulling her from her wonderment.

She looked up to find a tall man with flawless light blue skin, wearing a bellman's hat, smiling at her. Raucous laughter erupted from a group of men and feathered people playing a dice game at a nearby table. Bet smiled at the players' laughter then turned her attention back to the man. "Um, yes. I could really use a room and a bowl of vegetable soup, if you have a vacancy, that is."

The man's smile broadened. "I do believe we have a room available. Step this way," he said, leading her to a fine mahogany reception desk. He opened the registry, dragging his finger down the list. "Where are my manners? Allow me to introduce myself. I'm Errel Handover, proprietor of this establishment. And you are?" He stood, holding a fancy quill pen.

"Bet. My name is Bet."

"Do you have a secondary name?"

Confused by the question, Bet guessed he meant a surname. The only last name she had ever known was Malweather, but she refused to accept a reminder of that horrible woman. She thought of her recently discovered last name of Clarenhart, but she wasn't sure if she should use it, with them having been convicted of crimes back home. "Just Bet."

"Okay, Bet. How will you be paying?"

"Um," she said, reaching into her bag, avoiding Pooch-kin and finding the pouch of coins Anna had given her. She pulled out a shiny bronze coin, holding it up. "Is this enough?"

Errel raised an eyebrow. "It's a good down payment if you intend to buy this place from me. Do you have anything smaller?"

"I'm sorry. I'm not from around here." She pulled out a silver slug. "Is this better?"

Errel Handover eyed her. "How long do you plan on staying?"

"I don't know yet. Tonight, for sure. Maybe longer."

Errel held up the coin. "This will cover you for several nights and all of your meals. I'll refund the difference if you decide to check out sooner. Sign here." He spun the registry around and Bet signed. Errel grabbed a key from the wall. "I'll put you in room two twenty-two. It has all the comforts of home."

"Home wasn't very comfortable. I'm sure it'll be better," Bet said with a smile.

Errel smiled and stepped from behind the desk. "This way." He led Bet through the eating area and up the stairs. "You're a recent arrival. It's been a while. I don't seem to remember there being a gateway anywhere nearby."

Bet shrugged. "It's a long story," she said, without elaborating.

"Here we are. Room two hundred twenty-two." He opened the door and turned on the lights, revealing a large living space with a plush burgundy sofa and a fireplace on the back wall.

Bet stared in wonderment. The front room alone was bigger than the whole of the Malweather house.

"The bath and sleeping quarters are through here." Errel opened the bedroom door, and Bet spotted a large and very comfortable looking bed. "Would you like a fire?" he asked.

"Oh yes, please. Thank you."

Errel went to the fireplace, placed three rounds on the rack, rubbed his hands together, and a fire sprang to life. "I trust you will want to bathe before dining."

"I would like that very much," Bet said through a travel-weary voice.

"Very good. Place your soiled garments in the basket outside the door. I'll have them laundered and returned to you by morning. Is there anything else you'll be needing?"

"A tall glass of your finest water," Bet laughed.

Errel smiled. "The kitchenette is to your left," he said, pointing.

"Thank you. Thank you so much."

"My pleasure," Errel said. "Ring the bell if you require anything else. Your dinner will be brought to you shortly."

"If you don't mind. I don't eat meat of any kind," Bet said.

"As I suspected," Errel said, looking at the bulge in her bag.

Bet's face reddened. "Thank you," she said with a guilty smile.

Errel nodded and exited.

Twenty-Two

Bet opened the bag to set Pooch-kin free as soon as the door clicked shut. "I'm hungry, too," he said before his feet touched the floor.

"I'm sure you are. Food will be here soon enough, but first, it's time for a bath."

"All right. I'll wait for you by the fire."

"Nope. You first," she said, reaching for him. "You smell like crow spit."

"It's fine. I don't smell it anymore," he said, squirming in her grip.

"But I do. Your stink will attract every Wood Rat and Pucker-bug in the region thinking something died in here," she said, struggling to hold the protesting Chook-chook.

"I'll eat the Pucker-bugs, but I can do without the rats."

"It'll be quick. We don't want to offend our host with the smell."

"You're one to talk," he said, resigning himself to the impending scrub down as Bet carried him to the bath.

"That's why you're going first. I don't want your stink on me after I bathe."

Bet gave her friend a good washing in a tub made of polished ebony stone. Pooch-kin did his best to act like he hated it, but Bet knew he was enjoying his bath. After partially drying him with a fluffy towel, she sent him to continue drying near the fire.

Bet stood watching the water fall from the brass shower nozzle and smiled, feeling like she was in her own private castle. Never had she seen such luxury. "Maybe we'll stay for more than one night."

After a long shower, Bet wrapped herself in a soft, warm robe and stepped into the front room to find Pooch-kin nestled on a pillow on the sofa. She went to the door with her travel-stained clothing and stuffed them in the waiting basket, making sure she had emptied her pockets this time. As she did so, she saw Errel pushing a silver cart down the hall, carrying several covered dishes.

"Perfect timing," he said as he approached.

Bet held the door, and hurried to the table behind Errel. Her host began laying out the settings, then pulled out a chair for Bet to sit. He spooned a healthy amount of soup from the crockery, uncovered a plate of bread, explaining the sweet meal bread was famous in the region, and placed a small, covered silver bowl to the side.

"This," he said, tapping the bowl with a spoon, "is not for you."

"Thank you again. You're too kind."

Errel smiled. "Will there be anything else?" he asked, motioning for her to dig in.

"I feel kind of guilty for asking, but do you have any deserts?" She cringed, fearing she was asking too much.

Errel looked at her out of the corner of his large gray eyes, pursing his lips. "Hmm, deserts. We do have an excellent butterscotch pudding. Will that suffice?" he said, the corner of his mouth raising to a smile.

"Suffice?" Bet exclaimed. "That's my absolute favorite. It's like you read my mind."

Errel laughed. "Reading minds is not my particular Talent, though it would be helpful at times. But a burden I wouldn't want. I'll bring your pudding before long," he said, excusing himself.

"Thank you," Bet called out. Errel bowed as he exited the room.

Bet grabbed a spoon, but curiosity got the better of her. She pulled the lid off the dish not designated for her, and smiled at the contents of meal worms resting on a bed of corn kernels, rice, and various grains. "Pooch-kin. Dinner is here."

Pooch-kin lifted his head. His burgundy feathers transformed back to their natural flaxen color, and he made a dash for the table.

Bet placed him on the table and pointed to the bowl with her spoon. "I believe that's for you," she said, removing the lid once again.

Pooch-kin looked at his banquet and eagerly plunged his beak in without saying a word.

Bet and Pooch-kin were enjoying their meal when Errel knocked and opened the door. "Pudding is ready." He walked to the table and looked at Pooch-kin. "A Chook-chook? I thought I smelled a crow."

Bet choked a laugh. "You're not far off the mark after what he went through."

"I trust it's part of your long story?" Errel said.

"It is," Bet said, smiling at Pooch-kin, who turned his attention back to the remaining morsels of grain.

"Perhaps someday, when you both have the time, you can tell me of your adventures. I'll transcribe them for posterity. I was quite the scribe in my youth."

"Youth?" Bet said. "You're what, thirty years old? That's not old."

Errel laughed. "Then I'd still be a child. I'm three hundred and sixteen years old. Middle age for most Andolans."

"Three hundred and sixteen? Wow! Wait, you're not human?"

Errel chuckled again. "The blue skin didn't give it away?"

"I just thought, you know, people came in all colors here. In this realm, I mean," she said, feeling a little embarrassed.

"Oh, they do. Humans generally range from pinkish white to deep brown. Andolans come in every color in the prism, depending on the region they hail from."

"Oh. I hope I didn't offend you."

"No, not at all. But you do have much to learn. I take it you didn't learn much of the Whist while living in the Din?"

"Whist and Din? I don't know what they are."

Errel patted Bet's shoulder. "The Whist and the Din describe the two realms. The Din call us Users. Users of what, I don't know. Probably sorcery or some other nonsense. You, us, our minds are still, relatively quiet, and we are in tune with our Talents. Those of the Din are concerned with fortunes, conquest, and greed, which makes the mind incapable of hearing what the earth has to offer. Not all in the Din are concerned with such things, same as not all in the Whist are disinterested in them, but their lineage prevents the ability. Does that make sense to you?"

Bet shrugged. "I guess so. From my experience, I'd say it's close to accurate."

Errel looked at Pooch-kin, who was cracking the last seed of his meal. "Was your meal satisfactory? It was a rather generic dish as I've had only so many avians as guests."

"It was a good meal. Thank you," Pooch-kin said.

Errel looked to Bet for a translation.

Bet stared at Errel for a moment until she figured what he was waiting for. "Oh. Yes. He said it was good and he thanked you. You don't understand him?"

"No. Like I said, we each have our own Talents. If you end up staying for a while, I can tell you what I know, or what you should know."

"I'd like that," Bet said as Errel turned to go. "Do you know about the war?"

Errel stopped and forced a smile. "I do. But I lived on the other side of the Maltese Seas for the duration and only have second-hand knowledge. That, like your story, is long, as well."

"Okay," Bet said, sounding disappointed, and again hoping she hadn't overstepped her bounds.

"Is there anything else before I take my leave for the night?"

Bet thought for a moment, looking to the ceiling. "Just one thing. I was told to seek someone out when I got here. Though I don't know where to start looking. They said his name is Bathezine. Do you know of him? Or know someone who would?"

Errel stood looking at Bet, his face losing emotion. "Are you certain of the name?" he asked stiffly.

Unsure of his reaction, Bet hesitated. "I believe so. Do you know of him?"

Errel forced a quivering smile. "Perhaps," he said, then excused himself rather quickly.

Bet watched the door close, then looked at Pooch-kin. "That was weird. What do you suppose that was all about?"

Pooch-kin shook his head. "Maybe he knows him and doesn't like him. Or maybe he's dead and doesn't want to tell you. Or maybe he's thinking of someone else. Don't worry about it too much. If everything you told me about Anna and Dalin is true, I doubt they'd send you here to meet a mad man or a criminal."

Bet nodded, her forehead wrinkled with concern, knowing her own parents had been considered criminals. "I guess you're right. But," she looked at the bowl of butterscotch pudding. "Nothing I can do about it right now." She helped Pooch-kin from the table, grabbed the bowl, went to the sofa, and sat watching the fire.

She freed her mind of any troubles and worries, enjoying her treat. Her eyes grew heavy, and the thought of the big comfortable bed tugged at her. Bet placed the bowl on the end table, and gathered Pooch-kin, who was already fast asleep. She wrapped herself in the robe, made sure the Chook-

chook was comfy on a pillow beside her, and let her body sink into the soft mattress and pillows, falling asleep in an instant.

Twenty-Three

The clank of a dish made Bet's eyes flutter. In her dream, she was caring for various animals on a ranch set against low hills, blanketed by grass of violet and green. Another clink of a dish, and she found herself back at Malweather standing in front of a sink full of plates and bowls, covered in days-old food. A third clink, followed by the sound of heavily protesting springs, woke her. She looked around and watched the shadows, cast by the fire from the front room, dance across her open bedroom door. She checked on Pooch-kin, who was still sound asleep.

Scraping against the dish from the other room made her sit up, heart racing. "Pooch-kin," she whispered, nudging her friend awake. "Someone's in the other room."

Pooch-kin lifted his head. "Can't you go more than a few hours without something trying to kill you?"

"That's not much help," she said with a frown.

The scraping of the dish and the creaking sofa continued.

"Come on," Bet said, swinging her legs over the bed and cinching her robe.

"It sounds big. How am I supposed to help? Should I hope to choke it when it swallows me whole?"

"Just come with me," she said, grabbing a small vase off the nightstand. She got up and crept to the door. As she drew closer, she could hear noisy slurping coming from the darkness. Whatever wild creature had gotten in was enjoying her leftovers. She peered around the doorway and muffled a gasp. A very large creature sat on the couch, holding the bowl to its mouth, finishing the remnants of her pudding.

Bet ducked back. "Okay," she said, trying to stay calm. "You saw what I did to the inquisitor, and I got this." She held up the vase.

"I think you should join me in hiding under the bed until it leaves," Pooch-kin said, then darted away.

Bet growled. She peeked around the corner. The creature was lowering the bowl from its face. Bet recognized him as the bear-like man she had seen earlier sitting near the band in the dining hall. Firelight flicked off the flat nose at the end of his hairy muzzle. His long mustache quivered as he sniffed the air. It was now or never. She sprung out and hurled the vase, hoping not to kill the intruder, but at least stun him until she rang for help.

Without looking, the bear-man extended a large paw of a hand and snagged the speeding projectile from the air. "This, little child, is a priceless artifact from the Kingdom of Halthecia. You could've broken it," he grumbled and gently set it on the side table.

Bet's eyes widened at the effortless catch. Suddenly regretting not taking Pooch-kin's advice, she turned and ran back to the bedroom.

"Oh, now just you wait. I'm not going to hurt you."

Bet didn't listen. She dove to the floor, snatching the bag that held her knife in the process. Crawling under the bed, she spotted Pooch-kin, who had changed color to match the wood flooring. "Distract him," she panted. "I'll make for the bell to call for hel—" She felt a large paw grab hold of her ankle and drag her from under the bed. Bet groped at the smooth floor, helpless to stop the attack.

The bear-man lifted her by the foot, dangling her upside down. "I said I ain't gonna hurt you or your bird. I coulda done that while you slept." He tossed her on the bed and lumbered toward the light.

Bet landed with a bounce and scrambled away, putting the bed between herself and the intruder. "Who are you? What do you want?"

He switched on the light. The bear-man looked even more intimidating up close. Bet couldn't decide if he was more bear or man. Short brown and gold hair covered his head and snout, and his shaggy white mustache and beard held traces of the leftover pudding. She watched him with caution as he stepped to the doorway. His seven-foot frame filled the entry. His arms and chest looked very human, but twice the size of any man she had ever seen, save the black-bearded inquisitor. His muscular, slightly hairy arms stuck out from a sleeveless green tunic, and spotty beige pants covered stout legs ending in distinctly bear-like feet.

He looked at her with brown round eyes highlighted by yellow irises. "Name is Bathezine. You were askin' about me."

Bet's eyes widened. "Bathezine? You're the one Anna wanted me to find?"

Bathezine snorted. "Anna? I remember Anna. She was 'bout your age, maybe younger the last time I saw her. An Oragoth like yourself. She stayed in the Din after the war to care for her family. She sent you?"

"Helped me escape more than sent," Bet said, relaxing slightly.

Bathezine went to the sofa and resumed his investigation of the bowl. "Inquisitors after ya?"

Bet followed him. "Yeah," she said and sat on the arm of the sofa, keeping her distance. "I almost didn't make it. They were going to kill me."

"Kill you? Usually they catch, convict, then kill." He gave up on finding any more traces of pudding and dropped the bowl back on the table.

"Well, I sorta almost killed one of them." Bet suddenly found the fire very interesting.

"Humph," Bathezine snorted. "That'll do it." He cocked his head. "How'd a girl your size almost kill one of them?"

"One of them was going to shoot Spiff—"

"Who's Spiff?"

"The Saureped. He gave me a ride to the gateway. I got scared… mad.

Really mad, and threw a rock at the man. I hurt him…badly." She lowered her head and turned away.

Bathezine raised his shaggy gold eyebrows. "That's some throw. Glad you didn't hit me with the vase."

"Yeah. I'm sorry about that. But you did break into my room. After all that's happened the past couple of days, I thought you were another creature trying to get me."

Bathezine studied the fire. "Oragoths usually don't have that kinda strength. Have you done it since?"

"Yesterday." Bet scratched her head. "I think it was yesterday. I threw something at a Floragad. But they were definitely trying to eat me."

"Floragad? What were you doin' out near the Waste? Better yet, how'd you get there? That's a long way from Azural."

"I was trying to get here."

"From Azural?"

"I don't know anything about Azural. When I stepped on the runes, a wave… Well not really a wave, more like a funnel of water hit me. I blacked out. I woke up when Her-Gad-Ishu put me down in the mountains."

"Her-Gad-Ishu? That idiot crow? How'd he end up with you?"

Bet shrugged. "I don't know. Like I said, I blacked out. It's all been rather confusing since I got here. They did find me in the Waste, though. They said something about the purple lady saying I wasn't ripe. Then they took me to the edge of town."

The hair on Bathezine's hackles bristled. "Purple lady? Curious," he said, and returned his attention to the fire.

Bet spotted Pooch-kin poking his head out from the bedroom. "It's okay. This is the one I was looking for."

"I figured that out," Pooch-kin said, keeping his distance.

Bathezine ignored the Chook-chook. "This is all very unusual.

Remember this: do not use your Talents in anger. It can lead you to a place you don't wanna go."

"Anna said something similar. What does that mean?" Bet asked, worry creeping into her voice.

"No more questions tonight," Bathezine said abruptly. "We have a long journey ahead of us in the morning. Ursians need their sleep, just like young humans do." He stretched out on the sofa, resting his head on the arm opposite the one Bet was sitting on.

"But," Bet began.

"Turn off the light on your way to bed," he said and almost immediately began to snore.

Bet stared at the sleeping Ursian. "Come on, Pooch-kin. I guess I'm done here." She got up and headed for her room.

"Light," Bathezine said between snores.

Bet rolled her eyes and went back to shut off the light. She headed to bed, closing the door behind her. "Let's try to get some sleep," she said, putting Pooch-kin on the bed.

"You can sleep with that vicious predator out there?" Pooch-kin said, watching the doorway. "You don't even know if he's who he says he is."

"You're right. I don't know. But he seems pretty straightforward. And all I want to do is sleep." She fell onto the bed. "Besides, I think we're safe as long as he doesn't think we're pudding."

"Still, I think I'll sleep under here tonight," Pooch-kin said and crawled under the covers. Less than a minute later he scrambled out, panting with his beak open wide. "How do you sleep under such suffocating things?"

Bet rolled to her side and pulled the blanket to her chin. "Like this. Goodnight, my friend."

Twenty-Four

Bet woke up to the sound of Errel and Bathezine arguing in the front room. "Now what?" she said, tying her robe.

"You should've rang," Errel said when Bet entered the room. "He violated our strict policy and entered uninvited."

"I wasn't uninvited. You said she was lookin' for me," Bathezine said, still stretched out on the sofa.

"Its fine, Mister Handover," Bet said through a yawn. "He gave me quite a start, but it's okay, really."

Errel frowned, while looking at the lounging Ursian. "If you insist. And please, call me Errel." He snapped his fingers. A maid entered the room and began clearing the dirty dishes. "What will you be having for breakfast? We have a wonderful apple turnover, served on a bed of crispy potatoes, lightly sugared."

"Ooh! I'll have seven," Bathezine said, handing the maid the bowl he had licked clean.

"I didn't ask you," Errel said with a heavy breath.

"Just put it on my bill," Bet said, shaking her head. "The turnover sounds great. And if you have any oatmeal, I'd appreciate that as well."

"We do. Would you like maple and cinnamon added, as well?"

"I would! And a touch of brown sugar, if you have any," Bet said.

"We do. From the cane fields of Downy," Errel said, sounding exceptionally proud. "I placed your laundry on the credenza." He followed the maid out.

"Thank you," Bet said, then turned to Bathezine after the door shut. "You seem to enjoy antagonizing him."

"Andolans and Ursians don't mix well."

"And your boorish behavior doesn't help," Bet said, spinning on her heel back toward the bedroom.

"Neither does his snootiness. Andolans were the architects of Azural. They act like the rest of the world owes 'em."

"He's been nothing but kind to me. So I'd appreciate it if you would try to be…nice."

"Nice? Haven't I been nice?" Bathezine said, sitting up and resting his head on the back of the sofa.

"Hmm. Let me see. You broke into my room, ate the rest of my pudding, and hung me upside down."

"That makes you a friend in Ursian culture."

"Remind me to never visit your home, then. I doubt I'd survive." Bet looked in at Pooch-kin, who was still sleeping despite the ruckus. She went to sit at the table.

Bathezine growled. "Go take care of your morning business and get dressed. We leave after breakfast."

"I'll wait until Errel brings the food. I want to make sure you don't eat it all."

"You should go now. You don't wanna wait 'til after I'm done. Humans are easily offended. Especially those from the Din."

Bet let out a long breath. "Fine. But be nice if Errel gets back before I'm done."

"How am I supposed to act nice?"

"I don't know. Smile or something." She grabbed her clothes from the credenza and headed to the bathroom.

Bet returned fully dressed, with her bags packed, ready to face the next adventure, just as Errel returned pushing a cart with several dishes. "It smells delicious. Thank you," Bet said with a smile.

"You've given me enough thanks to last a lifetime. Now, no more of that. It's my pleasure," he said. "But you are welcome."

Bathezine finally got up from the sofa and stood near the table, bearing his teeth, with his upper lip quivering, making his droopy mustache twitch.

Errel looked at the Ursian, then back at Bet. "What's with him?"

Bet raised an eyebrow at the Ursian's best imitation of a smile. "He…he has to use the restroom."

Errel raised his hands, then dropped them to his side. "You're free to do so. Our plumbing should be up to the task."

Bathezine's forced smile faded back to his natural state. "There'd better be something to read in there. I'll be a while."

"Charming," Errel said and began to set the table. "Will your little friend be joining you?"

"He had a hard night. I thought it best to let him sleep." Bet sat at the table, taking in the spread. Her broad smile faded. "I sure could've gotten used to this."

Errel's mouth compressed into a forced smile. "I take it you'll be leaving, then?"

"After breakfast," Bet said through a long sigh.

"I'm sure the… Bathezine will guide you well. He knows these parts far better than most. Despite his abrasive nature, I believe he has a good heart and will watch over you well until you find your way."

"I hope so. This place has been, I don't know, challenging, I guess you'd say."

"The wilds can be trying even for those who know the land. There is good and bad in everything. The trick is to be aware of the bad and seek the good."

Bet nodded. What Errel said was true. She had found Pooch-kin at Malweather, making a bad situation much better. Even the Old Man had shown some hints of good in the end. Whether it was selfishly motivated or not, she wasn't sure. The Fangor proved to be a help, as had the fallen tree. Anna and Dalin definitely were on the good side of things, along with Bathezine and Errel. Her-Gad-Ishu, she classified as decidedly neutral. For better or worse, good or bad, this was her life now, and it was far better than what she had known on the other side.

Just then, Pooch-kin hurried out of the bedroom. "Something awful is going on in the bathroom. Terrible noises, and the smell… I believe something is being butchered alive in there."

Bet shook her head. "It's only Bathezine."

Errel walked to the bedroom door. "Open a window and spare us your defilement," he called to the adjoining bathroom.

"I'm otherwise preoccupied. Can't reach it. Can you take care of it for me?" Bathezine said through growling laughter.

Errel closed the door. "What he lacks in tastefulness, he makes up for in… I don't know yet. I'm sure something will present itself someday."

Bet laughed. "I hope you're right."

"Well, young lady. This is where I take my leave. I must see to breakfast and morning check-outs. The remainder of your balance will be waiting at the reception desk." He lowered his head.

"Keep it. I hope to stay here again one day." Bet got up and went to Errel.

"You're too kind. We'll consider it a credit, then."

Bet grabbed him in a tight embrace. "I know I've said it far too much, but thank you. Thank you for everything."

Errel held his arms aside then slowly brought them down to return the hug, patting her on the back lightly. "Please do return. I have that story to write, remember." He pulled away, resting his hands on Bet's shoulders. "Be safe, be kind, and be true to who you are." He turned away, and quickly left the suite.

Bet watched him leave. She lifted Pooch-kin to the table and uncovered the silver bowl. "Ooh, look at that. Lotsa worms and stuff this time."

Pooch-kin dug in without comment.

Bathezine came out of the bedroom and immediately went to the table. "Why're the doors closed, keepin' me shut in like that?" he said, stuffing a whole turnover in his mouth. "Like you had me in quarantine or something." He eyed the bowl of pudding.

"To save us our appetites," Bet said, grabbing the bowl and taking a helping of pudding before Bathezine could grab it.

Twenty-Five

As they exited the Dining Inn, Bet waved to Errel, who returned a smile before looking back at a diminutive fuzzy orange and white creature wearing a tricorn hat.

Bathezine walked to the Rhinodon, untying it from the hitching post. "This is Jangol. Jangol, this is Bet. I don't know what the bird's name is."

"Hi again," Bet said, looking at the large animal's bottom tusk, which protruded upward, covering his mouth and most of his flat nose. "The Chook-chook's name is Pooch-kin."

The Rhinodon grunted.

"Let's get you some feed. We're gonna need a wagon," Bathezine said to Jangol, whose head drooped at hearing the news. "It'll be a light load. Just hauling these critters and some supplies, not rocks."

"Where're we going? You haven't told me yet," Bet asked, walking alongside Jangol.

"Getting' supplies at the end of town," Bathezine grunted.

"Okay, I get that. But after that. I know a long journey doesn't end at the edge of town." She looked back. "C'mon, Pooch-kin." The Chook-chook sniffed at something in the dirt road and hurried to catch up.

"I suspect I should take you to Azural. Mokep the Black should know what to do with you."

"Mokep the Black? Who's that?"

"He's the brother of Mokep the Gray, Mokep the Orange, Mokep the Brown, and Mokep the Yellow. Sons of Mokep the White and Daria the Sly."

"I didn't ask for his lineage. What does he do that you need to take me to him? And what is he? I'd like to know what the different kinds of people are called here. There're only humans where I come from."

"Pooch-kin's not a human," Bathezine said through a grumble again.

"I mean the ones who had jobs, and run businesses and government and stuff."

"Horses don't have jobs? I thought pulling wagons was work. Same for oxen."

"Well, yeah, but… You know what? Never mind. You know what I mean. If you don't want to tell me, I'll ask Jangol," Bet said, increasingly annoyed at Bathezine's surliness.

They arrived at a shop with a weather-worn sign reading Supply Hut, which looked exactly like its name suggested. Six strong columns lined up in rows of three supported log beams covered in tin-metal sheets and plywood in an old post-and-lintel design. Rows of shelves held every manner of supplies and materials.

Bet examined the building. "No walls? How do they keep thieves out when they're closed?"

Bathezine laughed. "If you try to steal from Old Babbers, she'll cut your fingers off and feed 'em to you. That's how."

"Oh," Bet said, pulling her hands close to her body.

"Wait here," he said. "And gimme some coin."

"You don't have any?" Bet asked, looking at the Ursian suspiciously.

"I do, but you don't have a wagon, or blankets, or a kettle, or a pan, or a decent hat, or food, or—"

"Okay, okay. I get it. How much do you need?" She retrieved the pouch of coins and emptied some into her hand.

Bathezine raised an eyebrow at seeing the stash. "Let's see... Do you know what these are worth?"

Bet shook her head. "Anna didn't have time to tell me."

"The small one is a single piece, this one is an eight piece, and this is a sixteen piece." He held up a copper coin. "Can you guess what this one is?"

"A twenty four piece," Bet answered with confidence.

"No. It's a thirty-two. And this is a sixty-four. And the sixty-four should cover it."

Bet held out a shimmering bronze coin. "What about this one?"

Bathezine closed her hand quickly. "That's a year's wages for most. You'll need it to get settled. So don't go showin' it off. Most in these parts don't concern themselves with avarice and thievery, but some ain't immune to it. Now wait here. I mean it."

Bet watched him walk into the Supply Hut and heard a pitchy voice call from between the rows of shelves.

"Bathezine! Come to talk me down on my already fair prices again?"

Bet spotted Old Babbers walking toward Bathezine. She was anything but old, looking human in appearance, with soft brown skin and long silky black hair hanging from beneath a very well-worn canvas hat. She gave the Ursian a scornful but not entirely serious glare.

"Just tryin' to protect you from your own rapacity," Bathezine shot back.

Old Babbers' eyes met Bet's, then she led Bathezine away. "Let's get to it, then."

Bet listened to the pair haggle and yell in the distance, with the occasional claim of extortion and robbery coming from either one. "I hope he comes back with all of his fingers," Bet said to Pooch-kin.

"He'd deserve it if he didn't," Pooch-kin said.

"Oh, come on now, Pooch-kin. I mean he's crude, abrasive, uncouth for sure, and maybe more than a little ill-tempered."

"As I was saying," Pooch-kin said.

"But," Bet stopped him from saying more. "I believe there's some decency hiding under that prickly exterior."

Pooch-kin's floppy ears raised a little. "Time will tell."

A pair of young men came out from behind the Supply Hut, pulling an old wagon made of weather-worn gray wood. They immediately got to the task of hitching it to Jangol, who grunted his displeasure. Finished with their work, the two hurried off without a word.

Bathezine reemerged carrying two large duffels and a wooden crate, trailed by Old Babbers. "Don't go telling anybody about the deal I gave you. It'd be bad for business," she said.

"Deal?" he barked, dropping is burden in the wagon. "I'm lucky I got out of there with my hide. Call that a deal?"

"Hello," Bet said to Old Babbers.

The woman looked Bet over. "You watch this one," she nodded toward Bathezine. "Else he'll eat your provisions before you reach Broke Tail Bend."

"I ain't got an appetite no more after that catastrophe of a so-called deal," Bathezine said, checking over the various attachments connecting the wagon to Jangol. "Well, don't just stand there looking empty-headed. Get your skinny arse up on the wagon. And don't forget your bird."

"You left out a few adjectives when you described him. But I don't use that kind of language," Pooch-kin whispered as Bet put him in.

"I heard you use that kind of language plenty of times," Bet said and climbed aboard, sitting on a wood plank of a bench in the box.

"Those were expressive chirps," the Chook-chook said.

Bathezine climbed onto the driver's bench, the wagon creaking in protest beneath the weight. "Thing's built for four-feathered touks, not a full grown Ursian. Get going, Jangol. We gotta make the ferry by nightfall."

The wagon jerked into motion. Bet smiled at Old Babbers, who walked away flipping the sixty-four piece in the air. "I take it you two aren't best friends?"

"Ah, we ain't enemies neither. Known her since she was a cub, back when her daddy owned the hut. She was as mean as a spit toad when she was younger; she's only slightly less meaner now. She's good enough in her own way, though."

"Seemed nice to me," Bet said.

Bathezine looked back at Bet and rolled his eyes without a reply.

Twenty-Six

They rode mostly in silence until midday. Bet took in the scenery, which transformed from the alpines of the mountains to low hills covered in tall yellow-gold grass and thick clusters of cork oak trees. Birds of so many varieties she couldn't count flew overhead, danced between branches, or scurried through the grass.

The road began to narrow, and Bathezine directed Jangol to pull over. "We'll stop here for lunch," he said.

"Yes," Bet exclaimed, stretching her thoroughly jostled body when the wagon came to a stop. She jumped to the ground and stretched again.

"Careful, there's Snappers. The grass is thick with 'em," Bathezine said stepping down from his seat. He grabbed a canteen, took a healthy swig and offered the rest to Jangol.

"What're Snappers?" Bet asked, searching the grass.

"You know. Whatchacallits. Snakes."

She examined the ground a little closer and shrugged. "Come on, Pooch-kin." She held out her arms.

"I'll stay on board and out of a Snapper's belly, thank you," Pooch-kin said, peering over the edge of the wagon.

"How far is it to the ferry from here?" Bet asked Bathezine, who had already gone to the rear of the wagon and was stuffing a sizable portion of the bean loaf in his mouth.

"A ways still. But we're makin' good time. Broke Tail Bend is just ahead, and I wanna have my wits. It can be tricky." He broke off a piece of bean loaf and tossed it to Bet. Then he reached in a burlap bag and pulled out a handful of seed and grain, which he put in a pile in front of Pooch-kin. Bathezine leaned against the wagon, watching the trees. "Mokep the Black is the Tally. He keeps record of all the newcomers like you and gets them situated. His kind is called Morval, and they ain't too fancy on wearin' clothes. So if you're offended by such things, keep your eyes averted."

Bet laughed. "I'll keep that in mind." She studied Bathezine. He seemed more relaxed being in the countryside.

He looked at her. "I ain't fond of towns and cities."

Bet raised her brow. "Is reading minds one of your Talents?"

Bathezine gurgled a laugh. "Ya ain't gotta read minds to know what someone is thinkin'."

"I like the country, too," Bet said, leaning against the wagon, as well.

Bathezine said nothing, keeping his eyes on a stand of oak in the field across the road, occasionally raising his snout, sniffing the air.

Bet followed his gaze. Her eyes lost focus. The birds grew quiet, and she could hear the rustle of leaves in the cool breeze. She heard the crunching of brittle grass beneath feet too heavy to be birds. There were several sets of feet from something she didn't know. The footsteps were moving stealthily closer. She felt aggression. The feeling snapped her out of her trance-like state. "What's out there?" she asked, looking up to find Bathezine staring at her.

He kept his eyes on her for a moment longer before looking back across the road. He raised his top lip and opened his mouth, tasting the air. "Creedans," he said through a whispered growl. "Best load up."

Bet did as instructed without delay.

"Let's get goin'," Bathezine said to Jangol, who was nervously shifting from foot to foot. He climbed to the driver's seat.

"What are Creedans?" Bet asked, holding onto the rail when the wagon lurched forward.

"Hill folk. Mostly peaceful people before the war. But they took a likin' to fightin' and never gave it up. They usually stay higher up in the hills, but things have been muddled up as of late. Probably just a huntin' party," he said, keeping his eye on the tree line. "Pick up the pace, Jangol. Just in case."

Jangol trundled along faster. Bathezine let loose of the reins; the Rhinodon knew where to go. "Watch it!" Bathezine yelled. Something almost imperceptible struck the side of the wagon. He reached to the sideboard just behind his seat where the object had struck and pulled out a six-inch quill.

"Stay down," Bet said to Pooch-kin, who had already changed color to match the gray wood.

"Like you need to tell me," the Chook-chook said.

Bathezine sniffed the dart. "It ain't poisoned. Maybe they ain't tryin' to kill us. Less the toads are outta season. Probably a warnin'."

"A warning against what?" Bet asked, squatting behind the railing.

"Who knows? They're simple-headed. Reach into the blue duffel. There's a box of iron bearings in there. Grab a pocketful in case this is a particularly stupid bunch."

Bet did as instructed, putting the open box at her feet. She had no desire to hurt anyone, but she'd do what had to be done to protect her friends.

"Now remember, if ya gotta throw, don't use anger. It's dangerous. Protectin' yourself is justifiable, but takin' pleasure in it ain't, and it can lead down the same path as being angry. Keep it in mind. Hopin' it won't come to that."

Bet could only nod. She was scared, and briefly longed for the time when all she had to worry about was Biscuit Head's slaps. At least she wasn't trying to kill her. Bet snorted. No, she'd rather meet her end out here, free from servitude, than live another day in that perdition.

They drove down the gulch just before Broke Tail Bend, and Jangol brought them to a stop. "Ah, hell," Bathezine growled at seeing a log block their way. "This'll slow us down. Bet, open the crate and grab the bolas."

"Okay," Bet said, her voice cracking. She checked on Pooch-kin, making sure he was hidden.

The pair hopped off the wagon. Bet stuffed the bearings in her pocket and dragged the bolas behind her, making sure to keep the braided cords with their heavy iron weights from getting tangled.

Bathezine turned to her. "Now remember what you did back there with the listening?"

Bet nodded, her mouth too dry to speak.

"Do it again."

"I don't know if I can. I didn't try to do it," she said, clearing her throat.

"You can. When a Talent shows, it doesn't go away. Let go of your thinkin'. I gotta move that log and I need you to keep watch. I don't know what they're up to, but I'm guessin' it ain't good."

"Do you think they put it here?" Bet said, watching the tall grass.

"Logs don't migrate. They put it here sure as it's day."

Bet let go of her thoughts and, to her surprise, she became acutely aware of her surroundings. She heard a Seed-mouse scurrying through the grass, and a Snapper, coiling to protect itself from the vibrations of footsteps. The footsteps, now five different sets, were edging closer. She felt the Creedans. Four were angry at one for missing the shot. Bathezine was wrong. They were here to rob them, and they'd kill to get whatever they were after. But she felt something else, as if they had been encouraged to do the deed.

"There're five of them," Bet said. "They're getting closer. Two ahead, beyond the rocks above the gulch. Three coming from behind. They'll kill us."

Bathezine grunted, pulling the heavy log with all his strength.

"Watch out!" Bet yelled.

Bathezine was already in motion. He batted one quill aside and neatly snatched the other from the air and threw it back toward the attacker. "Bolas," he yelled.

Bet tossed them to him as best she could.

The powerful Ursian swung them once overhead and flung them with incredible speed.

Bet heard two voices cry out, then fall silent. She heard the three coming up from behind. A dart whistled past her head, and a second stuck her left arm. She cried out and fell. Her arm burned, but there was no time to worry about it. She saw them now. No more than four feet tall, their skin as white as snow, with round eyes spread far apart, and slits for nostrils. Their faces were smeared with brown paint or mud, and they dressed in fur and leather. The leader carried a stone axe.

Bet stood, pulling the quill out and clutching her arm. She grabbed a bearing from her pocket, feeling the weight in her hand, and fear mixed with a primal rage in her heart. She drew back and threw. The iron ball flew so fast from her hand it couldn't be seen.

The leader's eyes widened. He looked down at the hole that went clean through his chest and collapsed. The two others looked at their fallen friend and back at Bet. They charged forward.

The bola flew in, wrapped the first one's neck, and the three weights clacked against its skull in rapid succession, dropping it immediately.

Bet pulled another bearing from her pocket, reared back, but a large paw gripped her arm, preventing her from throwing. She looked up to see Bathezine staring down at her with wide eyes.

The remaining attacker screamed in an unnaturally high pitch, and came at them brandishing a stone club.

Bathezine let go a roar so loud it hurt Bet's ears, and rushed to meet it. He grabbed the Creedan by its head, spun around and flung the hapless creature across the field, watching it crash against a tree and fall limp into the tall grass. Quickly, he retrieved his bolas and finished pulling the log from the road.

Bet stood motionless, in shock from the horror at what she had done.

Bathezine returned, softly resting his bear-like hands on her shoulders. "Come on, little one. More will be comin'." He guided her to the wagon and gently lifted her in. "Let's go, Jangol. Move." The wagon jolted forward, with the Rhinodon pulling them at a run.

Twenty-Seven

After traveling for no more than a few minutes, Bathezine told Jangol to stop, pulling back on the reins to make sure he understood. "Bet," he said.

Bet stared at the floorboards, unresponsive. He called her name again, and she lifted her head toward him.

"Listen, we're not out of this yet. We're at Broke Tail Bend, but it's more of a switchback. I'm gonna need your help."

Bet's eyes shifted.

"I need you here with me. Okay? Jangol's in a bit of a nervous mood, and this turn is tricky for a mule. To make it worse, part of the road's been washed out since I last came through. Do you understand?" He rested his meaty paw on her shoulder, looking in her eyes to make sure she got the picture.

Bet nodded.

"Okay. Good. There's a good-sized gully to the right, and I won't be able to see it from the seat. If'n the wheels get too close, we could lose the load, then we'll be in a heap of trouble. You need to get out and keep an eye on it."

"But what if those…the, the Creedans come back?" she said, eyes wide and pooled with tears.

"That's why we need to stay alert and make sure we keep on the road."

"I'm not sure I can do it."

"We ain't got no choice. We're still a good clip from the ferry, and there ain't no turnin' back. Always forward."

Bet hesitated.

"We don't have much time."

"Okay, okay," Bet finally said. She hopped from the wagon and walked to the rear. "Is here okay?"

Bathezine watched her. "That'll do. Now here it is. Keep a close eye."

The road cut back sharply almost in a V. Bet watched the spoked wheel bounce and roll over the rocky ground. "Left. Hard left," she said, seeing the wheel roll up a large rock that looked like it might drop off to the gully side.

The road narrowed more, and the left wheels scraped against the rocky embankment, with the right hugging the edge. Bet looked into the gully. It was no more than ten feet deep, but it might as well be a mile if they went over. "Keep it hard left," she shouted, seeing another significant bump ahead.

"We're as hard left as we can get," Bathezine shouted back.

"Then go fast as soon as you feel the back wheel rise."

"You heard the girl," Bathezine said to Jangol. The back wheel rose. "Now!" he said, and Jangol took off at a run, with the edge of the road giving way beneath the weight. The wheel began to sink, but the Rhinodon's strength pulled it free. He kept up the quickened pace until the road straightened out a few yards ahead. Once safe, they came to a stop and Bet climbed back in.

"You did good," Bathezine said as she sat. "Don't think it'll be passable after the next rain. Why nobody's thought to build a bridge there is beyond my thinkin'."

Bet returned to her silence.

"Climb up here beside me," Bathezine said, scooting over as far as his girth would allow, making room for her.

"No, thank you," Bet said in a quiet voice.

"I wasn't askin'. Now plant yourself up here."

Bet sighed. She looked under the bench for Pooch-kin, finding him curled up next to the box of bearings.

"Are you all right?" the Chook-chook asked.

Bet looked at her bloodied arm. "It's sore, but it didn't go that deep."

"That's not what I meant," Pooch-kin said.

"Yeah," she said, her face expressionless. She climbed onto the driver's bench, having just enough room to squeeze next to Bathezine. "I know what you're going to say. I didn't have a choice; it was going to kill me."

Bathezine urged Jangol forward. "No. Wasn't going to say that at all. Now pull your arm outta the sleeve and let me take a look at that wound."

"It's fine."

"You don't know that. And like I keep sayin', it ain't a request."

Bet did as she was told and Bathezine examined the injury. "Lucky it wasn't poisoned. But you'll need to clean it up. There's some salve in one of the bags. Grab it when the road evens up."

They rode in silence for a few minutes before Bathezine spoke. "Now 'bout what you done back there."

"I know. It was in self-defense. But that doesn't make it any better," she said, staring across the landscape.

"No, it doesn't. And no words I can say or anybody else can say will make you feel any different. I know it's not any consolation, but if you'd wounded him, his clan would've killed him anyway. That's what they do."

"You're right, it's no consolation," she said flatly, staring out at the road.

"What's done is done. But what's troublin' is you using your Talents in anger. You can't do that."

"Yeah, you keep saying that. But who cares? The results are the same. Why does it matter?" she snapped.

"The end result won't be for you. That's why," Bathezine bit back. "The inquisitor, the Creedan. You keep actin' out of anger, you'll become one of the Foul."

"I've acted out of anger plenty of times before and I'm not foul. Whatever that means," Bet said, annoyed with the conversation.

"That's because you were in the Din. Haven't you noticed how things are different with your Talents here? The people there, always busy and worrying about possessions and hating others because they're different, it makes their minds hum, like bees, and they don't even know it. And like a buncha bees in a hive, it makes a buncha noise. It gets in your brain, your mind, and you can't hear what the livin' world is telling you. In the Whist, the buzz is quiet, and you can hear what you have in you. And if you have anger, jealousy, greed and so on, it ruins your balance 'til all you feel are those things. You become the Foul. You get what I'm saying? It ain't a good thing."

Bet stared ahead. Everything he said made sense. She did feel like a veil had been lifted since crossing over, and the veil was still being lifted every day. "What happens if you become the Foul?" She was sure there must be a way to redeem one's self if you messed up too badly.

"You stay that way," Bathezine said plainly. "There's a course to redemption, but most give into it, the lure becomes stronger the farther you fall. Some try to make their way back, but die before they get there." Bathezine looked to the sky. "There's the Fair and the Foul. Good and evil, some call it. Look at it like two wheels spinning toward each other. One is the Fair and the other is the Foul. They push against each other, with neither one getting nowhere. Which is how it should be. If you move from one to the other, everything you know gets thrown into chaos. You go the opposite way."

"If you can cross from Fair to Foul, why can't you go from Foul to Fair?"

"Look at it like this: if you spill blackberry juice on a white shirt, you can wash it and scrub it all you want, the stain might fade, but it'll always be there. And those emotions I warned you about, are like drinkin' that juice. Every time you use them, you chance spillin' it on you."

"Okay, let me get this straight; the Foul is berry juice I don't want to spill it on me. Can't I wear an apron, or a bib or something? Won't stain me then."

Bathezine growled. "The berry juice has acid in it, too, then. Is that better?"

"Why would I be drinking acid to begin with?"

"Exactly my point."

Bet laughed for a moment then turned away, feeling guilty for laughing.

Bathezine gave her shoulder a soft squeeze. "It's good that you feel bad, that you feel horrible. Shows that you ain't goin' over. Hold on to the good in your heart, the happiness you feel when you're with Pooch-kin. Those are the things that matter most."

Bet didn't reply. She knew Bathezine actually cared and was trying to help. She'd do all those things he had told her. But it didn't change what she had done. It would be easier if she could make the Creedans seem like something less than an animal, pretend that its differences somehow made it less deserving of life, but like all living things, it had feelings and a desire to live, albeit on a base level. Even a predator like Tuft could put aside instinct, see reason and care for her young. The feelings she got from the Creedans were somehow rotten, corrupted. Like they were tools being prodded to act. She jerked her head toward Bathezine. "Are the Creedans Foul?"

The big Ursian looked at her out of the corner of his eye. "That, they are. Like I said, they took a likin' to killin' during the war. But even though they've become what they've become, they almost never rob passersby, at least not with intent to kill. Somethin's muddled up here. Been gettin' that way for nearly a year now."

"Well, if killer mushrooms, carnivorous dirt eels, bands of bandits, and three-headed crows dropping newcomers in the middle of nowhere means muddled, I agree with you. Not to mention some purple woman in my dreams and hearing her when I'm awake. Speaking of which, do you know who she is?"

Bathezine shifted. "Jangol, I hate to say it, but you should probably pick up the pace. Don't want to be stuck on this side of the Plece River 'til mornin'."

Bet bounced around on the bench. "How're you doing back there, Pooch-kin?"

"Thoroughly shaken," Pooch-kin answered.

"Same here," Bet said, turning her attention back to Bathezine. "Why won't you answer my question?"

"Persistence is annoying," Bathezine grumbled.

"So is dodging questions."

Bathezine's body sagged. "The purple one, if it is who I suspect, is Fealist-Marsh, a Seventy-Two."

"Seventy-Two? What, there's seventy-two of her?"

"No. She's a Seventy-Two, better known as an Omia Temporian. You see, there are seventy-two known Talents. Most people have one or two. Some have nine or even eighteen. In a rare case, people have been known to have twenty-seven. But a Seventy-Two has 'em all. The chances of it happenin' are so low it's only happened twice in the last five hundred years or so."

"What, is she like the queen here?"

"No," Bathezine said quickly. "She's more of a hermit. She's rarely seen. In fact, no one has seen her since the end of the war."

"How come I can hear her?"

"Don't know," Bathezine said, shifting in his seat, clearly uncomfortable with the conversation. "You say she speaks to you?"

"No. It's more like I'm eavesdropping on her, kind of like she's talking to someone but not me."

"That ever happen with anybody else? Where ya hear 'em?" Bathezine's face wrinkled.

Bet pursed her lips, looking to the sky. "Nope. Not that I'm aware of. Do I have another Talent?"

Bathezine shrugged. "Could be. Could be somethin' else. Mokep the Black should be able to tell you more."

"You seemed to know a lot about other stuff," Bet said, unsatisfied with the answer.

"I've exhausted my knowledge on the subject."

"Or have you exhausted your willingness to talk about it?"

Bathezine studied the deepening colors of the sky. "C'mon, Jangol. Have to speed up a little more. We gotta make that ferry. I'll give you oats and honey when we get there."

Jangol's quick trot turned into a full-on run, ending any further conversation as Bet had to hold tight to avoid being tossed from her seat.

Twenty-Eight

They came around a slow curve that overlooked a river so broad, Bet swore it was an inland sea. Night had nearly fallen, and the distant ringing of an iron bell sang from a lighthouse near the shore, signaling the imminent departure of the ferry.

"Grab a light and flash it three times," Bathezine said. "Hope Tiny Nat will wait on us."

Bet climbed and fell into the back, and retrieved her light. If Bathezine didn't want to spend the night out here, she was sure she didn't want to, either. She raised her hand high and did as instructed. "Is that good?"

Bathezine kept his eyes on the lighthouse. "We'll see." A moment later a green light flashed from ahead. "Yup."

Jangol pulled the wagon with a huff and came to a stop before a gate in front of a wood ramp leading to the barge of a ferry. A very tall insect-like creature came and stood beside the wagon.

Bathezine climbed down and looked up at the creature, who wore nothing but a leather satchel across his thorax. "Thanks for waiting, Tiny. 'Preciate it."

"If we had known it was you, we would have left," Tiny Nat said, his voice coming through a hum from his pointed mouth.

"And leave poor old Jangol and the girl out here through the night?"

Tiny Nat extended his jointed arm and stroked the Rhinodon's back. He brought his two-fingered hand back to Bathezine. "Twenty-four."

"Twenty four?" Bathezine protested. "The last time I came through it was only eight."

"We had to wait," Tiny hummed.

"We had enough trouble with the Creedans trying to rob us. And now you?"

Tiny Nat scanned the low hills overlooking the river. He returned his attention to Bathezine, wiggling his two segmented fingers.

"Fine," Bathezine muttered, then turned to Bet. "Pay him so we can get going."

Bet fumbled through her coin pouch, pulling out a thirty two piece and placing it in Tiny's hand. "My deepest thanks for waiting on us."

Tiny Nat looked at the coin and placed it in his satchel. "It is good to see that the company you keep understands appreciation, Bathezine," he said before lifting the gate.

Bet climbed down with the aid of Tiny Nat's arm. She stretched her arms and rubbed her aching backside. "Let's go, Pooch-kin." She reached in, lifting her friend out.

Bathezine leaned into Bet. "You should learn to save your money."

"You should learn to be nice to others," she said with a mocking smile.

"Right this way, young mistress. We'll arrange a meal to aid in your recovery from the road," Tiny Nat said, looking at her arm after they boarded.

"Can Bathezine join me?" She motioned toward the Ursian, who was giving Jangol his promised treat.

Tiny Nat buzzed, which Bet took as a resigned sigh. "If you insist."

"Let me grab my bags." She went to the wagon. "We have a place inside."

Bathezine looked at the tall cabin amidships. "Hmm. Never rid in there."

Tiny Nat stepped to Bathezine. "Tell us about the Creedans."

"Things attacked us just before Broke Tail. They weren't there just to rob us neither. They was aiming to kill. They even laid a trap. Never heard of them goin' through that much trouble."

"This troubles us. They have become more aggressive."

"Maybe. Or more desperate. But they ain't no smarter." Bathezine patted Jangol on the rump. "I'll be back."

"We care little for you, but what little we do care, we do not wish harm to fall on you. Especially the Rhinodon," Tiny Nat said, looking over Jangol.

"Heartwarming sentiments, Tiny. And the feelin's mutual."

"Why would you take the old road from Illguard and not the Sumter Flats Highway?"

"The Flats is a half day's longer travel. The girl is a newcomer, and she needs to see Mokep the Black as soon as possible. That idiot crow, Her-Gad-Ishu, got her and dropped her off in the wild. Strange arrival." Bathezine looked at Bet for a moment, then grabbed a pack from the wagon.

Tiny Nat studied Bet, who was milling around the deck with Pooch-kin, looking at various pack animals, making their acquaintance. "Curious. We shall watch over her."

"C'mon, girl," Bathezine said, following Tiny Nat to the cabin.

Bet excused herself from a conversation with a Spring Boar and hurried to join them at the door.

Tiny Nat led them to a cozy parlor filled with rough-hewn tables and plush reclining chairs upholstered in fine green velvet. "You may sit anywhere you wish," he said, and turned his attention elsewhere.

Bet hopped into the seat nearest the front window and thanked her host. A shorter, paler yellow version of Tiny Nat hummed into the parlor, placing a plate of food and a carafe of juice in front of Bet, and left as quickly as it had arrived. A second insectoid, nearly identical to the first, repeated the act, leaving a bowl of grain on the table for Pooch-kin. They came and went so fast, she didn't have time to thank them. As she took her first bite of the foreign vegetables laid out before her, she heard a gruff voice call out from the back of the room.

"Bathezine! You old tic magnet. I didn't smell you coming in."

Bathezine growled beneath his breath. "Yep. Took to bathing every so often. How ya been, Tambor? What're you doin' this side of the Maltese Seas? You wear out your welcome in Talisburg?"

The burly man chuckled. "Nah. Had to tend to a pyre for my uncle Ando, and sign over his estate."

"Sorry to hear that, Tambor," Bathezine said. He sat in the chair next to Bet, looking around for his plate of food.

"Ah, only met the man once. Ma's too old to make the journey so it fell on me. How 'bout you? Still hauling rocks?"

"On occasion. Girl's family here hired me to charter her to Azural. Thought Jangol could use the break, and it pays well enough." Bathezine met Bet's eyes. "Her family's in the Blue Caste."

Tambor came around the table. He smoothed his black tunic, and a broad smile lifted his pork chop sideburns. "Tambor's the name. Pleased to meet you."

Bet looked up, meeting his bright green eyes set against his deep brown skin in a vivid contrast. "I'm Blair. Likewise." She offered her hand.

Tambor shook her hand, examining it. "Rough hands for a Blue Caste."

Bet gave a curt smile. "Grandfather taught me that hard work would give me a greater appreciation of my education." She pulled her hand back and returned her attention to the food.

"Your grandfather sounds like a wise man. Good to see they ain't soft with privilege," he laughed. "Back when I was—"

Tiny Nat stepped in, interrupting the man. "Mister Tambor, our guests have traveled far. The parlor is for quiet recovery. If you please," he indicated for Tambor to return to his table.

"Oh yeah, yeah. Sorry 'bout that." He flashed a broad grin at Bathezine. "Good to see you again. Remember, I still have a spot for you in Talisburg."

"I'll keep that in mind," Bathezine said, watching Tambor walk away. He looked at Bet, nodding his approval. "You're a quick study."

"Had to be, where I came from," she said through a mouthful.

Another insectoid hummed in and placed a loaf of bread and platter of fruit in front of Bathezine, and darted away. Bathezine tore off a bite of the loaf big enough for three men. "Well, don't get to used to it. There're some who can see through nearly any ruse."

"I'll keep that in mind," Bet said and let the conversation die.

After finishing her meal, she brought Pooch-kin to her lap, reclined her chair, and stared off through the window, watching the plumes of steam rise from the barge's engines, and dissipate against the moonlit sky.

Twenty-Nine

Bet sat in a darkened room. Faint light came from somewhere unseen, lightly illuminating wisps of fog hugging a black floor. No walls could be seen, but she felt encapsulated nonetheless. She realized she was in a dream, and she waited for the voice to come. When the voice came, it wasn't who she expected. It was a man's voice, deep, baritone, carrying with it malevolence, seeped with a burgeoning violence. The threat in the man's voice shocked her, nearly wakening her. She concentrated, forcing herself to stay in the dream.

"Kill the chieftain for the clan's failure." There was a pause, and Bet felt another presence enter the dream, but the unknown entity never spoke. The man continued. "Her Talents double with each passing day. Tell him to do what he must. I want that—"

The voice cut off abruptly and Bet found herself sitting on a patch of soft green grass, surrounded by a shimmering sea of sand as far as she could see. White clouds swirled and danced against a canopy of vibrant blue.

"I know you can hear me," the familiar woman's voice said, coming from everywhere at once. Bet tried to wake, knowing her eavesdropping had been found out.

"He knows what you hold. Protect it at all cost."

Bet attempted to speak, but her words wouldn't come.

"He will try to take it. He will destroy you to do so."

Bet fought against the sleep paralysis holding her words in her throat. *Who will?* she tried to say, the words left in her mind. She concentrated in the dream state, and her mouth opened. "What will he take?" she said, feeling a rush of freedom at being able to speak.

The woman's voice didn't answer, seeming to hesitate. "The Facet of the Din. Only you can free me."

"What do you mean? How can I free you? Free you from what?"

"He comes now. Awake, Bethany. Awake!"

Bet's eyes shot open. Her breath was calm. Everything was quiet and still. Bathezine slept with his head on his chest in the seat next to her, and Pooch-kin was asleep on her lap. She looked out the window. It was night still, but the ferry's steam engines had gone quiet. She looked to the next table to find Tiny Nat slumped over in a chair. Her eyes caught movement in a reflection in the window. Tambor stood behind her.

"What do you want?" she asked, and his body jerked in surprise.

Heavy boots walked around the table. Tambor's dark eyes narrowed. "How are you awake?"

"I'm a light sleeper, I guess," she said, looking at her friends. "What have you done to them?" She gently laid Pooch-kin on the table.

"They'll be fine. Just gimme your bag and nobody'll get hurt."

"Why do you want my bag?" Bet asked, stalling and hoping to find a way out of her situation.

Tambor looked at her sideways. "C'mon, girl. You know what I want, so just give it to me."

"Actually, I don't know." She unslung her satchel. "You won't hurt anybody?" She held out the bag.

"If you really don't know, you should probably keep it that way." Tambor dumped the contents of the bag on the table. He sifted through her belongings, pushing aside the pouch of coins, vials, and the knife. "Where is it?"

"Where is what?" Bet asked, shifting in her seat.

Tambor's fist clenched and his voice dropped. "You know what. The facet. That piece of rock you're carrying."

"Oh, that," Bet said, scooting to the edge of her chair. "I lost that back at Broke Tail Bend."

"Don't lie to me, girl! I can see through your deceptions. He wouldn't have sent me otherwise." He wiped the contents of her bag from the table.

Bet sprang from her seat, putting the chair between her and the man. "Who sent you?"

Tambor snorted a laugh. "Just give it to me and I'll let you live." He reached behind his back, drawing a shimmering stiletto.

Bet stared at the nine-inch blade and scooted to the next table beside Tiny Nat. "I kind of like that rock. Why does your master want it?"

"It doesn't matter why, all that matters is that he wants it." Tambor circled around the chair. He squeezed his fist tight and extended his fingers quickly. "Sleep!"

"I'm not tired anymore," Bet said, moving to the other side of her sleeping host, edging her way closer to the door. If she could make it outside, she was sure she could outrun the man and get to the wagon. Once there she would grab a bearing or two and the odds would be evened. Unless he could throw like her, then all she would get was a knife in the back for her troubles. It was a chance she had to take. She stepped closer to the door. To Bet's surprise, the man lowered his weapon.

Tambor looked at Bathezine, then to Pooch-kin. He snatched up the Chook-chook, dangling him by his feet, and held the stiletto to his throat. "Give me the stone or I'll kill your friend and have a good meal to boot." His face showed a toothy, humorless smile, and his eyes grew darker.

Bet shook her head. "No! No, I'll give you the stupid rock. Just don't hurt him."

Tambor pressed the knife against Pooch-kin's neck. "Now, no more games or I swear I'll cut off his head and then I'll kill the Ursian, too."

Seeing her friend hang helpless in the man's grip ignited a spark of rage in Bet. Pooch-kin was in danger again because of her. She would do what she must to protect him. She dug her hand into her pocket feeling for the pouch. She felt it, but she also felt an iron ball she had put there during the Creedan attack. Her eyes narrowed. She palmed the bearing, covering it with the pouched stone. She pulled her hand out and withdrew the shiny rock, showing it to Tambor, distracting him from what her other hand was doing. "Is this what you want?"

"That's the one. Now set it on the table and back away."

"Put him down first," Bet said, adjusting her grip on the iron bearing.

Tambor laughed. "I think I'll take him with me. Make sure you don't try anything stupid."

"Stupid? You mean like this?" She drew back her arm and threw.

Tambor's eyes widened. He dropped Pooch-kin, and dove out of the way of the projectile faster than Bet thought possible. The bearing hummed through the air, putting a hole in the parlor wall, continuing on its path.

The man rolled to his feet. "Yeah. Just like that." He rushed toward Bet.

It was all she could do to get out his path before he hit. He crashed into the chair Tiny Nat slept in, knocking him to the floor. Bet dove beneath the table, just out of reach of his groping hand. She scurried across the floor, searching for something else to throw. She considered the stone, but if she missed again, it would be gone forever. She continued to crawl and found the contents of her bag Tambor had swept from the table which included her knife.

"Shall we try this again?" Tambor said.

Bet peeked over the table top to see the man holding the knife to Bathezine's neck, the tip of the blade puncturing the skin, drawing a trickle of blood. She unsheathed her knife, keeping a cautious eye on the man. "Yeah, let's try it again." She stood, drew back her arm, then brought it forward, but didn't release the blade.

Tambor reacted as he had before, falling for the feint. He rolled out of the way and jumped back to his feet. Bet threw her blade as he stood, taking a little off the throw. His mouth went agape when the knife struck him in the chest and disappeared into his body, not coming out the other side. He stumbled back, falling against the door.

Bet watched him. She grabbed a teacup from a nearby table and followed him when he threw open the door and fell outside.

Tambor got to his feet and staggered across the deck until he reached the railing. He turned back toward Bet. "More will come," he rasped. "You haven't gained anything. They'll keep coming until you and your friends are dead and he has what he wants."

"Well, now there's one less I'll have to worry about." She threw the cup, watching it shatter to dust against his forehead. Tambor tumbled over the edge, splashing into the river.

Bet stood shaking and looked at the shiny rock in her hand. "I hope you are worth it." She pocketed the stone and headed back to the cabin.

Thirty

Bet went straight for Pooch-kin, gathering him from the floor, holding him close as she checked on Bathezine's wound. She searched the room, found a linen napkin and pressed it against his neck. Moments later, Pooch-kin stirred. "Take it easy, my friend," she said with a breath of relief when his eyes opened.

"I feel unusually sore for taking a nap," he said.

Bet set him on the table and gave him a half smile. "Well, you kind of took a fall."

Bathezine's head popped up and he stood with a jerk, knocking his chair over. "Where is he?" he demanded.

Tiny Nat awoke with a similar reaction.

Bathezine grabbed his neck. "What happened? Where'd that scummy little pig's arse go?"

Bet started gathering her things from the floor. "He had an accident and fell overboard," she said, pointing to his neck. "Keep pressure on that."

Tiny Nat's carapace turned from pale green to burnt-orange. "Are you injured?" he asked Bet, his usual stoic voice sounding menacing.

"I'm fine." She put the remainder of her items on the table and looked at Bathezine. A tear rolled down her cheek.

"We will look for his body," Tiny Nat said. Bet pointed in the direction Tambor had gone.

Bathezine stared at Bet and the tension in his body eased. He scooted around the table, wrapping a big arm around her. "There, there, little one. You're safe now."

Bet fell against his chest and broke down. "He was going to kill Pooch-kin…and you. He was going to kill me, too."

Bathezine guided her to her chair, pulling his chair to face her. "Now why was he wantin' to do that? Did he say?"

Bet nodded, pulling the shiny rock from her pocket, holding it out to him. "This. He wanted this."

"Probably should have left that in the creek," Pooch-kin said, drawing a sniffly laugh from Bet.

Bathezine studied the stone. "Where did you get this?" He folded her hand over the rock, directing her to put it away.

"I found it in the creek near where Pooch-kin and I used to live. I just thought it was interesting. She told me in my dream. She warned me, made me wake up," Bet rambled.

"Who warned you? Fealist-Marsh, the purple woman? I thought you just listened, eavesdropped on her?"

"Yeah, I did. It was different this time. There was a man's voice. He sent the Creedans after us, and Tambor. Then his voice disappeared and her voice came. She said I had to protect it at all costs and that I'm the only one who can free her." Bet started crying again. "I don't want this. I don't want to hurt anyone again. I just want to be left alone."

"I know, I know. Most of us do, but I ain't figured out how to do that just yet. Did she tell you what the rock was?"

Bet shrugged. "Not really. Something about the Facet of the Din. I don't know what that means. Do you know?"

Bathezine sat back, stroking his mustache. "Don't know for sure. There was talk at the end of the war. Somethin' 'bout the Staff of the Din and the Staff of the Whist. Don't know if that plays into this. 'Spect we'll find out soon enough, or at least try to. In the meantime, we need to keep you safe."

Tiny Nat came back in, looking slightly wet. His color had returned. "Are you certain he fell overboard? We found no traces. Was he injured?"

"Yes, I'm sure. And yeah, he was injured. I stuck a knife in his chest." Bet looked at the table.

"Maybe the Sheep-loggers got him already," Bathezine said.

Bet looked up. "What're Sheep-loggers?"

"Big fish. They eat stuff," Bathezine said, looking at Tiny Nat.

Tiny Nat seemed to consider the idea. "Perhaps. Or perhaps he pulled the knife out and swam away."

"No. The knife was in his chest. Inside. And I hit him in the head with one of your cups, too. I'll pay you for the broken dish, and the hole in the wall," Bet reached for her pouch. Bathezine put his hand on hers.

"Broken? You must be mistaken. Our dishes are made from unbreakable Chanswick stoneware." Tiny Nat examined the hole in the steel wall.

"Well, it shattered against his head when I threw it at him," Bet said, scratching Pooch-kin, not looking at him.

Tiny Nat was about to object when Bathezine stopped him. "Girl's got quite an arm."

Tiny stuck his finger in the hole in the wall. "We see your meaning."

"Speaking of the girl. I need services only the Vivicons can provide," Bathezine said. "She needs protectin'."

"I'm afraid our services are not for hire any longer. Not since the war," Tiny Nat said.

Bathezine dug into his pocket, pulling out a sparkling gold coin. "She really needs help." He put the coin in Tiny's hand.

"We have a ferry service to run."

"Didn't ask you to quit. Just need your hive mind to keep an eye out and give us warnin' if'n someone comes for her. With this, you can afford another ferry, doubling your business." He indicated the coin with a nod. "Who knows, maybe even buy a balloon for special customers like they do in Sultane."

"We seem to remember their balloon catching fire and killing twelve occupants."

"Okay. Forget the balloon. What do ya say? You know it ain't easy for me askin' you," Bathezine said, scratching at his ear.

"Where did you get this coin? We don't want stolen money," Tiny Nat asked, his lidless eyes staring at him.

"Since when?" Bathezine said, turning away.

Tiny Nat cocked his head. "Where did you get it?"

Bathezine sighed. "That business up in Walesburg durin' the war. They feel they owe it to me. I ain't got need for that kinda money. It's an annual payment. A tribute, they call it."

"You killed seventy-nine soldiers of the Din and saved the lives of a village of one thousand and twelve. This is one of two reasons we accept you."

Bathezine's eyebrows raised. "I won't ask what the second reason is. Well, ya gonna help?"

Tiny Nat shifted his segmented frame. "We will accept your offer. Where will you be taking her?"

"Takin' her to see Mokep the Black. I could use some guidance on the matter, too."

"Tell us what the matter is," Tiny Nat said, looking at Bet, who was doing her best to act like she wasn't listening.

Bathezine hesitated, looking at Bet as well. He took a deep breath. "The girl's got somethin' somebody wants. And I believe she's communicating with Fealist-Marsh."

"The Omia Temporian? How is this possible? We thought she died at the end of the war." Tiny took a seat at the table.

"Well, ya thought wrong. I heard she became a hermit. Looks like I heard wrong, too. As far as talkin' to her, the girl talks to her in dreams."

"Then she could be dead, and she speaks to her residual energy." Tiny Nat looked at Bathezine. "We have heard of such things."

"Nah. I heard of it, too. But they talk. Actual conversation. Never heard of a Remnant doin' that. And there's more." Bathezine leaned his elbows on the table. "You know anything about the Staff of the Din?"

Tiny Nat sat stiff for a moment. "Only rumor. It is a relic from a forgotten age."

"Well, the girl could be holdin' a piece, and that's what somebody wants."

"If this is true, we would not suggest going to Mokep the Black, or going to Azural at all."

"You got a better idea?" Bathezine asked. He eyed Bet, who looked away.

"If she has truly been in contact with Fealist-Marsh, we must find the Charge of Danthbrook. She can lead us to the Ancient One."

"The Charge of Danthbrook. You mean that overgrown hamster of a card cheat, Mandi-lyn?"

"The very same," the Vivicon said. "Do you know where she is?"

Bathezine's body slumped in the chair. "Yeah, yeah. I do. She was stayin' at Handover's back in Illguard."

Bet perked up at hearing the name. "Can we stay at Errel's?"

"Don't have a choice. Unless you wanna camp out in the wagon," Bathezine said, getting up. "How we gonna do this? You gonna turn the ferry around?"

Tiny Nat shook his head. "No. We have an outrider on this island. We will take that. It is large enough to fit Jangol and your wagon. Might we suggest taking the Sumter Flats Highway to Illguard?"

"I'll take it under advisement." He walked to the door. "So, you're coming along, too?"

"Yes, we are."

"When you say we, do you mean you or the whole bloomin' swarm?" Bathezine asked, returning to his surly form.

Tiny Nat struggled with the question. "The swarm, as you call us, will not. Only us...me, as an individual Vivicon, will physically travel with you."

"Great. I'm gonna go check on Jangol," Bathezine said, throwing open the door.

After Bathezine had gone, Bet looked up at Tiny Nat. "I'm glad you'll be joining us," she said with a smile.

Tiny Nat stood and looked down at her. "You are the second reason we tolerate the Ursian."

Thirty-One

The ferry had docked to a long stone terminal in the waning hours of the night. A low fog hugged the ground beneath a sky revealing the first hints of dawn as Bet, Pooch-kin, and Bathezine strolled along the walkway, keeping a wary eye for any threats. "Where are we?" Bet asked.

"Pallas Steep. This is the halfway point across the Plece River, more or less," Bathezine said, watching the Vivicons load Jangol and the wagon on the outrider.

"There's not much to it," Bet said, surveying what little landscape she could see through the fog and dim light, wrinkling her nose at the smell of mud and rotten vegetation at the river's edge.

"There's even less during the rainy season. You can just see the top of the lighthouse when the Plece floods." He pointed to a lighthouse at the end of a long causeway. "You can take a skiff from here upriver to Port Lexing. That's about all it's good for."

"Do you suppose that's where Tambor was headed if he got the stone?" Bet asked.

Bathezine turned to her. "Didn't think that much into it. But you might not be far off the mark. We ain't got time for investigatin', but I'll ask Tiny if his kind can poke around there a bit. I wouldn't mind knowing who was after you."

"All I know is he has a deep voice. He said something about killing the chieftain for failing. I'm assuming he meant the Creedans."

"Likely. That'll throw 'em into turmoil for a spell. Least we know they ain't actin' on their own accord."

Tiny Nat hummed his way toward the three, carrying several tranluscent bladders filled with a brown liquid and a canvas roll. "We will leave now. Ed will drive." He pointed to another Vivicon bringing up the rear. Bet stepped aside as Ed buzzed by her to the head of the wide flat boat, which looked like a smaller version of the ferry. Tiny Nat drew up the landing ramp. Another Vivicon untied the outrider from the moorings. A small steam engine chugged to life and two outboard paddle wheels started to spin. As soon as the outrider cleared the dock, Ed cut it hard a port and the wheels began spinning with such speed they buzzed like a hive of angry insects. The boat took off so suddenly, Bet had to catch herself to keep from falling.

Unfazed by the motion, Tiny Nat unfurled the roll on the deck. "We brought weapons for defense, if needed."

Bathezine kneeled down, grabbing a chain mace, what looked like a very large shuriken, and a blow pipe. "These're mine, I take it."

Tiny Nat nodded. "We seem to remember your proficiency with such weapons." He looked at Bet, handing her a multi-pouched belt. "This is yours. Fill the pockets with the iron balls."

Bet shook her head. "I don't think I should. I don't want to hurt anybody else."

"Whether you want to or not is irrelevant. Your life may depend on it, as well as ours. And take this," Tiny said, handing what looked like an ice-climber's pick. "You won't always have the benefit of distance."

Bet complied, frowning down at Pooch-kin, who watched the goings on from between her feet.

Tiny Nat grabbed an atlatl and a quiver of two-foot-long spears. He took a bandolier containing several throwing knives and strapped it around his torso.

"What's that?" Bet asked, pointing at the atlatl.

"It's a spear thrower," Bathezine answered before Tiny Nat could. "Tiny can put a spear through your eye at a hundred yards. You might take some throwin' pointers from him."

Bet stared wide-eyed at the Vivicon. She could imagine the strength such a large creature could put behind a throw. "And what're those, bombs?" She pointed at the liquid-filled bladders.

"It is nectar. We need to eat on our journey," Tiny said, adjusting his weaponry.

Bet hoped 'we' didn't mean her, too. The thought of drinking the brown fluid was unappealing at best.

"I can't help but feel like I should have a weapon, too," Pooch-kin said.

Bet shook her head. "I doubt they make weapons for Chook-chooks. Just keep changing colors and hide if needed."

Pooch-kin snorted at the comment. "Maybe I can trip somebody, or get stepped on and sprain an attacker's ankle."

"Now you're talking," Bet laughed.

Bathezine checked his gear and raised a bushy brow at Tiny Nat. "What's got you buzzin? I haven't seen you this worked up since before the battle of Sou Hill."

"We have learned of a gathering of clans among the Creedans. A chieftain has been killed—by whom, we do not know. The elders have united and are moving toward Ultum Seam."

"Ultum Seam? What've they got to do with that dot of a town?" Bathezine asked, feeling the heft of his mace.

"We are uncertain. They may yet change course; the town does lay in the hills south of Illguard." Tiny Nat folded his legs and sat.

Bet lifted Pooch-kin and put him in the wagon, giving his ear a reassuring squeeze. "Do you think they'll go to Illguard?" Her forehead furrowed with worry for her new friend, Errel.

Tiny Nat didn't respond.

Bathezine shrugged. "Don't know why they would. But if they did, Old Babbers won't hesitate to give 'em hell. Might even sell their hides after she's done with 'em."

"I'm more worried about Mister Handover."

Bathezine shook his head. "Don't let his fancy ways fool ya none. Andolans are more than capable when pushed to it. I wouldn't worry. 'Sides that, I don't think even the Creedans are fool enough to get the Andolan Guild involved. They got enough resources to mash most challengers, and they hold markers over a fair share of others who got what they don't."

Bet leaned against the wagon. The thought of how everything seemed to be turning so chaotic over a stupid rock made her want to toss it in the river. In fact, she wished she would've left it in Silt Creek to let somebody else deal with it a hundred years later. "What if he turns Foul, or Old Babbers, if they're forced to fight?" She swung her satchel in front her, and began rummaging through the contents.

"It's a risk we all take, and it's all in our choices. And I ain't ever heard of an Andolan turning Foul. Far as I know."

"Still," Bet said. She pulled the light from her bag, absentmindedly turning it off and on. "I'd rather none of this happened."

"Ain't no use concernin' yourself with what can't be changed or what you wish hadn't happened. There's plenty to worry 'bout with what is."

Bet shrugged, dropping the light back in her bag, which clinked against her glass vials. She pulled out the potions and handed them to Bathezine. "These were given to me. What are they?"

Bathezine took them, examining the wax seals. "Elixirs. Where'd you get them?"

"The old man, Harrelle. He gave them to me before I left Malweather. I don't know what they do."

Bathezine handed her one with what looked like a lightning bolt impressed in the wax. "That's for energy and stamina. It'll give you a boost when you need it."

"Oh, that's the one he gave me when I was sick to get my strength back. It really works."

The Ursian made a sideways nod. "That, it does. Just don't drink it all at once. You'll stay awake for a day, and it can make your heart explode."

Bet stiffened. "Good to know," she said, putting her hand against her chest.

"This," Bathezine continued, showing her one with a flower on the seal, "is for healing. It'll fix up superficial wounds and some illnesses."

Bet took the vial, tempted to try it on the injury she received from the Creedan dart. She thought better of it and it put it away.

Bathezine handed her the last vial, which had a swirling circle on the seal. "This one is an antidote. It works on just about any poison, even the poison from those Floragads you're so fond of. But I suppose you'd have to eat one."

"I didn't know they were poisonous." She put the vial back in the bag.

"Mushrooms are poisonous. Most people know that." Bathezine rolled his eyes. "Don't plan on gettin' anymore. So use them wisely."

"Why can't I just buy more?"

Tiny Nat raised his head. "They are illegal. Too many became addicted to the stimulant. Most elixirs were outlawed."

"Oh, like the smoke users back home...I mean in the Din. The city had a lot them," Bet said.

"Seeing as how it has the unfortunate side-effect of heart poppin', there ain't many addicts left here," Bathezine quipped. He looked at Tiny Nat. "I thought you was meditatin' or whatever you do."

"We were getting several points of information at once. We had to concentrate," Tiny Nat answered. "The Creedans continue to gather near Ultum Seam, but even more concerning is that the Mastives are also headed that way. It could be a tribal dispute between the two, but we are unsure as of yet."

"What are Mastives?" Bet asked. She dragged the box of bearings close to her and began filling her pouches.

Bathezine growled. "Big ugly critters. Have tusks that hang down out of their mouths 'bout this long." He put his hand on the middle of his chest. "If you thought Creedans were simple-headed, the Mastives are twice as much. They usually keep to themselves up in the Farrows."

Tiny Nat stood. "We will monitor the situation."

Bathezine stretched and patted Bet on the head. "You know, Tiny, ya might wanna have someone give the residence a warning."

"They are aware of the danger and have already made preparations to go underground."

Pooch-kin clucked, getting Bet's attention. "Going underground might be a good idea."

Bet nodded in agreement. "Pooch-kin's right. Why don't we hide out? Go underground, too. At least until this whoever he is looks elsewhere or gives up."

Bathezine snorted. "If this mystery man of yours knew you were on the ferry, chances are it won't take long for him to figure out we hid in the tunnels of Ultum Seam. 'Sides that, we got this Fealist-Marsh puzzle to figure out, and we can't do it by hidin'."

Bet let out a long breath. She leaned back to Pooch-kin. "Sorry, my friend. Looks like we're staying above ground."

Pooch-kin changed colors to match the wood. "Let's hope it stays that way, then."

Thirty-Two

Bet leaned on the edge of the outrider, watching the water churn, trying to get her mind off the chaos of her thoughts. She tried to connect to Fealist-Marsh again and hopefully get some answers, but had no luck. They docked at the unnamed terminal they had left the night before shortly before midmorning. Bet walked along the shore with Pooch-kin, watching Long-tailed Blue Doves flutter against a cyan sky striated by cirrocumulus clouds, and envying their carefree life.

Hearing Bathezine and Tiny Nat argue over who should drive the wagon brought her back to reality. She watched the two war veterans bicker; both seemed equally concerned with Jangol's wellbeing. "For two people who fought together in a war, they sure don't get along very well," she said to Pooch-kin.

"I don't think Bathezine gets along with anybody," Pooch-kin said.

"True," Bet said. Something caught her eye, and she kicked at the soft ground. She picked up a piece of rose quartz, rubbed the mud off on her pant leg, and dropped it in her bag.

"You should really stop picking up strange rocks."

"I'm sure this isn't endued with mystical powers. It's just pretty," she said, turning her attention back to the arguing pair. Watching them, a thought occurred to her. "You know what, Pooch-kin? They both fought in the war. I think it's time somebody gave me some answers. I'm about sick and tired of being treated like a child or an outsider. Let's go."

Bet stomped off toward the two with Pooch-kin following, doing his best to stomp, as well.

"Get your bird on board and load up," Bathezine said when Bet approached. He looked at Tiny Nat. "I'm driving."

Bet didn't budge. "Tell me about the war," she said straight to the point.

Bathezine ignored the statement and climbed onto the driver's bench. "Get loaded. We need to make Paskersville by sundown."

Tiny Nat deftly hopped in the back.

"I'm not going anywhere until somebody tells me about it," she said, standing firm.

"Another time, girl. We've got other things to concern ourselves with, at the moment." He shifted in his seat to get comfortable.

Bet shook her head. "No. If all of this is somehow related, I need to know. We can sit here all day for all I care." She looked to Tiny Nat for support.

"Now don't go gettin' selfish on me, girl. Tiny's sacrificin' quite a bit to help out, not to mention me," Bathezine growled, sounding more cross than usual.

"You don't think I should know?" Bet said, becoming increasingly exasperated by the Ursian's avoidance.

Bathezine lowered his head. "Giyyup, Jangol," he said, and looked at Bet.

Bet quickly grabbed Pooch-kin. "Stop, Jangol," she said, and the Rhinodon stopped.

Bathezine gurgled a curse. "Oragoths…" He shook his head. "Get in. We'll talk."

Surprised he'd relented so easily, Bet climbed aboard, sitting next to the Ursian. She put Pooch-kin back, next to Tiny Nat, then looked at Bathezine, waiting.

Bathezine looked at her from the corner of his eye. "It's not that there's anything being kept hid from you, it's just that…"

Tiny Nat clicked and buzzed, sounding like he was clearing his throat. "Bet, to many of those who fought in the war, the price was very high. War is not a natural state for those in the Whist. What minor conflicts we had were never on such a scale. Bathezine paid a high price for his part."

Suddenly feeling as selfish as Bathezine had said, Bet slumped in her seat. "I'm sorry. I didn't mean to… I don't want to upset you." She put her hand on the Ursian's big paw.

"Nah, nah. You're right. You need to know about those who took part and what took place." He whistled, and Jangol started off at a trot.

"You don't have to. Like you said, it's not that important right now," Bet said.

"There's a lot to say, and not a lot. A lot if you consider what went into it, a not a lot, when you look at the business of it. By that, I mean it was just fightin, and killin, and all the horrible things that go along with such insanity."

"How'd it start?" Bet asked.

"Not entirely sure. 'Spose you'd get a different answer dependin' on which side you asked. Most people say the conflict lasted five years. But that ain't the whole of it. It started eight years prior to beginnin' of all-out fightin'. And you can even say it's still goin' on since no one never signed no peace treaty or armistice. But there's a lot I don't know, at least with any certainty." Bathezine looked at the sky and urged Jangol to pick up the pace. "Back before you was born, there was one realm, though we— the Whist, that is—stayed clear of the Din for the most part, 'cept for trade and such. About twenty years ago, there was a series of killins that happened on the Isthmus of Tong. And King Dalverious' court accused it of being perpetrated by Users. Though there weren't no proof of it, it did seem peculiar in the manner the victims died."

"What do you mean by peculiar?"

"Peculiar," Bathezine repeated without elaborating. "Point being, the king appointed a special team of investigators. You know 'em as Dalverians, or inquisitors. They caught a Lasoom, reptile-lookin' bunch, tried him and executed him on five or six counts of murder. They never even showed motive for the killin', from what I understand. Though if it was me going about doing such things as murder and causin' general havoc, I'd be more inclined not to use my Talents so as not to arouse suspicion. Anyhow, Dalverious decreed that Users were to be banned from the Isthmus of Tong, and they was all forced to leave. It didn't sit well with many, and a certain resentment arose amongst the Whist who lost their homes and businesses."

"I can see why," Bet said. "It doesn't seem fair that a group had to suffer for the actions of one."

"True. It wasn't long before the same thing happened in the Surrol Plains. The king said it was retaliation, and the Whist were driven out of there, too. And they was mostly farmers, prosperous ones at that. Wouldn't you know it, the throne took control of the farms and their prosperousness." Bathezine sighed. "Thing is, this kept up. Same thing over and over. Before long, the Whist started pushin' back against being pushed out. As you might suspect, the king's forces started pushin' harder, and bad turned to worse."

"That's when the actual war started?"

Bathezine nodded. "See, the Whist weren't as ill-prepared as the king thought. Over a thousand years before something similar happened and they formed the council. Whatever happened before wasn't nearly as bad, and it was over land disputes. Anyway, the council gathered the Whist: Ursians, Vivicons, Andolans, Humans, Creedans, you name 'em, they were there, ready to protect their lands. Things escalated and the fightin' was horrendous. Lotta people died on both sides. And many in the Whist turned Foul. That's when things took an ugly turn. Abominations sprang up, like the Floragads and worse, created by the Foul. When that happened, the balance between the Fair and Foul was lost. We were winnin' the war, but losin' ourselves.

"That's when Fealist-Marsh showed up. Nobody really knows where she came from or where she'd been up to that point. Whatever the case, she did something that put an end to the fightin'. I don't know how. But the king's forces made a push deep into the land of the Whist, despite the Foul and their victory at all costs ideas. She stepped onto the battlefield in the hills north of Illguard, and when she was done, the land was laid flat and the realms were separated. The fightin' ended that day, and that, as they say, is that."

Bet sat in silence for a minute trying to digest everything she had learned and make a connection to the current situation. "Whatever she did, is that where the Waste is?"

"So, they say," Bathezine answered.

"How'd she do it? I'm sure someone had to see, or knows."

"Not sure. Thing is, she was the only one to walk outta there. It's said she was seen walkin' out of the woods and nobody never saw her again. She disappeared. And disappearin' like that circulates a lot of rumors."

Tiny Nat joined the conversation. "There are some rumors she wielded both the Staff of the Din and the Staff of the Whist. We are not certain if that is true."

"If she's so powerful, why does she need me to free her? And who's strong enough to imprison an Omia Temporian? If it's this phantom, why doesn't he just do the same thing to me? Something isn't adding up." Bet looked at both of them, waiting for an answer.

"These are questions we do not have answers for," Tiny Nat said. "Perhaps the Charge of Danthbrook will help us with this."

"You might wanna get one of your—one of you into Illguard. Flursh don't sit still for very long, and Mandi-lyn ain't no exception," Bathezine said.

"We are on the way now," Tiny Nat said.

"I know we're on the way, but we ain't gonna get there 'til tomorrow," Bathezine snapped. He looked back at the Vivicon, who returned the gaze with a cocked head. "Oh, ya meant 'we' as in you and your hive."

Bet shook her head at the Ursian, climbed in the back of the wagon and lay down, resting her head on a duffle. She watched the clouds and a flock of towne geese pass over against the cerulean sky. "You know, Pooch-kin, the more questions I ask the more questions I get in return."

"I have a question," the Chook-chook said. "Did you bring anything for me to eat?"

"You always ask the important questions," Bet said, sitting up to get her friend some seed.

Thirty-Three

The Sumter Flats Highway provided Jangol with even ground to pull his burden, and the group arrived on the edge of Paskersville well ahead of sunset. All along the journey, Bet watched travelers on the broad highway ride in a wide variety of vehicles, ranging from eight-team Riding Elk pulling carriages of commuters to single person sail carts zipping past at incredible speeds. She even saw the occasional motorized bike chug by coughing out billows of steam. She vowed that after her adventures were over, she'd get a sail-cart for her and Pooch-kin, and they'd travel this new world without the worry of deadly encounters.

Adobe homes painted in outlandish colors covered the hills surrounding Paskersville. The highway was lined with shops and diners of all sorts. Each sparked Bet's curiosity to see what treasures could be found inside.

Bathezine guided Jangol off the thoroughfare, along the access road to the seediest inn in sight. Bet hopped out of the wagon as soon as the wheels squeaked to a stop. She looked up at the dilapidated plywood sign painted white with red lettering. "Beds and Foods?" she asked, shaking her head.

"This is the place," Bathezine said, climbing down.

"We're staying at a place called Beds and Foods?"

Tiny Nat stepped off the wagon and seemed to share Bet's opinion of the establishment. "Ursian taste is less refined than most of civilized society's."

Bathezine scowled at the two. "We can stay down the road at some highfalutin place and pay three times as much for doin' the same thing we're gonna do here, which is grabbin' a bite and sleepin'. 'Sides that, this place has stalls round back, outta sight of the highway, and we might be wantin' to be inconspicuous."

"I guess you have a point," Bet said. "As long as we don't catch anything from the beds."

"They're clean enough for ya. I'll see if I can get us a room."

"We are certain they'll have vacancies," Tiny Nat said, drawing a laugh from Bet.

Bathezine tossed his mace in the back and secured his shuriken to his back. "If'n anybody asks, we're huntin' tree-cats in the wilds. On account of the weapons and all."

Bet let Pooch-kin down and watched Bathezine walk to the lobby. "He's trying to be nice. I know he doesn't like towns and crowds."

"There are many things he doesn't like," Tiny Nat said. "But you are correct. He does seem to be trying to be cordial." He scanned the roadway and surrounding hills.

"What?" Bet said, noticing his cautious gaze.

"We are at both ends of town. We will know if anyone comes for you."

"That's good to know. I learned I can sense intentions, but I obviously have a long way to go before I master it. With what happened with Tambor and all."

"Talents take time to master. Two beings may have the same Talent, but one can be stronger than the other in its use. You will learn your strengths over time."

Bet watched Bathezine through the window; he appeared to be arguing with the receptionist. She snorted a laugh. As she watched him, a certain sadness came over her. The Ursian did have a good heart, but he had gone through a lot during the war. She frowned when a thought occurred, and turned to Tiny Nat. "Did Bathezine turn Foul during the war?"

Tiny Nat glanced at her and walked to Jangol, checking on the harnesses. "Many did during that time. But we would advise you not to breach the subject with him. It is not something most wish to discuss, whether they did or not. Needless to say, he must act with caution in certain situations, lest the path to salvation be lost."

The office door of Beds and Foods swung open with a loud creak, followed by a louder slam. Bathezine stormed across the dirt lot, looking as angry as ever. He approached Bet, giving her a wink, then going to Jangol. "C'mon, I got you a nice covered port next to our room," he said to the Rhinodon.

Bet trailed behind Bathezine, with Pooch-kin hurrying along beside her. They reached the covered port, and the Ursian and Tiny Nat began freeing Jangol of various harnesses. Bet looked at the roof of the so-called covered port, which consisted of sagging boards and well-aged thatch. She examined the sky through a hole in the ceiling. "You call this covered?"

"Yep. Got this and the room for an eight piece and a single. Tried to charge me a sixteen. Bathezine's eyes followed Bet's to the hole. He cleared his throat. "Well, it ain't s'posed to rain."

"Where's our eight-piece suite?" Bet asked. "Sorry, eight plus one."

Bathezine frowned at her, fishing a key on a braided cord from his pocket. He pointed at the small cottage next to the port.

Bet raised an eyebrow at the shanty of a structure. She stepped on the wood porch and cautiously pulled the rusty hinged screen door open. She took a breath and unlocked the door, swinging it open with a jerk. She peered inside. There were no dead animals or people inside, like she had imagined. However, the room did reek of ashes, stagnant water, and what she guessed was lingering foot odor from its previous occupant. Two large beds were separated by a rickety table to her left, and a single chair leaned against the wall to her right. The bathroom was to the rear. The walls were unadorned except for what she hoped were various water stains. She poked her head around the door jamb. "You paid how much for this? I think you were taken."

Bathezine glared over his shoulder at Bet. "Get to unloadin' the wagon.

Dinner is about to be served."

Bet grabbed a duffle. "I can't wait. If the foods are as nice as the room, we're in for a treat."

Bathezine and Tiny Nat carried in loads, followed by Bet carrying another duffle. Tiny Nat ducked below the room's single hanging light. "You know there are inns where one doesn't have to hide all of their belongings for fear of theft."

"You, too?" Bathezine said, flopping on the bed closest to the door.

Bet looked at the other bed. "Does this mean one of us has to sleep outside with Jangol?"

"Nah," Bathezine answered. "Vivicons don't really sleep. He don't get a bed."

"And if we did, it wouldn't be here," Tiny said.

Bet laughed. "I almost envy you."

"All right, that's enough. Let's get some food before we miss out." Bathezine tossed his shuriken on the bed.

"We have our food here." Tiny Nat pointed to a nectar bladder.

"Once again, I envy you," Bet said with a laugh. "Yeah, let's go get some foods."

"What about me?" Pooch-kin asked, hopping up on the low bed.

"You didn't have enough already?" Bet said, grabbing a box of seed. "Stay here. It'll be safer."

"C'mon, girl. I'm hungry," Bathezine said, holding the door open.

"Our foods await. I shall ask the maître d' for a table near the kitchen," Bet said, hopping toward the door.

"You'll be lucky if you get a menu," Bathezine muttered below his breath.

Thirty-Four

Bet and Bathezine returned a short time later to find Tiny Nat sitting in the room's lone chair with his legs drawn up and Pooch-kin asleep on the bed.

"How was your cuisine?" Tiny Nat asked.

"I think the chef believes that vegetables of all kinds are permanently out of season. But the bread was a late vintage and gave my jaw a good workout," Bet said, falling on the bed beside Pooch-kin.

"Any news on the Creedans?" Bathezine asked Tiny Nat, ignoring Bet's dining review.

"Yes. It is as we feared. The Creedans and Mastives have joined forces. This is unusual."

"This whole stinkin' mess is unusual. Are they on the move?" Bathezine went to the room's porthole-like window, trying to see through the hazy glass.

"They have made camp no more than a mile outside of Ultum Seam, but the Creedan scouts have bypassed the town and are headed toward Illguard."

Bet sat up. "We shouldn't stay here. We should go there tonight."

"It ain't gonna do nobody no good if we're too exhausted from lack of sleep. Jangol needs the rest, too. We'll leave before sun-up. And I'm sure

Old Babbers is aware of 'em. Nothing gets past her. They'll be ready if there's danger."

"I still think we should go," Bet said, looking to Tiny Nat for support.

"Remember where you are, girl. You ain't the only one with Talents here. There's plenty of people who got Talents you ain't even heard of. They'll be fine. We'll be in Illguard by midday. You just quit your worryin' and try to rest." Bathezine sat on his bed, grabbed a pillow, beat it into a ball, and lay back.

"Bathezine is correct. They'll be safe in Illguard for the time, and you should rest," Tiny Nat said. He turned off the light. "You will sleep better in the darkness."

Bet fluffed her pillow in frustration, though without the vigor of the Ursian. She squirmed to get comfortable on the uneven mattress. "Looks like we're here until morning," she said to Pooch-kin, who was already back asleep. A moment later she heard Bathezine's snoring. She remembered Dalin's advice about eating and sleeping. She took a deep cleansing breath and tried to relax.

Closing her eyes, Bet let her mind drift. She felt the presence of Pooch-kin, nervous even in sleep, Bathezine, who was surprisingly calm, and Tiny Nat, who was as alert as he had been all day. She avoided trying to delve deeper into their thoughts and emotions, feeling that would be a betrayal of their friendship.

Bet continued to drift, seeking out other presences. She became aware of various insects crawling around the room and had to suppress a shiver of disgust. Woodworms ate at the frame of the cottage, and she wondered if the owner even cared. She decided Beds and Foods should change their name to Bugs and Filth.

Her mind drifted outside to Jangol, who was feeling lonely in the stall by himself. Seed mice scurried in the shadows, busily seeking out scraps and insects. She felt the sudden terror of a mouse as its life was taken by a Screech-hawk, and she felt the hawk's satisfaction in finding food for its young. The curiosity of feeling life instead of simply seeing it kept her thoughts free from worry. She stayed in the meditative state for an hour, feeling all the life around her, until her mind began to tire.

On the edge of sleep, a new feeling swept through her mind. Something odd; a void in the sea of existence. The emptiness was moving, disturbing insects and frightening small creatures as it passed on the outskirts of the inn's lot. She focused on the life around the void, feeling it move from cottage to cottage. The emptiness stopped just outside of Jangol's stall. The Rhinodon seemed to sense something. Bet felt his nervousness.

Bet sat up slowly, keeping her mind focused on what wasn't there. "Tiny," she whispered.

"Yes," Tiny Nat said, matching her whisper.

"Something's outside of Jangol's stall. He's nervous."

"You can feel it?" he asked, quietly standing.

"No. But I can feel what's around it, reacting to it. It's like an emptiness. A bubble of nothingness." A chill ran up her spine.

"Usually only one steeped in the Foul can develop such Talents. Are you certain?" He ran his hand along his bandolier, feeling the knives.

"I'm sure of it. What is it?" She reached for her belt.

"A Vapid. One who can mask his presence. Not common, and rarely good." Tiny Nat crept to the door. "Rouse the Ursian."

Bet kneeled beside the bed. "Bathezine," she whispered, lightly touching his shoulder. He grumbled and rolled over. She said his name again, shaking him.

"What do you want, girl?" he said, too loud for Bet's taste.

"Quiet. There's a Vapid outside, near Jangol's stall."

Bathezine's eyes snapped open at hearing that. He scooted off the bed, slow and careful, making sure the mattress didn't creak, then grabbed his blowpipe and a handful of darts. "Is it moving?" he asked in a voice so low Bet had to strain to hear him.

"No. Jangol knows it's there, but he can't see or hear it." She covered

Pooch-kin, who knew to stay quiet.

"How do you wanna handle this?" Bathezine asked Tiny Nat.

"It could just be a robber. We don't know his intentions."

"I don't think so. It checked the other rooms before coming here," Bet said. "Hold on. I lost it."

Bathezine and Tiny Nat stood in silence, listening for any movement.

"It's on the step, just outside the door." Bet pulled an iron bearing from a pouch.

"Tiny, unbolt the door. Bet, get back in bed. We'll let it come in. When it's clear of the door, you let us know. Tiny will close it and we'll trap it inside." Bathezine slowly lay down again, careful not to make a noise.

Bet didn't like the idea of letting a potential assassin inside, but trusted Bathezine and did as instructed. Tiny Nat unbolted the door with extreme care and positioned himself along the wall.

The door knob turned, slow and quiet. Only the slightest of pops from sticking in the frame was heard. Nearly a minute passed until the intruder braved pushing it farther open. Every few seconds, inch by inch, the door opened.

Bet could feel the dust mites being disturbed with each step the prowler took. The Vapid stopped at the foot of Bathezine's bed. Bet opened her eyes, seeing a shadow against the darkness. "Now!" she yelled.

Tiny Nat slammed the door shut, bolting it closed. Bathezine rolled from the bed, brought the blowpipe up and shot.

The Vapid dove to the ground, with the dart sticking in the wall where its head had just been.

"It's on the floor. On the floor," Bet said.

"Where?" Bathezine yelled back.

"I don't know," Bet yelled, with panic in her voice.

Tiny Nat began throwing knives at the ground, hoping for a lucky hit.

Bet felt roaches scatter and reacquired the target. "It's crawling toward the bathroom." She drew back to throw, but Bathezine flew in front of her, landing on the intruder.

The Vapid cried out as the Ursian grappled with shadowy limbs, trying to get a grip. "Lights," Bathezine yelled.

Tiny Nat flicked on the light revealing a charcoal gray, almost black human form struggling against Bathezine's powerful grip. It reached for one of the throwing knives stuck in the floor.

"Watch out," Bet warned, pointing to the knife.

Bathezine saw what the man intended. He rolled to his back, holding the Vapid tight and swung him into the wall head first. The Vapid grunted and crumpled in his arms, unconscious. The man changed from dark to a pallid gray. He was wearing only tattered shorts.

Bet felt his presence at once. She exhaled and let go of her concentration.

"You did good, girl," Bathezine said, easing the thin-framed man off him. "Your Talent of Touch is gettin' stronger."

Tiny Nat tossed Bathezine a rope from the supply box and began retrieving his knives, examining each blade for damage. "Impressive for one so new. We wonder what else you'll be capable of."

"Thanks, I guess," Bet said. She pointed at the unconscious man. "Now what?"

Bathezine finished hogtying the man and stood. "Well, guess we should try to get some information before we decide that." He opened a canteen and poured water on the man's face, saving a drink for himself. Then he tossed the canteen on the bed.

The man groaned and coughed, then opened his eyes. He twisted and jerked, trying to free himself, until finally collapsing back. His wide, dark eyes stared at the huge Ursian and even taller Vivicon. "I didn't know there was a bug with you. I would've fumigated the place first."

Tiny Nat pulled a knife, touching its tip with his other hand, and stared at the man in silence.

"You're not in the position to be insultin' anyone," Bathezine said, picking up his mace. "Next thing that comes outta your mouth better be answers to my questions, else your mouth won't be fit for nothin' but bleedin.'"

The man opened his mouth, saw the Ursian swing his mace, and promptly shut it.

"Tell me now, what'd ya break into to our room for?"

The man eyed the three. "I was just looking for some easy loot from travelers," he said, keeping his eye on Tiny Nat.

"He's lying," Bet said, looking at the man. "I can tell."

The man glared at Bet, closed his eyes, and began to turn dark again.

"He's hiding. I can't sense him," Bet said, unsure how to get around his defenses.

Bathezine looked at Bet, then back to the man. He grabbed one of the Vapid's fingers and snapped it.

The man howled in pain, writhing on the floor.

Tiny Nat took a pillow case and shoved it in the man's mouth, muting the noise.

Bathezine watched until the man stopped moving. He leaned close to him. "You can't focus on hidin' through the pain, can you? Now I'll ask again, and if ya lie again, I'll snap two more. Ya got it?"

The man nodded.

"Okay. What were ya doin' in here?" he asked, pulling the pillow case from the man's mouth.

"A rock. I was hired to steal a rock from the girl," the man said through ragged breaths.

"Who sent ya?" Bathezine asked.

"I don't know. A man with a black beard. Never got his name."

Bathezine looked at Bet, who nodded. "Where's this man with the black beard?"

"I met him in a tavern in Brighthill," the man said.

"Lying," Bet said, grimacing at what was about to come.

Without hesitation, the Ursian reached for the man's hand and snapped another finger.

The Vapid roiled and yelled, receiving the pillow case in his mouth again for the trouble.

After several minutes, Bathezine pulled the fabric from the man's mouth. "Now I took it easy on ya and only broke one. You wanna try again?"

The man nodded. "It was in the Din. In a dive just outside Hammerton. Said he'd pay me three hundred shackles and a gold piece after I crossed over if I did the job."

"The Din?" Bathezine said, turning to Tiny Nat.

"Someone on the other side knows." Tiny looked at Bet.

Bet shook her head. "Only one person knew I had it and she would never betray me. She sent me here to escape the inquisitors. There has to be another way." Her heart raced. What if someone had gotten to Anna and hurt her, forcing her to tell? But how would anyone on that side even know? Her mind spun with panic.

Bathezine put his hand on her shoulder to calm her. He turned back to their captive. "Who's your contact here? How'd you know where to find us?"

The man hesitated, seeming to contemplate another lie, but thinking better of it. "I didn't get that name either. I was told to meet a Loren in Raymor. She told me what to look for. I'm a tracker."

"A female. Can't be your mystery man," Bathezine said to Bet. He glanced at Tiny Nat, who was keeping a steady eye on the man, then turned to the Vapid. "Who does she work for?"

"I don't know. She didn't tell me." He looked at Tiny Nat. "But if I'd known there was a bug, I would've killed it free of charge."

Tiny Nat didn't react.

"He's telling a half truth," Bet said. She didn't flinch this time. If this man had anything to do with Anna and Dalin possibly getting hurt, he deserved what was to come.

Bathezine reached for another finger.

The man tried to roll away. "It's the Reacher. He can cross the divide. You should've given me the stone, girl. Now he'll stop at nothing to get it. He'll kill you and anybody who tries to protect you. The Reacher knows."

"Who's the Reacher?" Bet asked. An ominous feeling washed over her.

"He is everything. Now he'll kill you."

"Shut up," Bathezine demanded.

"Or what, Ursian? You'll kill me? You can't do that, can you? I hope I'm there to watch you die."

Bathezine put his knee against the back of the man's neck, and tied the pillow case around his head, gagging him. He stood and looked at Tiny Nat. "So, what do we do with him? We can't turn him loose and…" he sat on the bed in frustration.

Tiny Nat walked over, made a fist, and a long stinger extended from his knuckle.

"No," Bet said. "You can't kill him. It's not worth it."

The Vivicon shook his head. "We won't kill him. This is a toxin. It will paralyze him temporarily. He will be left in a comatose state for at least a month." He looked at the man. "We understand it feels like fire when injected. But he will soon be unconscious and will eventually awake unharmed, like hibernating. Though he will feel like he was beaten by a

Gar Sloth, from what we've been told."

"What do we do with him in the meantime?" Bet asked, surprised at almost feeling pity for the criminal after all he had done.

Tiny Nat stuck the man in the stomach, holding the stinger in for several seconds. The Vapid writhed from the delivery of the toxin then went limp. Tiny Nat stood, swaying on his feet, then sat.

"I'll pay the manager for a month's stay and tell him not to service the room. Benefits of staying in a place like this," Bathezine said. He tossed the limp man on the bed, removed the gag, and went to the door. "We'll load up and get underway when I get back."

After Bathezine left, Bet went to Tiny Nat, resting a hand on his arm. "Are you okay?"

Tiny Nat nodded. "We will be fine. Stinging is taxing on us. But we will recover soon."

"I'm sorry I got you involved. I didn't know all of this would happen." She patted her pocket and collapsed on the bed, putting her face beside Pooch-kin.

"You did not get us involved. We volunteered. Do not carry an extra burden that does not exist." He expanded his thorax and appeared to be rejuvenated. "We fear this Reacher has more nefarious plans beyond acquiring the facet. We fear we were too hasty in stinging him. He could've told us more."

"No. He didn't know any more than he told us. He's just a hired thug."

"We must find Fealist-Marsh. She can reset the balance."

"Wherever she is," Bet said and began scratching Pooch-kin's ears. "Are you okay, my friend? I seem to be asking you that a lot lately."

"I could be worse," Pooch-kin said. "I could be in Biscuit Head's pot."

Bet hugged her friend. "You have a point. We'll get this figured out. I promise."

Thirty-Five

Old Babbers stood in the middle of the road, hands on her hips and a scowl on her face, as the wagon pulled in to Illguard.

"Aye, this can't be good," Bathezine said. Jangol came to a stop in front of her without instruction. "This woman is the only thing that scares me."

Old Babbers' scowl eased when Jangol snorted at her. She tugged at his tusk playfully. Her sour disposition returned when Bathezine climbed from the driver's seat. "Whenever there's trouble, you seem to be part of it," she said, placing her hands back on her hips.

"Good to see you again, too, Old Babbers. And so soon." The Ursian holstered his mace.

"What's this about with the Creedans? I caught one of 'em sneaking about on the edge of town. Got out of him that you put a hole in a hunter's chest. That true?"

Bathezine put his hands up in defense. "Wudden't me. They attacked us with the intent to kill at Broke Tail Bend. The girl's got a strength Talent. Put one of them bearings right through him."

Old Babbers regarded Bet, who was climbing off the wagon. "Hmm," she snorted. "I 'spose someone has to deal with the troubles you cause. We heard about the attack. And if you weren't so brick-headed, you woulda listened to me and not gone that way."

"Ah, your advice ain't so valuable. What'd ya do with the Creedan? I'd like to do some interrogatin' of my own."

Old Babbers pulled off her hat and ran her hand through her hair. "Had him locked up in the waste bin. But he broke loose and went about tryin' to bite me and some customers."

Bathezine's shoulders slumped. "Where's he now?"

Old Babbers swooshed her hand to the side. "Fed him to the hogs."

"That ain't no help to us. Tiny, is Mandi-lyn still at Handover's?"

"Yes. She is playing chips."

"Tiny Nat," Old Babbers said. "Thought that was you. I'm surprised to see you lowering your station in life by associating with this bear."

"We will be rewarded with a second ferry."

"Hope you got the money upfront," she said, taking the Vivicon's hand in greeting.

"Of course we did."

"Nice," Bathezine grumbled at the pair. "Bet, why don't you and the bird go see about gettin' us a room at Handover's?"

Bet's face lit up. "Sure thing! C'mon, Pooch-kin." She lifted her friend from the wagon and started off. Old Babbers put an arm out to stop her.

"I heard you got a Talent for throwing," the woman said, squeezing Bet's arms.

"Yes, ma'am."

"Ma'am?" Old Babbers laughed. "I like that. But you can call me Babbers or just plain Babs. The old part is for these wannabe traders. Makes them feel like they're my equal."

"Okay, Babbers. I mean Babs," Bet said with a smile.

"Tell me, ya done anything else with your strength aside from throwing? That don't usually come alone."

Bet looked to the sky. "Well, I did tear a handle off a door once." Her eyes shifted from Old Babbers to the ground.

The woman raised her eyebrows. "That's a start. Stick with me. I'll teach you how to use and control it, and not just when you're scared or mad. That Ursian has it, too. But it's different for them than humans. Ursians are already strong."

Bet's face brightened. She felt like she would finally learn something more than just lectures on when to use her Talents. "I'd like that very much. Thank you."

Old Babbers gave her a warm smile. "Okay. Go on now. We'll meet up later."

Bet ran off, urging Pooch-kin to keep up.

Old Babbers watched her leave then turned to Bathezine. "So, what's this trouble you got into have to do with her?"

Bathezine shook his head. "Can't get nothin' by you."

"You got something right for once," she said, mocking surprise. "Tell me what's going on."

Bathezine laid out the whole course of events ending with the incident in Paskersville.

"You stayed at Beds and Foods? I'll need to take you out back and have you washed down with lime and alcohol."

"Is that all you took from this?" Bathezine growled.

"Let's see. You've been attacked three times in a day or so, on account of some stone. I get that. But what else is going on? You're holding back. It ain't that simple."

Bathezine leaned close to the woman. "The girl's been in contact with Fealist-Marsh."

Old Babbers' countenance turned serious. She leaned against the wagon rail. "You sure about that?"

"Sure as I can be. What's more, the one after her is known as the Reacher. From what we gathered from the Vapid, this Reacher fella can cross the barrier to the Din. That accounts for his interest in the stone. We think it's a piece of the Staff of Din." Bathezine waited for her reaction.

Old Babbers stared at the ground, her face twisted in thought. She raised her eyes to the Ursian. "If this phantom Reacher, whatever he is, finds a way to bring down the barrier, it'll be war all over. Where's the Omia Temporian? If she's really still alive, we might be able to stop it."

"That's another story. Apparently she's bein' held prisoner or trapped somewhere. Don't know where, why, or how. She told Bet that she's the only one who can free her. Don't know how she's supposed to do that either."

The woman nodded. "You need to talk to the Charge of Danthbrook."

"That's why we're here," Bathezine said.

"You figure that's why the Mastives and Creedans teamed up? They know something we don't? That union smells like trouble in a sack of problems."

"We believe that is the situation," Tiny Nat said. "We have been watching their movements near Ultum Seam."

Old Babbers nodded again. "All right. I'll gather the boys and we'll set traps in the valley between here and there. If they come this way, that'll slow 'em up."

"What about the forest critters? Don't want 'em springing the traps before they get there. If they come this way, that is." Bathezine looked to Tiny Nat, who seemed to agree.

"I'll take Fiskers. He's an Oragoth. He'll warn the critters." Old Babbers looked up and down the road, as if expecting to see a marauding ban of invaders.

Bathezine seemed satisfied. "Before I forget. We're gonna need a sturdier wagon. Something light and with rubberized wheels for crossin' rough terrain if'n we need to."

"I'll put it on your tab," Old Babbers said with a mischievous smile. "What're you gonna do now?"

"We're gonna go see Mandi-lyn. Once we have her, we'll set out in the mornin'. Maybe even draw that coalition's attention away from town. Being as how that Reacher seems to know where we're headed."

Old Babbers laughed. "That old fur ball ain't one for adventures. You'll have a hard time pulling her away from the tables. And an even harder time issuing the edict. She ain't gonna sit around and listen."

Bathezine looked at Tiny Nat. "I'm sure we can convince her. The two of us can be a persuasive team. And I'll get the words out before she can scurry off."

The woman snorted. "Good luck with that," she said and hurried away.

Thirty-Six

Bet leapt over the steps leading to the Dining Inn, yanked open the door and rushed inside. She scanned the nearly empty room looking for Errel Handover. Not seeing him, she walked amongst the tables and handful of patrons. In the corner to her right, she spotted a Vivicon sucking on a bladder full of nectar. To her left two men discussed their bean crops over matching plates of ham and eggs. She let her mind drift to see if she could feel any malicious intent in the men, only to find their minds were actually absorbed by thoughts of their crops. Eyeing the plates, Bet snatched up Pooch-kin, who knew it was time to hide in the crowded bag again.

She looked to the back of the dining hall, in the room where music played on the night of her visit to find it mostly empty and quiet. Sitting at one of the gaming tables, she saw the furry creature wearing the tricorn hat, who she now knew was the Charge of Danthbrook. Bet ignored her. Bathezine would deal with that situation. She hoped the Ursian had a better relationship with her than he had with practically everybody else they encountered, but she didn't invest much hope in that possibility.

Disappointed in not finding Errel, she went to the reception desk. "Excuse me," she said to the Andolan behind the counter, who was busy looking over the ledger.

The Andolan raised his head from the book, seeming surprised. "Oh! Good morning, young mistress. My apologies. How may I help you?"

"Hi. Is Mister Handover in today?"

The Andolan smiled. "Mister Handover is always in. Who may I ask is calling?"

The swinging door to the back office swooshed open before she could answer. "Bet, my sweet child. Back so soon? I was worried about you after hearing of the incident with the Creedans."

"Errel!" Bet exclaimed. She hurried to him, embracing him in a tight hug.

Still noticeably uncomfortable with displays of affection, Errel patted her back, stepped arm's length back, and smiled down at her. "What brings you back? Had enough of that Ursian already?"

"Nah, he's okay," Bet laughed. She looked around the room. "Does anyone in here have, you know, like a super hearing Talent?"

Errel laughed. "That's not quite the name for it. But as far as I know, no one has. And if they did, it wouldn't matter, an Audiad's range can be a half mile or more."

Bet shrugged. "Okay. Well, since you already know about the Creedans, I'll fill you in on what else has happened. Oh, and we'll need two rooms."

Errel looked to the other behind the desk. "Have rooms two twenty-one and two twenty-two prepared at once. And mark them as unregistered."

Bet grabbed a seat at the nearest table and motioned to her bag, getting Errel's approval to let Pooch-kin out. Once Errel took a seat across from her, she exhaled and leaned in. "Before I begin, there's a couple of things I don't know if I should tell you yet. It's not because I don't trust you, I just don't want any trouble coming to you."

"You seemed to have aged ten years in the time you've been gone," he said through a sigh. He patted his open hand on the table. "And troubles and trials are inescapable parts of our lives. I don't fear them, nor do I back away from them."

"Yeah, well, not troubles like this." Bet looked at the table for a moment, letting out a tired breath. "You're right. I do feel like I've aged ten years since yesterday. But we were attacked twice more after the Creedans, and I found myself in a situation where I had to defend myself or die."

Errel frowned. "I am very sorry to hear that. I can't imagine what you must feel. So young and so new to this place, and yet the hardships seem to be growing with you. Do you know the motives behind the attacks?"

Bet swallowed hard. "I have something somebody wants. But I don't know if you should know what it is. I really don't want you in danger, though it seems like it's on the way."

"The Creedan and Mastive union? I doubt they'll attack an Andolan. Most know that such trespasses are met with swift and total retribution by the Andolan Council."

"I don't think they care."

Concern crossed Errel's face. "What makes you think that?"

Before Bet could answer, Bathezine and Tiny Nat burst in. "Errel Handover, I'm sure you're happy to see me again," the Ursian proclaimed.

Errel stood. "I wouldn't use those words, but you're welcome, of course. Tiny Nat, good to see you." He looked at the Vivicon sitting in the corner.

"Errel, our pleasure, as well," Tiny Nat said. The other Vivicon got up and left.

"You get us a room?" Bathezine said to Bet. He looked at Mandi-lyn in the gaming parlor, who paid him no mind.

"You'll be staying in room two twenty-one," Errel answered for her. His eyes followed Bathezine's to Mandi-lyn, then fell on their weapons. "You're expecting trouble?"

"Something ill is afoot, Errel," Bathezine said, not pulling his eyes from Mandi-lyn. "Go open my room, will ya, Bet?"

"C'mon, Pooch-kin," she said, not wanting to be part of whatever the Ursian had planned.

Errel snapped his fingers at the man behind the desk, motioning for the key and indicating the room number. He turned back to Bathezine and Tiny Nat, and cocked his head. "Will there be a...ruckus?"

"I'm hopin' not." He leaned close to Errel's ear. "We need the Charge of Danthbrook. Lock the door, if'n you wouldn't mind. She's skittish about helpin' others."

"She's a paying customer, and she alone practically keeps the chip table in business."

"Funny how she always comes out ahead, though." Bathezine watched Tiny Nat, who had taken a seat at the dice table across from the chip table. "We'll just be borrowin' her for about a week or two. I'll deliver her back."

Errel looked at him doubtfully.

Bathezine went to the gaming parlor and took a seat at the crescent-shaped chips table next to Mandi-lyn. He threw down a twenty-four piece in front of the dealer.

"How would you like it?" the dealer, a reptilian-like Lasoom, asked.

"Four circles, twelve triangles, and eight squares," Bathezine said, glancing at Mandi-lyn.

Mandi-lyn's pink nose and long whiskers twitched. "Such a high roller," she said with sarcasm.

"I ain't got your kinda luck," the Ursian said. He studied the green felt table top with a pattern of twelve orange circles arranged in a diamond embroidered in the fabric.

"Your bet, Bathezine," the dealer said.

"Don't rush me." Bathezine scratched at his beard. He looked at the diamond for a moment longer and placed his eight square chips on the tip of the diamond closest to him. "Eight fours on nadir one."

Mandi-lyn adjusted her leather tricorn hat and placed a tall stack of circle chips on the opposite tip of the diamond. "Twenty two on zenith one."

With no one else at the table, the dealer turned the crank on a wood barrel tumbler next to him three times. The ceramic chips inside pattered against the cushioned interior. A small hatch at the bottom of the drum opened. "All bets in," said the dealer. He reached in and pulled a bright green diamond shaped chip from within, and placed it on the table in the center of the diamond of circles. He flipped the chip, revealing a cursive Z. "Zenith one wins."

Mandi-lyn's pink hairless hands pulled all of the chips to her. "You can't walk up to a table cold and expect to win on a one."

The dealer slid a blue diamond chip to Mandi-lyn. "Place your bets."

"Let's try this, then," Bathezine said, placing his remaining chips on the circles nearest the bottom point. "Twelve threes on nadir two and four ones on nadir three."

Mandi-lyn snorted. "I'll see that." She placed an equal amount on the same spots on the zenith side.

The dealer repeated the same actions as before, pulling a green diamond chip and placing it on the table. "All bets in." He flipped the chip, revealing a cursive Z with the number three beside it. "Zenith three wins."

Bathezine growled. "Got me again."

"You never were much of a gambler. Stick to dice next time," Mandi-lyn said, gathering her winnings.

"If you're finished," the dealer said, motioning for Bathezine to leave the table.

"Did I say I was done?" He pulled a silver piece from his pocket and flicked it to the dealer.

The Lasoom's forked tongue licked the air. "How would you like it?"

"Four blue octagons."

Mandi-lyn's nose twitched. "You must do well hauling rocks."

"At times," Bathezine said. He studied the table and placed the chips on the left point of the diamond after the dealer called for wagers. "Four eights on west."

Mandi-lyn stared at the Ursian, drumming her fingers on the edge of the table.

"Wagers, please," the dealer said.

"Okay, okay," she said. She slid her entire stack on the opposite point. "One thousand twenty-four on east."

The dealer's eyes narrowed as he cranked the tumbler. He reached in, pulling out a bright red diamond chip, and placed it on the table. "Triple pay out. Loser must match half," he announced, looking between the two. "Can you cover or will you withdraw?"

"I'm in," Mandi-lyn snapped.

Bathezine tapped the table with his thick finger, indicating the dealer to flip.

The dealer turned the chip showing a black double-u. "West wins."

Bathezine gave Mandi-lyn a crooked smile. "Maybe you should stick to cards."

Mandi-lyn pounded her fist on the table. "Shenanigans! There's no way. You cheated!"

Bathezine held his hand to his chest. "Such accusations."

"Don't give me that. You're not that lucky," she yelled. The dealer watched the exchange, showing little care.

"All right. Don't get your fur in knots. I'll spot you your wager and tell ya how it's done," Bathezine said still sporting his grin.

Mandi-lyn looked at him with suspicion. "I'm listening."

"Good," he said, leaning close to her ear. "I sequester the Charge of Danthbrook to my reque—"

Mandi-lyn's black eyes widened. "No!" She pushed away and bolted from the table.

Tiny Nat spun away from his seat and snagged her in his long arms.

"Unhand me, bug!" she squealed, her legs kicking at the air.

Bathezine walked to them. "Do I really have to say it three times?"

Tiny Nat nodded. "For it to be legal, yes."

Bathezine sighed. "I sequester the Charge of Danthbrook to my request."

"I'm not listening," she screeched, squirming against Tiny Nat's grip.

"I sequester the Charge of Danthbrook to my request," Bathezine said again.

Mandi-lyn squirmed harder, breaking free. Falling to all fours, she made a dash for the door.

Errel stepped in front of the door and locked it. "Are you trying to flee from a loss?"

"Conspiracy!" she yelled, and made for the kitchen.

Bathezine was there and met her with a tackle, bowling over a chair. He pinned her to the floor. "I sequester the Charge of Danthbrook to my request."

Mandi-lyn went limp, shaking her head. "No. I don't want to go. See the Charge of Fassian. He'll be willing."

"Fassian is on the other side of the Malt Seas. We are pressed for time," Tiny Nat said.

Bathezine stood, helping her up and pushing her hat against her chest. "I'd rather not use you, but like Tiny said, we're in a bit of a rush."

Mandi-lyn took her hat and put it on with a jerk. "What is it you need?" she asked, her voice filled with resignation.

"I'll fill you in upstairs," the Ursian said, then turned to Errel. "Make sure she gets her wager back. I won on a triple. Get me my wager, too, and take the rest back. That'll cover the cost of the chair."

Errel raised an eyebrow. "Perhaps you're not as bad as I thought."

Bathezine coughed a laugh. "Well, the feeling ain't mutual."

"I stand corrected," Errel said with a laugh.

"And we could use a meal. The grub at Beds and Foods left something to be desired."

Errel shuddered. "I'll bring a meal to you shortly. Then we'll see about getting you deloused."

"Nice," Bathezine mumbled, then took Mandi-lyn by the arm. "C'mon, hamster."

Thirty-Seven

Bet sat on the plush red sofa in her room, happy to be bathed and enjoying a bowl of butterscotch pudding, while Pooch-kin munched on his usual fare. Errel had been kind enough to bring the snacks without request, but with the dual purpose of finding out more of her adventures. He explained the circumstances of the Charge of Danthbrook's servitude and informed Bet that Mandi-lyn's kind were known as Flursh, and that the term hamster was considered offensive, though Bathezine didn't seem to care.

As she listened to Bathezine's deep voice reverberate through the walls, Bet wondered what would come next. Having spent most of her life looking forward to a better life, something beyond the loneliness of the orphanage and then beyond the misery of Malweather farm, this wasn't the future she had hoped for. Even though change had been thrust upon her in unexpected and dangerous ways, she was happy. The growing group of people she had fallen in with made her feel like part of a family for the first time in her life.

Despite the feelings of contentment, she couldn't shake a sense of foreboding, a feeling that change was coming, and it wouldn't be for the better. Bet laid her head back and let out a long breath. "I'm worried about what's to come. So many people are helping me, but their help is putting them at risk. It doesn't seem right."

"Tomorrow doesn't exist, only now. Worrying about it will only serve to make your now miserable," Pooch-kin mumbled.

"Is that a Chook-chook philosophy?"

"No, just advice."

"Right now, I could use a nap." She closed her eyes, letting the stress leave her body, only to have it interrupted by Bathezine pounding on the wall.

"Get in here, girl," his burly voice boomed from the next room.

"So much for that. C'mon, Pooch-kin." She stood and stared at her belt of weaponized balls. She patted her pocket, making sure she still had the facet, and grabbed her belt and satchel.

Pooch-kin stretched. "Why do all of your summonses include me, too?"

"Because I don't want some crazed assassin dumping a crate of Snappers in here without me around to protect you."

The Chook-chook stared at her. "Why does it have to be snakes? I don't like snakes."

"Okay. A crate of weasels. Is that better?"

"No. No, it's not."

Bathezine pounded on the wall again. "Okay, I'm coming," she shouted. "Don't get your shorts in a wad."

"You know you're starting to sound like that bear," Pooch-kin said.

Bet growled. "C'mon, bird," she said with a smile.

"See?"

〜〜〜〜

Bet and Pooch-kin entered the room, which was half the size of her own and not nearly as lavish. Tiny Nat stood at the window, staring out at the forested landscape, Mandi-lyn sat in a wicker papasan chair, and Bathezine stood in the center of the room with his hands on his hips.

"Finally. Any longer and I'd have sent a search party," the Ursian said in his surly manner.

Bet threw up her hands and rolled her eyes. She looked to her left, surprised to find Errel sitting at a small table in the corner. He gave her a slight nod.

Bathezine waved his hand at her. "Bet, this is Mandi-lyn, the Charge of Danthbrook. Tell her 'bout what you dreamed."

"Pleased to meet you," Bet said, offering the other her hand.

Mandi-lyn wiggled her nose, sniffing at Bet.

"Flursh don't shake hands," Errel said from the corner.

"Oh. My pardon," Bet said, hoping she hadn't offended her.

"Enough of the cordialities. Tell her 'bout what Fealist-Marsh told ya," Bathezine interrupted.

"Right. Well, I don't know what Bathezine has told you, but I've heard her talking to others in my dreams, and sometimes when I'm awake. And recently she spoke directly to me and warned me of the attack on the ferry."

"Yes, yes," Mandi-lyn said, not masking her impatience, her whiskers twitching.

"She said I have the Facet of the Din and that I'm the only one who can free her now. Though she didn't tell me how or even where she is. She also said that he will destroy me to get it and I should protect it at all costs."

"If she said you are to free her, she's still alive. Is this person she said will destroy you the one known as the Reacher?"

"I'm assuming he is. I heard him speaking before I heard Fealist-Marsh last time."

Mandi-lyn shifted in her seat. "What did he say?"

"He ordered someone to kill the Creedan chieftain, and that my Talents grow with each day, then he said something about wanting it. That's all I heard before I lost contact. That's when I connected with Fealist-Marsh."

Mandi-lyn's beady, dark eyes scanned the room, not looking at anything in particular. "What else can you tell me? Did you see anything? Objects, a building, anything."

"I only saw darkness when the Reacher spoke. But when I spoke with Fealist-Marsh, I was sitting on a patch of green grass in the middle of what appeared to be a vast desert, though it wasn't hot. It was very bright, and her voice sounded like it came from everywhere at once."

"That sounds like the Transcendent Plane, but the grass could be a clue." Mandi-lyn got up and pattered around the room, stopped, stared at nothing, then returned to her chair.

Bet looked to Bathezine for an explanation, who returned a shrug.

"You must find Fealist-Marsh. May I see the facet?" Mandi-lyn said after settling in her chair.

Bet looked at Bathezine again, who nodded his approval. She pulled the stone from her pocket and held it out between her finger and thumb.

Mandi-lyn studied the shimmering quartz-like stone for several seconds before speaking. "The Staff of the Din was created by the Omia Temporian, along with the Staff of the Whist."

Tiny Nat turned to the conversation. "Fealist-Marsh? It was our understanding that these were ancient relics."

Mandi-lyn adjusted her hat, whiskers twitching. "Are you broadcasting this to the whole hive? This is a private conversation."

"It is only heard by those in this room," Tiny Nat answered.

Mandi-lyn hesitated. "It was not created by Fealist-Marsh. The Omia Temporian come and go through the ages, though rarely in succession. From what I know of them, there was a time many generations ago when two existed at once. They saw the avarice and potential for violence and conquest in the hearts of the Din and created the staffs as a safeguard…a last resort for protection should the consequences of the Din's greed come to pass. As we well know, they did."

"Are you saying the wall of separation was created by destroying the staffs?" Errel asked, scribbling notes on a paper.

"Precisely. The facets were scattered to the winds. That this Reacher is seeking them is concerning, as the staffs can only be wielded by an Omia Temporian."

"Do you think this Reacher is one, also?" Bet asked. She met the others' faces, who carried the same worried expressions.

"I don't know," Mandi-lyn said. "It could be that he is holding Fealist-Marsh captive by some means, compelling her to reconstruct it."

"How could a person capture someone as strong as Fealist-Marsh?" Bathezine asked.

"The breaking of the staffs would require great energy. She may have been weakened temporarily by doing so. But that is purely speculation. What we know is that she's alive and we must find her." Mandi-lyn broke off the conversation, grabbed a large lasher nut from the table, and began gnawing on it.

"Why am I the only one who can free her? It doesn't make any sense," Bet said, feeling the weight of her task.

Mandi-lyn shrugged. "We must first find an Ancient One. Only one of them would know where she could be. Maybe then you'll have your answers."

"And that's why we have the fur-ball here," Bathezine said, patting the Flursh on the shoulder, who jerked away. "She knows where they are."

Bet looked at Mandi-lyn, waiting for an answer.

"There are three known to be alive after the war. One is a wanderer, making it difficult to track. Another is far beyond the Malt Seas, north of the Karish Ocean in Arcticalia. It would take two months to travel there. The other was last known to be in the Caves of Moth. I would rather find the wanderer than go there."

"This doesn't sound good," Bet said, holding Pooch-kin close.

Tiny Nat buzzed, pulling the group's attention from the subject. "There is worse news. The Creedans and Mastives have broken camp. They are on a path to Illguard."

Bathezine growled. "Immunuh check to see how Old Babbers is comin' along with the traps." He hurried from the room.

Errel patted Bet's shoulder in a rare gesture and headed out, as well, with Mandi-lyn trailing him. Tiny Nat followed them out.

Finding herself alone, Bet sat on the papasan chair. "Guess the conversation is over, Pooch-kin."

"I kind of wish it never began."

"Boy, I'm with you on that, my friend."

Thirty-Eight

Bet sat in the chair for several minutes contemplating what she had learned. Too antsy to sit still, she got up and went to the door. "Let's go see about getting you something more comfortable to ride in besides this old bag."

She opened the door and was surprised to find Tiny Nat on the other side. "Back already? Did you leave something?" Bet said, noticing he wasn't wearing his bandolier.

"Bathezine doesn't want you alone. You should stay here." He pushed his way inside and closed the door behind him.

"Oh, well, okay. How far away are the Creedans?"

"One day and one half at their current pace," he said after some hesitation.

"I'll be fine, then. I have to go to the Supply Hut and pick something up." Bet reached for the knob.

Tiny Nat stepped in front of the door. "I will accompany you, then. But before we go, there is something we need to tell you the others do not know yet."

Bet studied him for a moment. She thought the group shared all information. Did he just say I? She reached out to get a sense of him, but couldn't feel anything. She didn't know how a Vivicon's mind worked, but she had always been able to sense him before. "Okay… What is it?"

"Please, have a seat." His eyes flashed a different color, but returned to their normal pale yellow.

Bet hid her surprise. She had never seen them do that before, not even when he was angry with Tambor. She turned her back on him and looked at Pooch-kin, motioning for him to go to the bedroom with her eyes as she put him on the floor. She sat on the arm of the sofa and waited.

Tiny Nat locked the door.

"Do you really need to lock the door?" She shifted her weight and tried to get a feel for his intent, but still couldn't read him.

"I don't want them walking in and disrupting what I have to say," he said, looking back at her.

"Oh, okay," Bet said, rubbing her hand along her belt. "Well, what is it? I really need to get to the store before things get too crazy here."

"First, is the facet safe?"

"Of course. Right here in my satchel, like always." She patted the bag.

"Good. Let me see it." He reached out, extending his pointed fingers.

Bet forced a smile, trying to stay calm. "Why? You've seen it before on the outrider. Remember?"

"Yes. But what I have to say has everything to do with it." He stepped closer.

"Oh. Okay." Bet stood. "Funny thing, though. I never showed it to you on the outrider."

Tiny Nat's head trembled and twisted. Bet watched in horror as the Vivicon's carapace cracked and split open, falling away and revealing a wasp-like head with black eyes and deadly mandibles.

"Give it to me!" the imposter hissed and leapt at her.

~~~~~

Bathezine and Tiny Nat hurried toward the Supply Hut, with Errel trailing them, telling everyone he passed of the impending danger. All along the road, shop keepers and home owners began closing storm shutters and barking orders to others.

They arrived at Old Babbers' shop to find her loading a wagon with spools of wire. "Let me guess, they're on the move." She wiped sweat from her brow with her sleeve and waited for a reply.

"That, they are. Your boys headed out yet?" Bathezine asked, looking at a line of people waiting for supplies.

"Getting loaded right now. How much time have we got?" She looked to Tiny Nat.

"We believe about…" Tiny Nat's voice trailed off. He walked away, his head moving in jerks toward the sky and ground.

Old Babbers turned to Bathezine. "What's with him?"

The Ursian's bushy eyebrows scrunched together, his eyes narrowed. "Dunno. Anyway, probably 'bout a day or so out."

"All right, then. I'll get them moving with what we got loaded. Looks like I'll have to stay here and mind the shop. Don't wanna get looted if Errel gets the whole town in a panic." She looked back at Tiny Nat, then nodded to Bathezine.

Tiny Nat's head continued to bob and tilt in different directions.

"Hey, what's goin' on, partner?" Bathezine said, stepping in front of him.

After several moments, the Vivicon looked at Bathezine. "There is a void in the hive."

"Someone die?" he asked. Old Babbers came alongside him.

"Yes. But the mind lingered. We are trying to pinpoint—" He stopped, standing motionless.

"What is it?" Old Babbers asked, edging closer.

Tiny Nat's head snapped toward Bathezine. "Bet is in danger."

Bathezine and Tiny Nat took off at a run. Old Babbers turned to a young man near the wagon. "Fiskers, mind the store," she shouted and sprinted after the others.

Errel Handover stood talking to an elderly woman, when the commotion pulled him away. "What?" he shouted at Bathezine when they passed by.

"Bet!" he shouted back.

Errel joined in the race, quickly outpacing the others with long strides. Beating them to the door, he pushed it only to discover it had been locked. He fumbled in his pocket for the keys.

A blur of motion passed Bathezine and Tiny Nat before they reached the steps. "Open it," Old Babbers yelled.

"Trying," Errel yelled back, finally yanking the keys from his pocket.

"Get out of the way," Old Babbers said and punched through the brass door plate.

Bathezine pushed them both aside and rushed to the stairs, taking them four at a time. Errel and Old Babbers followed close behind, with Tiny Nat taking up the rear, trailed by several Vivicons, which seemingly came out of nowhere.

The hallway walls were peppered with holes from Bet throwing iron balls at her assailant. Bathezine reached for the knob, finding it locked. He stepped back and kicked the door from its frame. When he stepped inside, his eyes widened with horror. The wasp creature, free of its Vivicon shell, stood over Bet with its stinger buried in her abdomen. Pooch-kin relentlessly pecked at the creature's leg to no effect.

The wasp rummaged through her satchel, turned its head, and bared its mandibles. "You're too late," it said, revealing the stone he pulled from the bag, and spread its wings.

Bathezine pulled his the shuriken off his back and let it fly in one motion. The wasp hissed just before the spinning blade severed its head from its body. The wasp fell dead, its wings fluttering against the wood floor.

Bathezine rushed forward, kicked the headless body aside, and knelt beside Bet. "No, no, no. C'mon, girl. Stay with me."

Pooch-kin went to Bet's ear, chirping repeatedly.

Bet's eyes were wide and unseeing, her lips a pale shade of blue, and frothy foam dripped from her mouth down her cheeks.

"Get her on the sofa," Errel yelled.

Bathezine laid her on the couch, checking for signs of life. "She's not breathing!"

Pooch-kin chirped wildly.

"Quiet, bird," Bathezine snapped.

"He's trying to tell you something," Old Babbers said from the doorway.

"What's he sayin?" the Ursian growled.

"I don't know," Old Babbers growled back.

"The elixirs," Tiny Nat said. Pooch-kin tweeted an affirmative.

Bathezine snatched up the satchel, tossing things from inside. "They're not in here," he said, casting the bag against the wall.

The group scanned the floor, eyeing the contents the wasp had thrown from the bag in its search for the facet.

"There," Old Babbers said, pointing to a vial near the far wall.

Errel grabbed the glass vial and tossed it to Bathezine.

"Not it," Bathezine said, placing it in his pocket.

Pooch-kin looked under furniture while the others searched the room. The other Vivicons entered to assist.

"It's gotta be here," Bathezine urged. He held her hand tight. "Hurry! We're losing her."

Tiny Nat kicked the wasp's body in frustration and another vial rolled from underneath. "Here," he exclaimed, and threw it to Bathezine.

"Let's hope it's the right mix." He bit off the wax sealed stopper and dumped the contents in Bet's mouth.

The group watched in silence, holding their breath, waiting for a sign. Nearly a minute passed with nothing happening.

Bathezine lowered his head. "I don't think it was the right mixture."

Pooch-kin moaned a quiet warble.

Bet coughed.

"Bet!" several of them shouted in unison.

She continued to cough, her breath coming in fits and rasps.

Bathezine squeezed her tight. "Thought we lost you, girl," he said, his eyes wet.

Bet groaned, but couldn't speak.

"What're you sayin?" Bathezine asked.

She moaned and her eyes went toward her stomach, tears rolling down her cheeks.

Bathezine looked at the angry puncture wound. "There's another vial somewhere 'round here. It's a healing potion."

The others resumed their search. "We can't find it," Old Babbers said after a couple of minutes of looking.

Bet shook her head and raised her trembling arm. She opened her hand, revealing the vial.

Bathezine gave his odd toothy grin. He uncorked the elixir, but hesitated. "This will sting a bit."

Bet shrugged.

"I know. Can't be any worse than what you already got." He sprinkled a few drops on the wound, and Bet's eyes widened while she moaned.

"Maybe it is."

Bet's skin sizzled and the injury closed, leaving a pink splotch of skin where a hole had once been.

Pooch-kin crawled beside her head and nuzzled close, making quiet purring noises. Bathezine pushed her hair from her face.

Bet closed her eyes and licked her lips. "Thank you," she whispered and passed out.

Bathezine snorted. "You're welcome." He looked at the wasp head lying on the floor. His body slumped.

Thirty-Nine

Tiny Nat pulled the shuriken from the wall and put it near Bathezine without speaking. He watched the Ursian for a moment, his large frame on the floor, leaning against the sofa, his head resting on the arm above Bet, staring at nothing.

Tiny Nat lowered his head and went to the fireplace. He searched for a flint or matches and found nothing. "Does anyone have a flint? We need a fire."

Errel walked over, squatted, rubbed his hands together and the fire sprung to life. "She might be more comfortable in her room. I can start a fire in there," he said, his voice still shaky from the ordeal.

"The fire is not for Bet. The attacker was a Troojian Wasp, a parasite. We need to dispose of the body to ensure its eggs die as well," Tiny Nat said. The other Vivicons began slicing the wasp, bringing small pieces to the fire. "Make sure the flame burns hot."

"Right," Errel said, trying to mask his disgust at the sound of the wasp being cut to pieces. He rubbed his hands once more and the fire burned white hot. "I have to check on my doorman."

Mandi-lyn bumped into Errel on his way out. "What happened?" she asked, surveying the damage caused by Bet's struggle.

"She was attacked again. This time by a parasitic wasp using one of Tiny's friends as a host. She was stung and almost died. Where were you?"

Errel said.

Mandi-lyn's whiskers bobbed and she took off her hat. "I went to buy nuts for my journey." She held up a large sack.

Errel rolled his eyes.

"I'll need to eat along the way, too," she said and walked to Bet. She kneeled beside Bathezine, who raised his head. She began sniffing Bet, who smiled in her sleep at the Flursh's tickling whiskers. "The toxins are nearly neutralized. Is this the wound?" She touched the pink skin.

Bathezine nodded. "Used a healing elixir to seal it up. Also used an antidote elixir for the venom."

"Those are illegal."

"The girl had 'em. Brought 'em from the Din. Good thing, too, else she'd be dead."

"The antidote was fine, but there is a piece of the stinger left in the wound. That's why elixirs are dangerous for novices to use. The wound must be free of foreign matter before closing. There is a risk of infection. Hold her tight. This will hurt." Mandi-lyn began making a chittering noise with her large incisors.

"Can't it wait a little? Let her recover a bit," Bathezine said. Tiny Nat walked over to see.

"There is no time," Mandi-lyn snapped.

Bathezine held Bet still and tight, and Pooch-kin moved to the arm of the sofa. Bet's face began to contort as Mandi-lyn's chattering grew louder. Moments later, Bet opened her eyes and screamed as the debris rose through her skin. The Flursh's chattering stopped. She held up a quarter inch piece of stinger, which Tiny Nat took and threw in the fire. Mandi-lyn pushed her hand on the exit wound and the bleeding stopped.

Bet panted, laid her head back, and passed out again.

Bathezine rubbed her forehead. "Didn't know you was a healer," he said to Mandi-lyn.

"Don't let it get out or I'll have a hundred people a day sequestering me to fix them, and I won't have time to take your money at the tables."

"I think I took your money last time."

"You cheated."

Tiny Nat picked up a rock near what remained of the wasp. He tossed it to Bathezine. "The Troojian had this."

Bathezine studied it and handed it to Mandi-lyn. "Is it anything important?"

The Flursh examined it, holding it up to the light. "It's common rose quartz. Nothing of value, unless you're a collector."

Bathezine laughed. "The girl's smart. Let's get her to her room. Smells like cooked wasp in here."

Old Babbers, who had been studying the damage in the room, found a wasp arm in the corner and handed it to a Vivicon. "She put up a good fight."

Bathezine carried Bet to the door. "She can do that. C'mon, Pooch-kin."

Babbers followed him to Bet's room and sat on the edge of the bed after the Ursian laid Bet down. "I wanna go with you on your little quest. Her Talents are raw. She needs training."

"What about the hut?" the Ursian asked, taking a chair in the corner.

"Fiskers can handle it. And I ain't had a vacation since Pop died."

"It ain't gonna be much of a vacation. Might be danger and fighting and such."

Old Babbers laughed. "I'm counting on it. I was younger than her when the Din forces came through Illguard. I made sure not many of 'em left. 'Sides, helping her will help me stay on the edge. Those of us who fell to the wrong side of things need to be selfless to keep from falling too deep."

"As ornery a critter as you are, you ain't too far gone." Bathezine looked at his feet, lost in thought.

"Hey there, bear-man. You did what you had to do. There's no fault in that. You did it outta caring for and protecting someone."

Bathezine shook his head. "I know. But I ain't done no killin' since the war."

"Listen, you're as unpleasant as anyone I've known, but you got a good heart. You can't beat yourself up to the end of your days by hauling rocks and giving your money away, and keeping everyone at arm's length over what happened during the war. It won't change nothin'. Pop knew you was good inside. I know it, too."

Bathezine took a deep breath and nodded. "I'm a-scared of what's in store. A-scared of what it can do. I ain't got many years left in me and… well. I'm just a-scared."

Old Babbers sniffed a laugh. "I'll be there, and we'll keep one another in line." She looked at Bet, who was beginning to stir. "And that's as mushy as you'll ever hear me talk. So, don't go getting used to it."

"If'n that was mushy, I'm a Flit-hopper." He looked at the woman with a half-smile, then went to Bet.

Forty

Bet's eyes blinked open to the blurry shapes of Bathezine and Old Babbers standing over her. She felt around and found Pooch-kin nuzzled close to her. "Are you okay?"

"I am. The question is whether you are," Pooch-kin said.

Bet looked around, tried to sit up, but fell back. "I feel like I've been trampled by a herd of Rhinodons."

"Just you take 'er easy, little one," Bathezine said. "You've had one hellfire of a day."

"What happened? Did you catch that thing?" Her eyes widened. She felt her pocket, then eased back.

"We found it, then it lost its head. You're lucky to be alive," Old Babbers said.

"I thought it was Tiny Nat at first, but it wasn't. I tried to fight, but it was so quick. Then it stabbed me with something." She touched her abdomen, and a tear rolled down her cheek. "I wanted to keep it from Pooch-kin, but I couldn't move."

"Don't worry none. You did good. But you're lucky that old man gave you those elixirs, else you wouldn't be here." Bathezine sat beside her and patted her leg. "Glad you're all right."

Bet rubbed her eyes. "What happened? You said you got it."

Bathezine explained most of what happened, leaving out some of the more gory details. "What's important is you're safe now. And I ain't leavin' your side again for a second."

"Does that include me using the bathroom?"

"I suppose I can afford you that privacy." Bathezine laughed.

"I see your sense of humor is wearing off on her," Old Babbers said.

"I ain't got no sense of humor," the Ursian grumbled.

"You got that right," Babbers added.

Bet smiled and rolled her head, loosening her tight muscles. Her smile faded. "What I want to know is how that wasp thing got inside of the Vivicon."

"What do you mean?" Old Babbers asked.

"Well, parasites usually start off small to infect the host. It had to get in it somehow. Maybe somebody put it in him."

The other two shared glances. "Good question," Babbers said.

"Coulda picked it up anywhere, I 'spose," Bathezine said, his voice telling her he wasn't convinced.

"And it just happened to be here and was after the stone? I doubt that very much," Old Babbers said.

"We'll talk to Tiny about it. And speakin' of stones..." Bathezine put the decoy quarts on the bedside table.

Bet gave him a sheepish grin. "I figured someone would come looking for it again. I almost gave it to the Vapid, but he seemed a little more intuitive."

"You should find a box full then," he said. He twisted toward Old Babbers. "If'n you're comin' with us, make sure we got the best supplies, not the junk you usually sell. And plenty of food, too."

"I'll get a second wagon, if only to carry your food," Babbers said.

Tiny Nat and Mandi-lyn entered the room. "How is she healing?" Tiny Nat asked.

"I'm doing good," Bet answered.

"We are glad to hear," he said through a buzz.

"We were wondering how your friend got infected," Bathezine said without preamble. "We're concerned someone put the parasite in him."

"A Troojian wasp usually paralyzes its victim and injects the larva, though it can also be ingested. The parasite cannot be detected by the host. We can detect it if we know the victim has encountered the wasp. The rest of the hive has already been checked. There are no other infections. But that is a lesser concern at the moment. The Creedan alliance is moving at great speed. At their current rate of travel, they will be here shortly after dusk."

Bathezine stood. "How? They ain't that fast. They steal motorized vehicles or somethin'?"

"No," Mandi-lyn interrupted, looking at Tiny Nat. "I believe they're using elixirs. It's the only thing to account for how fast they're moving on foot."

"Won't their hearts explode or something?" Bet asked, sitting up.

"Probably. But if they're being compelled, they won't care. If they intend to raid the town, they have to know it will be a one-way trip for most of them. And the Mastives aren't affected by elixirs as most are," Mandi-lyn said.

"We believe we should leave soon to protect Bet," Tiny Nat said.

"That's the plan, ain't it?" Bathezine said, sounding irritable. "What do ya think, Mandi-lyn, is she well enough to travel?"

"I'm ready to go. Don't worry about me," Bet said before the Flursh could answer.

"She should be well enough to travel, though she might feel weak. But her strength will return shortly." Mandi-lyn paced about the room. "If this

Reacher has trackers or can sense where we are—or where we're going, as the Creedan and Mastive advance seems to suggest—we should make for the Caves of Moth with haste. He may have already anticipated our next move."

"I thought only the Charges know where the Ancients Ones are." Old Babbers said.

"We don't know what the Reacher is capable of. If he can cross the barrier, whether physically or mentally, who knows what he can do," Mandi-lyn said.

"We know he can't physically travel here. Or else why wouldn't he just come for Bet and get the facet himself?" Old Babbers said. "He must Presence travel."

Mandi-lyn nodded. "Very true. Perhaps he is connected to staffs as well. But we can only guess, and only an Ancient One would know the answers."

Bet swung her feet over the edge of the bed. "Listen, I'm fine to go. Really. Mandi-lyn is right, we need answers. I have a feeling, a sense of… I don't know, foreboding. Like there's a darkness or shadow growing. And if we don't find Fealist-Marsh soon, things will get worse, much worse. It's like we're standing on the edge of doom, and if we hesitate…" Bet stood on shaky legs, catching herself on the bed post.

Bathezine gave her his hand; she waved it away. He studied her for a moment. "Is what you're feelin' the same as what you felt when you sensed the Creedans and the Vapid?" he asked, still keeping his hand extended in case she needed it.

"I don't know. Kinda, but it's different. It's more of an undercurrent of darkness. Thinking about it, it seems like I've felt this since before I left the Din, but I wasn't aware of it. If that makes any sense."

"You're more in tune with your Talents in the Whist, so yes, it does," Mandi-lyn said. She went to Bet, leaned close, her whiskers nearly touching her. "You need sugars. It will help counter the after-effects of the venom and antidote."

"You don't need to tell me twice," Bet said. A smile eased across her face.

"There's still some pudding in the other room."

"Natural sugars. Fruit," Mandi-lyn added.

Bet shrugged. "That'll work, too."

Errel walked in the room. "Good to see you up so soon," he said, seeing Bet on her feet.

"She needs fruit. You got any fruit?" Bathezine snapped.

"There's some on the dining table," he said, shaking his head at the Ursian's gruff manner. "Mandi-lyn, I hate to bother you, but is there anything you can do for Walt the doorman and the chip dealer, Le'lel? They appear to have been stung, as well. They're both unconscious downstairs."

"If I had antidotes, yes. Otherwise, it will take me hours we don't have."

"If they were stung before the Troojian hatched, it would be Vivicon venom. We can reverse the effects," Tiny Nat said. He followed Errel out.

Old Babbers tossed Bet a yellow fruit from the bedroom doorway. "I'm gonna get the wagon loaded. Hope Fiskers hasn't sold out the store yet," she said and hurried off.

"I'm going to pack," Mandi-lyn said. "Eat your fruit."

"Ya ain't thinking 'bout runnin' off, are ya?" Bathezine said.

The Flursh stopped and turned to him. "You know I can't. Even if you were to release me of my sequester, I'd still go. This is too important to be concerned with self. It must be stopped."

Satisfied, Bathezine turned back to Bet. "How ya feelin?"

She took her last bite of fruit and tossed the core at him. "Let's go find this Ancient One."

Bathezine sniffed the core, shrugged, then popped it in his mouth. "To the Caves of Moth, it is," he said, his voice lacking enthusiasm.

Concern crossed Bet's face. "What are the Caves of Moth?"

"If'n I told ya, ya'd probably wanna stay here and fight the Mastives."

Forty-One

Bet followed behind Bathezine, carrying all of her belongings and Pooch-kin, as the burly Ursian pushed his way past the crowd at the Supply Hut. They spotted Old Babbers directing people to make a line.

Bathezine pressed forward, and when a man refused to budge, he picked him up by the shoulders and set him aside.

The man looked like he was about to say something he shouldn't but Bet stopped him. "Probably not wise to upset him."

The man looked at Bathezine's hulking frame, and agreed.

"You 'bout ready?" Bathezine said, finally freeing himself of the throng.

"Yeah," Old Babbers said with a huff. "Both wagons are out back. I hitched one to Alice, my Fleet Ox. She's a bruiser and seems to like Jangol. How're Walt and Le'lel?"

"Tiny fixed 'em up. Speakin' of, have you seen him?"

Old Babbers pointed down the road. "He was down at the west end of town last I seen him."

"C'mon, girl," he said.

"Hold on," said Bet. "Babbers, do you have a bag I can carry Pooch-kin in? He doesn't like the satchel, and I don't want him getting trampled out here."

"I can take care of myself, you know?" Pooch-kin said.

"I know, but I need to keep you close."

Old Babbers looked at the satchel. "Can't say I blame him. Come with me."

Bathezine watched them go and threw up his hands.

"I'll only be a minute," Bet said to ease his impatience.

Old Babbers led her to the back of the shop where various linens hung on racks. "How ya feeling? You up for this?"

Bet shrugged. "I feel fine. I don't know if I'm up for this, though." She held Pooch-kin close, scratching his ears.

Babbers pulled a canvas shoulder bag off a hook. "It's wool-lined. They're used for carrying pop-melons, but it's roomy enough for a Chook-chook."

Bet showed Pooch-kin the bag and draped it over her shoulder. "Climb in, my friend," she said, holding it open.

Pooch-kin looked inside. "It'll do. Your arms get sweaty."

"They also get tired. Hop in."

Once Pooch-kin got settled, Old Babbers took her to a hat rack. She took down a brown, floppy-brimmed, suede hat and put it on Bet's head, studied the girl for a second, then took off her own canvas hat, tossing it aside, and put the hat on her own head. She grabbed a similar hat, only black, and put it on Bet, and smiled. "You know, nobody's ever ready for what's happened or will happen. But I want you to know, I'll be with you every step."

"Thank you. That means a lot. You know, I never had a family, and through all of this, it kinda feels like I've become part of one now. Though I wish the circumstances were a little better."

Babbers sniffed a laugh. "Sometimes circumstance is what brings a family together."

Bathezine poked his head from behind a shelf. "If you two are done playin' dress-up, we gotta get Tiny and hightail it outta town."

"You ain't got a tail, bear," Old Babbers snapped back.

"That's 'cause I ain't a bear."

"So you keep telling me," Old Babbers said. "You two get going. I'm gonna weapon up, and close shop. I'll bring the wagons around when I'm finished. And so ya know, I loaded mine with shell bombs in case something needs persuading with a boom. Don't go starting a fire or nothin'."

Bathezine raised his brows. "What else ya got in there?"

"Little bit of everything. Now go. Tell Tiny we're all set."

Old Babbers squeezed past them, and Bathezine watched her go. "That woman thinks of everything."

Bet smiled, looking at him. "You care about her, don't you?"

Bathezine scratched his ear. "Like I said, she's good enough."

Forty-Two

The pair found Tiny Nat on the edge of town, where the road wound into the wooded countryside, watching the western sky. "Hey there, Tiny. Wagons are loaded. We best be off," Bathezine said.

Tiny Nat put up a finger and continued to stare westward.

"He's communicatin'," Bathezine told Bet.

"I kinda figured that out," Bet said with a sardonic tone, to which the Ursian raised an eyebrow.

"See? I told you. You're starting to sound more and more like him," Pooch-kin said, his head poking out of the bag.

"Quiet, you," Bet said, playfully scratching at the bag.

"Whatcha got?" Bathezine asked, stepping beside Tiny Nat.

After a few more seconds, Tiny Nat turned to him. "We believe there is a new threat coming."

Bathezine growled. "Ah, what now?"

"We have spotted a flock of Thorn Eagles headed this direction."

"What are Thorn Eagles?" Bet asked.

"Birds of prey. Got thorny hooks in their tail feathers for catchin' fish.

As if their talons ain't enough," Bathezine said, then looked back at the Vivicon. "What's the threat in that? There's plenty of them things about."

"They are carrying objects."

"Still ain't seein' your point."

"Do you remember the battle of Gaunt Ridge?" Tiny Nat said.

"I wasn't there. But I remember it was a rout in our favor."

"Falcons were used during the fighting. They carried bombs made of hollowed-out eggs filled with petroline."

"Oh," Bathezine said. He gripped Bet's shoulder. "This is a problem. How far out are they?"

"Five minutes for the first wave. Approximately twenty birds. The second group is ten minutes away. We can't say this is the case with any certainty. They could simply be migrating. Perhaps we are being overly cautious."

"Then we should err on the side of caution. Let's get back and warn the others. And see if one of your boys can knock one down. If'n it explodes, we know."

"Drones are neither boy nor girl," Tiny Nat said.

"Ya know what I mean," Bathezine said, jogging back to the Supply Hut. "Keep up, girl."

Bet stared at the sky a moment longer, then ran to catch up.

By the time they reached the shop, Tiny Nat had confirmed that the threat was real.

"Bad news," Bathezine said when they found Old Babbers shuttering up the store.

"That's usually all you have," she quipped. "What is it now?"

Bathezine put up his hand. "Tiny, have them take out as many as they can before they get here."

"We will do our best," Tiny Nat said.

Bathezine turned back to Old Babbers. "Thorn Eagles. And they're carryin' bombs."

"What's next, Thunderpods?" the woman grumbled. She handed Bet a leather pouch.

"What's this?" Bet asked, feeling the weight.

"Pea gravel. Throw it by the handful. Better chance of hitting than a single rock or ball or whatever. And when you do throw a ball, hold it loose in your hand, focus on your target, step towards it, point your elbow where you want the ball to go, bringing your arm over the top, and throw."

"Okay. Got it." Bet looked for a place to carry the heavy pouch. Already burdened with two bags and Pooch-kin, and weapons, she put the strap over her head.

Old Babbers smiled, patted her on the shoulder, took the pouch, and looped it around Bet's belt. She headed off to warn the crowd still milling around the road.

Forty-Three

Bathezine guided Bet along the road, dodging panicked townsfolk rushing to make preparations for the oncoming assault. "Now I want you to stick close. I know you can handle yourself, but if'n we meet the Creedans full-on, it'll be something like you've never experienced. And, well, I have."

"I'm more worried about the people here. It's my fault these attacks are coming," Bet said, looking to the sky.

Bathezine stopped and took Bet by the shoulders. "It ain't your fault. There ain't no blame being put on you by anybody. If ya feel the need to place blame, put it on this Reacher fella, or even King Dalverious for startin' the whole confounded mess. Blame his parents for raising such a fool. While you're at it, blame his great-grandmother."

"Well, that's just stupid. How would his great-grandmother be to blame?"

"That's my point. Don't go feelin' guilty for somethin' you had nothin' to do with. It's a waste of time and energy, and it robs you of livin'."

"You're right," Bet said after some consideration. She couldn't change anything that led up to where she was, and there was no way to know what was to come with any certainty. She looked at the Ursian. "You should take your own advice."

Bathezine gave her a sideways glare. "My advice is for me to give, not to take."

"Just saying…" her voice trailed away as she stared at the east end of town. "The Creedans are here. They're waiting on the eagles."

"What? What're you sayin'? They ain't gonna be here for at least another hour or more."

"A small band. Twenty of them." Her eyes widened. She dug into the leather pouch, grabbed a handful of gravel, reared back and threw it straight up. "Watch out."

Bathezine craned his neck, looking toward the sky. "What're doin', girl?"

"Wait for it," Bet said. A moment later three balls of fire erupted high above. "They're diving."

Bathezine grabbed her by the arm. "Get inside."

Bet pulled away and threw another handful. Four more fire balls exploded a fraction of a second later. "Now we get inside."

They ran for the building next to the Dining Inn, and barreled through the door, taking cover just as the first bomb impacted.

Fire rolled over the road where they had just been. People screamed when the flames overtook them.

Tiny Nat burst in. "Are you okay?"

"We're fine. Where's Old Babbers?" Bathezine said, pulling his blow pipe and a handful of quills.

"At the store. We couldn't see these ones. They were too high."

"At least we had some warning," the Ursian said looking at Bet.

Bet stood and looked at the burning building across the road. Citizens of every kind helped the injured and sought cover. Anger rose up inside her, and she fought to control the feelings of rage at seeing the town that almost felt like home burn. She took another handful of gravel and ran outside before Bathezine could stop her.

Bet let her senses extend past the fear and confusion and felt the next wave of Thorn Eagles approaching form the west. She saw several explosions in the air and knew right away that Old Babbers was using the same technique to stop them. Bet let loose another volley and took out what the woman had missed.

Mandi-lyn rushed from the Dining Inn loaded down with a pack and an armful of leather tubes. "Where's the wagon?"

"Old Babbers is bringing it," Bet said, watching the townsfolk unfurl long hoses and attach them to iron pumps. She turned to Bathezine and Tiny Nat. "The Creedans are coming."

"We know," Tiny Nat said. "They are still an hour out."

Bathezine shook his head. "There's a party of twenty or so on the edge of town your boys missed."

"How could we have missed them?"

"Watch it!" Bathezine said. He twisted and knocked an arrow from the air. "Don't matter. Here they come."

Twenty Creedans, covered in dried mud and leaves, rushed down the main road, making high-pitched calls, attacking everyone they saw.

Tiny Nat threw a knife and Bathezine fired a dart, both taking down their targets.

Bet swung Pooch-kin's bag behind her, grabbed an iron bearing, and focused on her target like Old Babbers had told her. The Creedan stopped and drew back its bow. Bet threw before it could line up its shot, and separated its leg from its body.

The remaining Creedans spotted her and attacked en masse.

"Oh no, you don't," Bathezine said, drawing his mace. He rushed to meet them. The first Creedan fool enough to confront the Ursian was met by a mighty swing of the mace, which sent it flying ten yards away through a boarded shop window. The second met a similar fate.

Errel stormed out of the burning Dining Inn. He surveyed the fight, grabbed the nearest Creedan by the head, and the squealing attacker burst into flames. Errel dropped the flaming creature and went for another. He reached for the next when an arrow struck him in the shoulder. He yelled out and fell.

"Errel!" Bet shouted and threw again. The ball hit the archer, leaving a hole where its slitted nose had once been.

Errel crawled out of the fray, seeking shelter alongside the boardwalk.

Le'lel, the reptilian chip dealer, burst from the inn, and in a fluid motion, coiled his slender body around the nearest Creedan, squeezing the life from it instantly.

"Woah," Bet said, surprised by the grace and quickness of the attack. "Glad he's on our side."

Bathezine took another attacker by the head and used it to beat yet another unconscious, then cast the weaponized Creedan body aside.

"Out of the way," a woman's voice called from behind.

Bet turned to see Old Babbers driving Bathezine's wagon up the road, beside another being pulled by the Fleet Ox.

"Save some for me," she shouted with far too much enthusiasm. Before coming to a full stop next to the group, Old Babbers leapt from the seat, over the Rhinodon, drawing her hatchets in midair.

"Fight's over," Bathezine said to Bet.

Tiny Nat threw another knife into the chest of an attacker and stepped aside.

The woman landed amidst the remaining Creedans, swinging her weapons. Bet watched the spinning ballet of glimmering hatchets twirl in a dizzying frenzy of motion. Creedans fell by the wayside as the whirling ball of energy that was Old Babbers cut them down. The display ended with her standing perfectly still, weapons ready for another target.

Bet stood with her mouth agape.

When no other threat presented itself, Old Babbers wiped the blades clean on one of the victims, and holstered them. She turned and gave Bet a crooked smile. "Focus and control."

"You've been training," Bathezine said, looking equally impressed by the show of skill.

The woman shrugged and adjusted her hat. "Every now and then. Now let's load up and get going."

"Errel's hurt," Bet said and rushed to where he rested against an awning post. She slid to the ground beside him and looked to Mandi-lyn, who was holding the arrow. "How is he?"

"I'm fine, Bet," Errel said and looked to Mandi-lyn, who nodded. He placed a finger against the open wound, and a quick flash of flame erupted, cauterizing the flesh. He grimaced. "See? Good as new."

Bet smiled. "We have to go. Will you be okay?"

Errel coughed a laugh. "I'll tell you along the way. If you have room, that is."

Bathezine walked over and offered him his hand. "We'll make room."

"Who's going to watch the inn?" Bet asked.

"Walt and Le'lel. If the fire brigade can save it."

With a lull in the fighting, the citizens resumed their rescue efforts and battling the fires.

"Hurry up, will ya," Old Babbers called to Bathezine from the seat behind the black shaggy-haired Fleet Ox. The bulky animal snorted her agreement, scratched the ground with her front hooves, and lowered her head, with large horns forward, ready to meet any challengers.

Tiny Nat helped Errel into a seat behind Old Babbers, and squatted, preparing himself for another confrontation.

Bet loaded Pooch-kin and watched Mandi-lyn climb in and curl into a ball on the floorboard beside the Chook-chook. She took hold of the rails to pull herself in, but stopped and looked eastward. "More Creedans."

"How is this possible?" Tiny Nat said. "We should have seen them."

The group looked down the road to see the mass of white-skinned marauders charging toward town. A cloud of dust rose farther down the road.

"What's that?" Bet said, pointing at the rising haze. She climbed aboard and quickly began restocking her weapon belt.

"Mastives," Bathezine growled.

"We need to clear a path," Old Babbers said, pulling back on the yoke to calm the antsy Fleet Ox.

Bathezine hopped down and pulled his shuriken. "I liked this thing." He spun his body like a discus thrower and let go of the star-shaped weapon.

The spinning blade cut through the front line of the Creedans with such speed none had time to react. The star continued to fly out of sight. A moment later they heard the distant roar of Mastives as the blade cut through that group.

"Giyyup!" Old Babbers shouted, and Alice the Fleet Ox charged ahead.

Bathezine climbed aboard, and Jangol matched the other's charge.

The tandem of beasts gouged, hammered, and trampled their way through the crowd of Creedans. Undeterred by the clobbering hooves and horns, the hill folk tried to cling to the wagons. Those who managed to grab hold were met by either Bet's fists or Errel's fire.

Tiny Nat buzzed loudly, and several dozen Vivicons raced in from the forest edge, descending on the remaining Creedans.

Bet leaned back, taking a breath, and watched the insectoids make quick work of the diminutive wild men. "He couldn't have done this sooner?" she said, surprised by the counter attack.

"Timing's everything," Bathezine said. He drove Jangol alongside the other wagon, and shouted over their thundering hooves. "We'll never make it past the Mastives."

"We'll take Aspen Trail," Old Babbers shouted back. "The growth is thick. It'll slow 'em down."

Bathezine urged Jangol for more speed.

Bet squatted behind the big Ursian, watching the dust cloud grow closer at an alarming rate. "How much farther?"

"Not far. You and Mandi-lyn lean against the side rail. We're gonna take this turn at speed and I don't wanna flip us."

"Which side?" Bet yelled, her voice shrill with panic.

"Right side. Now!"

She grabbed Mandi-lyn and they clung to the rail. Bet gasped when the first of the Mastives came into view. She could see froth dripping down their tusks and a primal rage on their faces, making the twelve-foot-tall beasts look every bit as intimidating as they had been described, if not more so.

Old Babbers cut her wagon hard left, followed by Bathezine.

Bet held tight, feeling the right side of the wagon rise up. She closed her eyes, willing the ride not to flip. The wagon slammed back level. She opened her eyes, watching the low branches of old forest streak by overhead. "That was close," she said to Mandi-lyn, who gave her a suspicious glance, then returned to her spot on the floor.

Forty-Four

The wagon team sped down the heavily wooded Aspen Trail, jarring the occupants with tooth-rattling impacts from the rutty old road.

Bet took a sigh of relief and looked down at Pooch-kin, who only shook his head without saying anything. She shook her head in return with a smile. The crashing of low branches not far behind them told her that her relief had been premature. "They're still coming."

"You didn't think it would be that easy, did you?" Mandi-lyn said from the floorboards.

"I was hoping," Bet said.

Tiny Nat pointed to the sky from the lead wagon. "Thorn Eagles," he cried.

Bet glanced up, but the Mastives giving chase and matching their speed kept her attention. She reached for a ball. "One thing at a time," she muttered to herself. With the jostling of the wagon, she had doubts about the accuracy of her throw. She decided to try a different approach. Bet focused and reached out to touch the Mastive's mind. The pure primal rage she felt nearly made her recoil. The intense single-mindedness of the creature was nothing like she had felt in the Creedans or Vapid. She tried to convince the beast to slow or even stop. But something else drove its desire to pursue. There was another presence in its mind. The shock made her pull away.

The surprise on her face was apparent. Mandi-lyn looked at her, whiskers bobbing wildly. "What is it?"

Bet shook her head. She looked through the forest canopy to see a Thorn Eagle tumble from the sky, taken down by one of Tiny Nat's knives. The bird spiraled downward, losing its payload, and she felt the heat when a ball of flame erupted in the nearby trees. "That was close." She felt a pang of pity for the animals caught in the blast.

Reaching for the Mastive's mind again, she once more felt the other presence. Bet focused, trying to push it from the gaining creature's consciousness. A dark force drove the Mastive to fulfill its selfish desires. The darkness gave off a sense of malevolent satisfaction, and Bet was pushed from the beast's head.

She fell back, frightened, but in a strange way in awe of the power she had felt. Bet knew at once it was the Reacher pushing these creatures, and that they wouldn't stop until they either caught their prey or died of exhaustion. Her heart filled with pity for the simple-minded beings, but she also knew she was powerless to stop them. "We're in trouble," she said, with Mandi-lyn watching her with wide eyes.

The eagles were nearly in position to drop their loads, and the lead Mastive was so close she could see the lust for destruction burning in the creature's eyes. She took a ball and again readied her throw. A dark form flying in from the northern sky caught her attention. She watched as it clashed with the eagle.

The Thorn Eagle let out a piercing screech, but the much larger newcomer silenced it immediately. Bet squinted through the tree limbs and saw the eagle's attacker. Her-Gad-Ishu swooped down, snagging the petrol-loaded egg mid-air. The three-headed crow flew above them, drawing even with the wagon, and dropped the bomb.

"What is it doing?" Bet said, wondering why the crow had attacked the eagle, only to continue its work. She watched the egg fall through the trees and realized what was coming. She pulled Mandi-lyn down just as the egg impacted against the Mastive.

The beast caught fire, but continued to run for several yards, before finally succumbing to the flame. The Mastive behind it tried to charge over its fallen comrade, but tripped, causing the one behind it to fall as well.

Bet watched the sky, catching glimpses of Her-Gad-Ishu down the Thorn Eagles and rob them of their weapons. The crow continued to turn the bombs on the Mastives. The ever-growing pile of flaming Mastive bodies clogged the road allowing their prey to quickly outpace them.

"What happened back there?" Bathezine yelled from the driver's seat, not taking his eyes from the road.

"Her-Gad-Ishu showed up," Bet said.

"That stupid crow again?"

"That stupid crow just saved us," Bet said, letting out another relieved breath, which wasn't so short-lived.

Forty-Five

The wagons rumbled along the Aspen Trail until daylight began to wane. Her-Gad-Ishu continued to pace the team, flying low, with brief intervals of rising high, before swooping back down.

They reached a wide clearing, and Old Babbers called for Alice the Fleet Ox to stop. Bathezine followed suit, bringing Jangol alongside the ox. He hopped off his seat and checked on the Rhinodon. "Sorry 'bout that, buddy. Didn't mean to run ya so hard. You did good." He rubbed Jangol's horn and offered him water from his canteen. Jangol snorted his appreciation.

"He said he knows we couldn't stop," Bet said, climbing down.

"I don't have to know what he's saying to understand him," Bathezine grumbled and went to Old Babbers, who was checking on Alice.

Bet shrugged off the Ursian's ill-temper and helped Pooch-kin down. "Stay close," she said.

"Where would I go? I'm sure there are a dozen things or more out here that would just love to eat me," the Chook-chook said.

"Not while I'm around," Bet said, twisting out her kinked back muscles.

"It feels good to use my legs again. I've been in one bag or another for so long, I feel like I'm back in the egg." He rustled his feathers to match the umber ground.

"At least you're not covered in yolk," Bet joked.

"True," Pooch-kin said, pecking at something unseen on the ground. "To be honest, though, I feel I should never have come here. I don't have much to offer, and I'm a burden to you. I fear I'm a distraction and you might get hurt trying to protect me."

"Hey," Bet said, kneeling next to him. "You're not a distraction or a burden. I need you. You keep me grounded—from going crazy in all of this madness. Was it your fault I got stung by that wasp thing? Did you cause me to get hit by that Creedan dart? Or get attacked by Tambor? Whatever happens will happen. It's not your fault or my fault. This is all on the Reacher. He's the cause of this insanity. You're my friend as long as we live, and I love you like a brother. A short, hairy-feathered brother, but a brother nonetheless. Don't forget that."

"I'm your short and hairy-feathered brother?" Pooch-kin said, feigning insult.

Bet laughed. "And I'm you're taller, pink-skinned, featherless sister. Is that better?"

Pooch-kin tilted his head. "I guess I can accept such an odd thing as a sister."

"Good," Bet said, scratching his back. "Because you're kinda stuck with me."

Mandi-lyn crawled out of the wagon. "Come with me," she said walking past Bet.

Bet stood and followed her to where the others were gathered.

"How're you holding up?" Old Babbers asked.

"I'm fine. Though a little bothered by how easy it's become to fight. I don't like it," Bet said, resting her hand on the Fleet Ox.

"Tell them what happened back there," Mandi-lyn said before the conversation could fall into a discussion of life and death situations and the nature of survival.

Bathezine looked at Bet from beneath scrunched, shaggy brows. "Did something happen we should know about?"

"I guess so," she said, looking at Mandi-lyn. "Back when the Mastives were close behind, I tried to enter the thoughts of the nearest one to convince it to give up the chase. I couldn't do it. It was incredibly focused and determined."

"It's hard to stop a determined Mastive," Old Babbers said.

"I figured that out. But it was more than that. There was another presence, driving it, pushing it to go. I felt it. The presence took pleasure in driving the Mastive beyond its limits. He knew what I was trying to do. Then he pushed me out. It was the Reacher. These creatures aren't doing this on their own accord, or using elixirs. They're being controlled."

"Ain't never heard of that before," Bathezine said, tugging on his beard. "Any of you?"

Everybody shrugged except Mandi-lyn. The Charge of Danthbrook stepped forward. "I have only heard of an Omia Temporian being able to possess such a Talent. If the Reacher is one, as well, then our troubles have increased."

"Wait," Bet said. "I can influence a mind. I know I can. If the Reacher hadn't been there, I could've convinced the Mastives to give up."

Old Babbers shook her head. "It ain't the same thing. Influence and control are two different Talents. Mind influence is temporary. Control is on an entirely different level. My Pop could influence with the best of 'em."

"Are we in danger of being controlled? Can he just telepathically tell Errel to set me on fire and take the facet?" Bet said, looking at the others with a hint of worry.

"It ain't like that," Bathezine said. "I reckon he could try, but the Creedans and Mastives, even the Thorn Eagles, they're simple-minded. They're easier to control."

"Bathezine is correct. It would take far too much effort to control the strong-willed," said Mandi-lyn as she paced in a circle. "Regardless, we must be aware, ever watchful, for odd behaviors among any of us. Bet, you've had contact with him twice. You will know."

Errel cleared his throat. "Let's not forget that this sort of Talent is of the Foul, as well."

The others nodded. "Do you really think there are two Omia Temporians? From what I know, that's not how it usually works, right?" Bet asked Mandi-lyn.

"I don't see how it could be. You said the voice you heard was a man's. I doubt we wouldn't have known about a second Omia Temporian. If the Reacher is of the Foul, he must've been gaining power since the war, keeping himself hidden until the right moment."

Bet stiffened at Mandi-lyn's words. Something about the word 'hidden' made her think of her time in the Din, when everything about the war had been erased from public knowledge. She wished she would've had the time to speak with Dalin about it a little more thoroughly.

"Why would he reveal himself now?" Errel asked.

"Questions perhaps the Ancient One could answer. Chances are he has the other pieces of the Staff already, and Bet carries the final piece." Mandi-lyn looked to the darkening sky. "In any case, we shouldn't tarry here any longer."

Bet patted her pocket, feeling the facet against her thigh. She opened her mouth to speak, but spotted the dark form of Her-Gad-Ishu fly overhead and alight just outside of their circle. "Maybe he… they can give us some answers," she said and marched to the crow.

"We're back," Her said.

"Returned," said Gad.

"Back again," Ishu followed.

Bathezine looked as if he was about to say something angry and offensive, but Bet stepped in before he could speak. "Her-Gad-Ishu. I'm glad to see you. Thank you for stopping the Mastives and Thorn Eagles," she said.

"Our pleasure," Her said.

"Not a problem," said Gad.

"It actually was a problem," Ishu followed up.

"Where's Fealist-Marsh?" Bathezine interrupted. "Did she send you?"

"Who's she?" Her asked.

"Don't play games with us, crow," Bathezine said. "You know? The purple lady."

"Oh, her," Her said.

"She's violet," said Gad.

"Lavender," added Ishu.

"Whatever," Bathezine growled. "Where is she?"

"We don't know," Her said. "She only talks to us when we sleep."

"Sound asleep," said Gad.

"Don't like getting woke up," Ishu followed, sounding irritated.

"Is he, or they, telling the truth?" Bathezine asked Bet.

Bet stared at the crow, her eyes darting between the three heads. Her face wrinkled in concentration. "I can't tell. They can block me."

"Hah!" cawed Her, followed by Gad.

"We're smart. Not stupid like some say," Ishu said, looking at Bathezine.

"I believe them, though," Bet said. "If they knew, Fealist-Marsh would just have them take me to her and save the trouble. Especially with the Reacher trying to kill me at every step."

Her-Gad-Ishu began to hop around, all three heads looking in different directions as if something was about to burst out of the trees. "The Reacher knows what she knows," Her said.

The crow's words caused a stir amongst the group. Bet's heart raced, and an icy wave passed through her chest. "Then he knows I can free her," she said. She bent down and picked up Pooch-kin, for her own sense of security more than his.

"You must seek out the Ancient Ones at once," Gad said.

"That's what we're doing," Tiny Nat said. "We are going to the Caves of Moth."

"The Caves of Moth?" Her said.

"Why so far?" said Gad.

"There's another one closer," Ishu finished.

"Where?" Mandi-lyn asked. "Do you know where the Wanderer is?"

"No," Her said.

"Nope," said Gad.

"Okay," Bathezine put his hands up, stopping the answer. "We don't need to hear no three ways. Where's the closest one?"

"In the Dead Woods," Her said.

"Across the Waste," said Gad.

Ishu looked at Bathezine. "What they said."

"Well, I wish I'd known all of this a little earlier," Bet said. "I seem to be traveling in circles. I made it as far as Pallas Steep and I've been doubling back ever since. I was just there a few days ago, after you dumped me in the mountains. It didn't occur to you to let me know before you swept me away to Illguard?"

"You weren't ready," Her said.

"You needed to discover more Talents," said Gad.

"We didn't know," added Ishu.

Bathezine threw his hands up. "Okay, so now we have to travel across the Waste with an army of determined, angry Mastives and Creedans after us. Do ya even know where this Ancient One is? And how about you, Charge of Danthbrook? You said there were only three."

"We know," Her answered for the other two heads.

"Then who is it?" Bathezine asked, sounding increasingly irritated.

"I think I know," Bet said before the crow. "It's the old tree, isn't it?"

Her-Gad-Ishu hopped in a circle. "That's the one," Her said.

"You can't learn from this Ancient One through words," said Gad.

"You must listen with your mind. You hadn't discovered that Talent. Now you must go to the tree before the knowledge is gone," Ishu said.

Bet raised an eyebrow toward Ishu. "That's the most I've ever heard you say."

Ishu clucked at her.

"The Charge Keepers believed the Crickshaw were killed during the war. When Fealist-Marsh created the Waste, they were felled," Mandi-lyn said.

"If the Crickshaw are the trees, then one is alive still. Sort of," Bet said.

"Yes," said Mandi-lyn. "There were four Crickshaw in the region. All were Ancient Ones, but few knew. What do you mean by sort of?"

"It's dying. It's been uprooted, and the beetles are eating it. He helped me escape the Floragads. I don't know what good he can do; his memory is almost gone," Bet said, looking back at the crow.

"The purple one said you must see him first," Her said without the other heads chiming in.

"Why doesn't she just tell me herself? I've had contact with her. We've spoke. Albeit in a dream," Bet said, sounding on edge. "I've spent the last I don't know how many days being chased by things that want to kill me, capture me, rob me, or just flat out eat me. Wouldn't this whole endeavor be just a little easier if she would come out and tell me where she is? Or how about tell me what to do while I'm hiding in the trunk of the one I'm supposed to talk to?"

"Makes sense," Bathezine said, nudging Mandi-lyn.

Mandi-lyn shrugged and shook her head. "This is all unprecedented. I'm sure there is a reason." She looked at Her-Gad-Ishu.

The crow hopped in front of Bet. Gad leaned close to the young woman. "To communicate with you openly puts her at risk. The trials you have faced thus far have caused you to realize your Talents and are necessary. You were born in the Din with no one to nurture you. Only your strongest Talent shone through the noise. Remember where you are now. You are in the Whist. Peace, thoughtfulness, and love are your allies. We fight only to preserve our lifecycle. Never for gain, power, or pleasure."

Bet stared at the crow, back-dropped by the looming night. She nodded and took a deep breath.

"It's easy to get caught up in the turmoil," Mandi-lyn added.

"Chaos begets chaos," Errel said from the edge of the group. "We are all vested in protecting Bet, but we have to remember the consequences of our actions."

Old Babbers pushed her way into the center. "We should probably seek shelter somewhere, unless you wanna travel through the night. We're not far from Fiverton, though. What's left of it, anyway."

"That old ghost town?" Bathezine asked.

"You wanna camp out instead? There's some places left standing we could use for cover," Babbers said, heading back to her wagon.

Bathezine eyed Her-Gad-Ishu. "You coming with us, crow?"

The three heads clucked at one another. "We will," Her said.

"Good," Bathezine said. "You can perch on top of one the buildings and help Tiny keep watch."

Ishu cackled. "They can keep watch. I'm sleeping."

"We'll take turns," Her said.

"You first," Gad said to Her. "Then me."

"And then you," Her and Gad said to Ishu.

"Unless the lavender one wakes me," Ishu said.

"Purple," Her said.

"Violet," said Gad.

Bathezine growled. "You can argue amongst yourselves while you're flying." He stomped to the wagon and climbed into the seat. "Load up."

Bet watched her friends climb aboard and smiled. A sense of peace flowed through her, knowing this was her family. She helped Pooch-kin in, then pulled herself up. She held her Chook-chook friend on her lap and closed her eyes, letting her mind feel the forest creatures begin their nocturnal foraging, while keeping alert for any threats.

Forty-Six

Trickles of light from the waxing moon filtered through a nighttime haze, vaguely illuminating the dilapidated gray wood of the few buildings still standing in Fiverton. Overgrowth of forest shrubs, young trees, and vines hid the windows and doorways of the abandoned town.

Bet stood beside the wagon, examining the dreariness of the remnant town. "Her-Gad-Ishu mentioned taking me here before they took me to Illguard. Why would they even consider this place?" she said, shuddering at the skeletal frames.

"At least they didn't take you to Napeville," Errel said, standing beside her. "That place was overrun with prickle-spiders after the war."

"I don't even want to know what those are," she said, not bothering to tell him Napeville had also been on the shortlist of destinations. She watched Her-Gad-Ishu alight on the withering rooftop of the tallest building, noticing Gad and Ishu immediately tuck their heads in to sleep while Her kept alert.

"It looks like the livery is still standing," Bathezine said, grabbing a hatchet from a supply chest. "That's where we'll camp."

Old Babbers took a machete and followed the Ursian to clear the brush from the entrance.

Errel scanned the dark tree line, standing stiff, while stretching his fingers and balling his fist repeatedly.

"How's your wound?" Bet asked.

The corner of his mouth raised in a half smile. "It's fine. Still a little tender, but fine."

"I'm glad you came with us," Bet said. "But I'm sorry about the inn."

"Andolans are builders. It'll be back in business before long. Speaking of," he said, turning to Tiny Nat. "How is Illguard after the attack?"

Tiny Nat raised his head, looking skyward. "The town was saved. The Creedans abandoned the fight. Several townsfolk were injured, but none died."

"That's some consolation," Errel said. "Any word on how your friend acquired the wasp?"

"We are uncertain as of yet. We would have known had he been stung. Are you certain you saw no Troojians near the town?"

"Somebody would've noticed, I'm sure. You don't see those every day."

"I didn't see any," Bet added. "In fact, your friend looked fine when I saw him at the inn when I got there. He was just sitting in the corner sipping on one of those nectar bags."

Tiny Nat nodded. "Then perhaps…" he paused, tilting his head in different directions.

Errel and Bet looked at each other, then stared at Tiny Nat, waiting for him to talk. Mandi-lyn climbed down and joined them. "Why are we looking at the bug?" she asked.

Errel put up a finger. "Tiny? What's going on?" He looked around wondering if there was an approaching danger.

Tiny Nat turned his head toward Errel. "Our scouts travel lightly with no provisions. Do you know where he got the nectar?"

"I'm sure it was from my kitchen. I try to keep a wide variety of foods stocked for all kinds. Why?"

"We believe that may be the source. Troojian eggs are very small."

"Wait. If you're suggesting I had anything to do with this…" Errel said, putting up is hands.

"No. We're not," Tiny Nat said. "Who is your supplier?"

"Falcid's out of Cadmia. He's the only distributer in the region," Errel said, pacing between the wagons. "I'm sorry if that's the case. I've always trusted him. Can you tell Walt to check the inventory?"

"We are doing so. You are correct. Falcid is usually trustworthy." Tiny paused again. "Your inventory was infected. We are investigating the supply route and headed to Cadmia as we speak."

"It would take great foresight to know you were headed to Illguard and infect the shipment," Mandi-lyn said.

"Perhaps the Reacher has an expanded foresight Talent," Tiny Nat said. "Regardless, it is a puzzle we will soon piece together."

Bet watched the Vivicon walk away to help the others. "Mandi-lyn, there's something that's bothering me I hope you can help me with."

The Flursh looked up at Bet and guided her to the rear of the wagon. "What is it?"

Bet stared at the ground for a moment before speaking. "Everyone said that the Reacher's ability to cross the realms is unprecedented, right?"

"As far as we know," Mandi-lyn said, cocking her head.

"But I heard Fealist-Marsh in my dreams while I was in the Din. What does that mean? Am I like the Reacher or does that mean Fealist-Marsh can cross the barrier as well? We didn't communicate, like talk. I just heard her."

Mandi-lyn studied Bet for a moment, then looked at Errel, who was leaning against a wagon, listening. "These are questions I have no answers for. And this is why we need to get to the Ancient Ones as soon as possible." Her whiskers twitched as she continued to watch Bet.

"I feel like maybe you know, or have an idea," Bet said, returning the other's stare.

The Flursh's whiskers bounced nervously. "I only have guesses, but we must go with what we know. To tell you my initial assumptions wouldn't serve us and could even veer us from our path. When we reach the Dead Woods, we will know more." She looked away. "I need to study," she said and climbed back in the wagon and unfurled a parchment from one of her leather tubes, not saying another word.

Bet looked at Errel, and the two exchanged shrugs.

Moments later Bathezine returned, grumbling about thorns, while Old Babbers chided him over not taking direction. "Let's get the wagons inside," the Ursian said, sounding more irritable beneath the woman's scolding.

Errel and Bet followed the wagons into the decrepit building while Tiny Nat crawled into the overgrowth, becoming perfectly hidden in the branches.

"All right, let's eat and get some sleep," Bathezine said, grabbing a handful of bread from a bag beside Mandi-lyn. "Tiny Nat will keep watch, and the crow's up top. We should have plenty of warnin' if'n anybody comes."

Errel climbed in the wagon, taking a seat beside Old Babbers. "I don't like being stuck inside with only one way out," he said between mouthfuls of cheese.

Old Babbers nudged him with her elbow, pointing to the barely visible back wall. "It's taken care of." She took a long swig from a leather flask, lay down, and was asleep in an instant.

"I wish I could do that," Errel said, listening to her heavy breaths. He too took a drink, put his head back, and waited for sleep to come while staring at the darkness overhead.

Bet munched on an apple, sharing bits with Pooch-kin. She could just make out Mandi-lyn's form, who was still studying the scrolls. "Do you need a light to read by?" she asked, reaching for her bag.

"Ya probably don't wanna do that," Bathezine said.

"Yeah, you're right. Don't want to attract attention," Bet said, trying to get comfortable on the wood wagon bed.

Bathezine snorted. "That and you don't wanna see what's in the rafters."

Bet looked up, stretching her senses toward the ceiling. "What's up there?"

"I don't wanna tell ya neither," he said. "Sides that, Flursh are nocturnal. They can see in the dark."

Bet couldn't help herself and let her senses continue upward. She felt the presence of a hundred primitive creatures, realizing what she felt were a colony of some sort of arachnid. "I should've taken your word for it," she said with a shiver.

Bathezine sniffed a laugh. He tucked his chin into his chest and followed Babbers' lead, falling asleep in an instant.

Bet lay with her eyes closed, listening to Pooch-kin's rhythmic breathing, Bathezine's gurgled snoring, and the occasional rustling of parchment as Mandi-lyn continued to study. She took a deep breath and stretched out with her mind, trying to sense any nearby danger. Finding none, she relaxed, scratched her friend's floppy ear, and fell into a much needed slumber.

Forty-Seven

Bet felt herself glide over a shimmering silver seascape. The blue sky held no trace of clouds, and the coolness of the air caressed her face, putting her at ease, with no worry of falling into the endless sea. A spot of green grass appeared below her. Her flight ended, and she felt her body slowly waft downward like a feather caught on the wind.

She touched down, bare feet cool against the plush grass. She knew it was a dream or a vision and sat cross-legged, waiting for the voice she knew was coming to make itself known. While she waited, she studied her surroundings. The sea appeared to be a vast desert. She took a deep breath and felt at peace.

The sky grew bright white, and the voice she expected came. "Bethany," the disembodied voice of Fealist-Marsh said, sounding at once mellifluous and commanding. "You've returned."

Bet felt a flash of confusion. "Did I come here on my own accord or did you bring me?"

"All that you do is of your own volition. I cannot take you where you do not want to go."

"So, everything that I'm a part of is my own decision?" Bet said, shaking her head. "I didn't have a choice when I was dumped in the mountains. Or with what's happened since."

"You were placed on the mountain for your own protection. Your strength brought you through and immersed you into the Whist. Your Talents have grown because of this."

Bet reached out, trying to figure out where Fealist-Marsh was speaking from. "Where are you? Why can't you tell me so we can end this trouble?"

"I can't tell you where I am because I don't know."

"Wait," Bet said, standing up. "I thought you were this powerful being, and you don't know where you are? Were you kidnapped or something? This doesn't—"

"I removed the memory. If the one you call the Reacher were to discover my location, your troubles will be worse. Pursue your current path. Your rapport with the Crickshaw will serve you well. Her-Gad-Ishu will act as your guide."

"I don't know if I can do this much longer. I understand what needs to be done, but the killing of these creatures, even if they are trying to harm us, I feel like it's making my heart sick and it's becoming easier. I don't like it."

"You are far from becoming the Foul, Bethany. Stay pure and protect those who protect you. Anger is natural, but hatred corrupts."

"There's so much I need to learn. I need your guidance. I'm lost."

"Listen to those who surround you, and your path will become clear. Remember, only you can find me." Fealist-Marsh's voice faded away. "Travel, Bethany."

Bet found herself alone once again. "Travel? What do you mean? I am traveling. I haven't stopped since I got here."

She waited, expecting to be wakened from the dream. But consciousness didn't come. Several minutes passed. Worry began to creep into the corner of her mind. What if I stay here? I'll be stuck in my mind forever, she thought, afraid to speak the words out loud for fear of making it real. Worry became panic. She forced herself calm. "No, this is happening for a reason." Remembering a book on meditation she'd read back at the orphanage, Bet closed her eyes, taking slow breaths, feeling her body rise and fall with each breath.

Her body felt light. Bet opened her eyes to find the sea and sky had gone, replaced with swirling prismatic color. Everywhere she looked, above and below, the colors swam past her. Her weightless body, guided only by her thoughts, fell into the vibrant maelstrom. "Travel," she said, remembering Fealist-Marsh's last words. At the command, Bet felt her languid movements explode into a burst of speed.

Bet sped through unknown places. Deep canyons and towering peaks swept past at dizzying speed. An ocean appeared beneath her, which soon gave way to vast sheets of ice. She wondered if this was the place where the other Ancient One had gone. The ice disappeared before she had time to think more about it, and she found herself on the other side the polar cap. The sky remained streaks of color, and she felt as if she could go anywhere she wanted. "I wonder," she said aloud. She closed her eyes and spoke the name. "Raisin Town."

Bet felt as if she were catapulted, and her dizzying speed increased to nauseating. The prismatic sky gave way to a milky gray. Her movement slowed. The air grew thick. Fear overcame her. She thought she had made a fatal mistake and would be stuck between realms for all time. Her mind raced, trying to think of a way out. No answers came. As hope slowly began to fade she felt the thickness ease. The sky returned, but it was different. No longer the color of a million rainbows, it became black and white, with shades of gray. Below her sat Raisin Town.

Bet descended onto the road in front of Anna's home. The rain fell, as it had the day she left, but she felt no moisture. She took a step then hesitated, feeling as if nothing had changed since she had gone. The splashing of feet to her right caught her attention. Spiff the Saureped ran to gate, moving in strange warps of speed and slowness. Dalin guided him to the barn, and Anna appeared, looking the direction the Saureped had come. A smile crossed Bet's face. Her friends were safe.

Motion sped up once again, and movement to Bet's left caught her eye. A Chook-chook dashed across the road. "That's strange," she said. "It looks like Pooch-kin." She was sure the strange movements of being in the Din were playing tricks on her vision.

The rattling of an iron carriage drew her eyes away. The inquisitors were coming. Panic set in again and she worried they might have some way of seeing her. Bet thought of Anna. Her instinct told her they were coming for Anna. She rushed to the door. Reaching for the knob, her hand passed through the door. She recoiled, startled by what had happened. Remembering she was still in a dream state, she braced herself and walked through the wood door. Spotting Anna near the fireplace, she yelled out. "The inquisitors are coming for you!"

Anna lifted her head and stood motionless. "Bet?" she said. The woman shook her head, then rushed out the backdoor to Dalin.

Bet stepped back. The room seemed to swirl around her. She ran back outside and saw the inquisitor carriage speeding to the house. The Chook-chook stood in the road, changed colors, and hunkered down in the mud. Seeing that the bird would be trampled by the hooves, she dashed across the road, snatched the bird, and leapt upward. The world began to swirl again.

The spinning scenery nearly made her retch. She had to feel the ground beneath her feet before she emptied her stomach. Bet held the Chook-chook close, not knowing what to do with him. She knew she couldn't take him back with her. The gateway, she thought.

Bet found herself back at the river's edge and her eyes widened in horror. The inquisitors were there. "How did they…" she said. Then she realized what she was seeing. She saw herself struggling to reach the gateway. The events unfolded just as they had a week before. She dropped the Chook-chook, realizing it really was Pooch-kin. Bet stumbled back, closing her eyes, not wanting to watch.

"What did I do?" she said. Bet looked at the negative colored sky and yelled. "Fiverton."

She passed through the milky gray in an instant and rejoined her body back in the wagon. Bet sprang up, gasping for air.

Bathezine was up in a flash. "What is it?" he said, taking her by the shoulders.

Bet looked at him, her body trembling. She checked on Pooch-kin, who returned her a curious stare. "I…I don't know. I had a dream. Maybe it wasn't. I don't know what happened." She looked at the Chook-chook again, confusion crossing her face.

Bathezine handed her a water flask. Bet took a long drink and caught her breath. "What happened in your dream? Did you talk to her again?" he asked, looking at Old Babbers and Errel, who had gathered at the side of the wagon.

Bet nodded. "Yeah, I did. But then I had a weird dream. But that's all it was. Is it morning yet?" she asked, looking for daylight.

Mandi-lyn looked at Bet, her wide eyes glistening in the faint light of the moon. "You've only been asleep for a couple of minutes," she said, keeping her gaze on the girl.

Bet scrunched her brow and took a deep breath. "I'm fine. It was only a dream," she said, petting Pooch-kin for reassurance. She lay back down. "I'm fine."

"Do you wanna talk about it?" Bathezine asked.

She shook her head. "Really, it was just a dream. No visions of doom or anything. I'm fine. Sorry about waking you. Let's just go back to sleep. We're gonna need it."

"If you say so," Bathezine said, not sounding convinced.

Bet listened to the others climb back into their wagon. Soon after, she heard the Ursian's heavy breathing. "It was only a dream," she told herself in a whisper. As she closed her eyes, Bet saw a glint of light in the Flursh's pupil.

"You'll have more answers when we reach the Crickshaw," Mandi-lyn said.

"I hope so," said Bet. She rolled over, keeping Pooch-kin close, knowing she wouldn't sleep.

Forty-Eight

Tiny Nat crept alongside the wagon, careful not to make any sudden noises. "Why are you creeping up on us?" Mandi-lyn said loud enough to wake the entire assemblage.

Bathezine shot up, grabbing his mace, and Old Babbers did the same with her hatchets. Errel followed suit, albeit at a more leisurely pace.

"We were trying not to startle the group awake. Most mammalians are easily spooked," Tiny Nat said, sounding as annoyed as he ever had. "The point is moot now."

"There's no immediate danger," Bet said, her voice scratchy from lack of sleep.

Bathezine holstered his weapon. "The why'd ya wake us?" he asked, stretching his burly arms.

"The Mastives are on the move," Tiny Nat answered. "Though Bet is correct, there is no immediate danger, they have regrouped and are no more than an hour away. The crow has gone to scout their movements."

"Then let's get up and moving," Old Babbers said. She stretched and twisted out her tight muscles, then checked on Alice.

Bet climbed down, helping Pooch-kin to the ground. She followed him as he meandered about, pecking at unseen objects on the dirt floor.

After a couple of minutes of Bet watching him in silence, Pooch-kin stopped his scavenging for grain and looked up at her. "What's wrong, Bet?"

Bet jerked out of her thoughts. "I don't know. I guess my dream kinda got me jittery."

Pooch-kin tilted his head. "I have a feeling that's only part of it."

"You're too observant at times." She dragged her bottom lip between her teeth and squatted close to him. "What do you remember about coming here? To the Whist, that is."

He scratched at the ground. "Like I told you, I made it to the gateway after you were swept away and I ended up on the stone. Then the crow took me."

"Yeah, I remember you saying that. But how about before? You said you went to Anna's. Do you remember anything at all about how you got to the river?"

"No, not really. I was outside the house, in the road, and the next thing I knew I was watching you fight off the men. I must have lost that memory from crossing over." Pooch-kin continued to stare at her. "Why?"

Bet hesitated before speaking. "In my dream, I spoke with Fealist-Marsh. That part wasn't a dream. I've always woken up after that. She told me to travel, and I guess I took it literally during the dream part. I traveled to the Din, to see Anna one more time. While I was there, I saw you, outside the house. The inquisitors arrived just after Spiff came back. You were in the road. The horse and carriage was about to run you over. I reacted. I grabbed you and took you to the river. From there, I guess you crossed over. It kind of freaked me out, and I woke up. But you don't remember going to the river. Anna never saw you."

Pooch-kin shook his head. "The inquisitors couldn't be in two places at the same time. Whether I remember it or not, being in two places at once is impossible, especially for the Din."

"Yeah, I suppose you're right. But what if I actually did travel there? What if I saved you from getting smashed under hoof?"

Pooch-kin chirped a laugh. "Maybe I died there and you died in the river, and we're all just spirits wandering through the afterlife and we don't know it. It was a dream. That's all. I dreamed I ate a giant worm, and my belly is no fuller than it was before the dream. You want to protect me, as I do you, and your mind creates ways to do that. Besides, I think I would remember being trampled to death."

Bet nodded and smiled. "I know you're right. It was just so vivid. Sometimes you make more sense than anything or anybody in this place. I don't know what I'd do without you."

"Consider me your spirit guide then," Pooch-kin said, warbling a laugh.

"Not funny," Bet said, standing. "C'mon, let's get going."

Pooch-kin followed, bouncing behind her. "Woo, woo, look at me, I'm a ghost. Woo."

"Not funny, bird," Bet said, trying to be serious.

"Yes, it is. Woo, I'm spooky."

Bet shook her head. "Why couldn't my spirit guide be a Moon Bear or a Flit-hopper?"

Forty-Nine

"You all set, girl?" Bathezine said. He helped her back in the wagon and handed her Pooch-kin, then stared at her in what remained of the moonlight until Bet shifted under his gaze. "Listen, I know you're havin' a tough time of things since ya came here. And I know I ain't always the easiest to get along with."

"You're not that bad," Bet joked.

"Thanks," Bathezine said, scratching beneath his beard. "I want ya to know, we're with you all the way. Me, Tiny Nat, Old Babbers, Errel, and maybe even the Flursh. We'll get this figured out with ya. Jangol and the bird, too, and I'm sure Alice. Whatever comes. If'n recent events means anything, the goin's gonna get rougher. It don't matter. We're here. I pledge it."

Bet smiled and took Bathezine's hand. "That means everything. And your pledge isn't one-sided. I'm with you, too. Whatever may come, whatever it takes, we're together."

"In Twiggian culture, that's a marriage vow," Mandi-lyn said, not lifting her head from her parchments.

Bathezine growled and Bet laughed. "Was that a joke?" Bet said. "It sounded like a joke. I didn't know you had it in you."

"Mm-hmm," Mandi-lyn said. She turned her head away from her studies and fixed her dark eyes on Bet. "I've found no precedent for the situation we find ourselves in. Perhaps after we see the Ancient Ones more will be revealed. What is clear is that your particular Talents are becoming very strong, exceeding the Talents of those who have been in the Whist since birth. While I'm not implying you are an Omia Temporian, I believe you will come into many more Talents."

"I take it I can't choose which ones come to me," Bet said, half serious.

"Not entirely false. You can choose which Talents you develop. It may be that by carrying the facet your Talents are intensified—only time will tell. I will give you the benefit of my knowledge to see this endeavor to its conclusion."

"That's not usually part of sequesterin' a Charge, is it?" Bathezine asked.

"My sequester notwithstanding, my interest is such that I must see this through. We are crawling onto unknown ground. The knowledge must be recorded. Which is not to say I am opposed to being in this circle of friends."

"That's as close and heartfelt as you're ever gonna hear from a Flursh. And because of it, I ain't gonna call her a hamster no more," Bathezine said.

"This is why we rarely express emotion," Mandi-lyn said, turning her attention back to the parchments. "Perhaps we should end this therapy session and get moving, before the Mastives catch us and render the discussion pointless."

Bathezine climbed into the driver's seat. "Can't argue with that logic. Time to go, Jangol." He shook the reins and the Rhinodon ambled forward.

Her-Gad-Ishu flew in from the south, gliding just above both wagons. "Continue on Aspen Trail until it forks at the edge of the Waste," Her said.

"I know where to go," Old Babbers said, sounding annoyed at the directions. "We'll follow the fork to Twist River and skirt the Waste to the Dead Woods."

"If you know where to go, I won't tell you that the Mastives have split and are in route to the river to prevent you from heading to the Caves of Moth." Ishu said, punctuating the statement with a caw.

Old Babbers didn't reply to Ishu's attitude. "What do ya think, Bathezine? Do we face them head-on or come up with another plan?"

"We don't confront 'em unless we have to," Bathezine yelled back over the galloping of Alice and Jangol. "How far to the Waste from here?"

"It's not far," Babbers said. "What're you thinking? I hope it ain't nothin' stupid."

"It probably is," Bathezine mumbled, looking back to Bet. "Check the crate for a black bag."

Bet crawled to the nearest box and checked the contents. "I don't see it."

The Ursian craned his head back. "No, the white crate. With the cookin' stuff in it," he snapped.

"You could've said that to begin with," Bet said, matching his tone. She sat on her knees, fighting to keep her balance in the bouncing wagon. After a moment of searching she pulled out the bag. "Found it."

"Good. Now hold tight." He jiggled the reins and Jangol's pace quickened.

Old Babbers did the same, and the caravan sped along the trail, forcing the occupants to grip the rails.

Mandi-lyn grunted her displeasure. "Who can study with all the bouncing?" She looked at the sky growing brighter in the east, rolled up a small leather map, and curled into a ball. "I'm going to sleep."

Bet wondered how she couldn't study under the circumstances, but could sleep. The ride continued at speed for another half hour, until the thick trees to their left gave way to the vast expanse of the Waste. The breaking day highlighted a haze covering the lower slopes of the mountains on the far side. Bet watched the peaks come into view, not wanting to go back. She had no desire to run into any Floragads again.

She closed her eyes, getting a sense of the surroundings. The forest creatures gave off a feeling of nervousness and were retreating deeper into the woods. The nervous feeling crept into Bet. She couldn't tell what brought on the anxiety, whether it was the byproduct of being in tune with the animals or something else. A cold sensation swept over her, followed by heat. The feeling continued, alternating rapidly, until finally giving way to a sense of emptiness. She forced a calm on herself and opened her eyes, realizing the wagons had come to a stop and everyone was looking at her. "What?" she said.

Bathezine nodded at her, indicating his nose.

Bet frowned and brought her hand to her face, touching a sticky warmth beneath her nose. She pulled her hand back, seeing blood on her finger tips. The idea of bleeding without reason disturbed her, though she didn't know why. "What? It's just a bloody nose. People get those all the time."

"If you say so," Bathezine said. "Just remember our talk. You can tell us anything, and we'll help you."

Bet shook her head. "Really, it's just a nosebleed." What could she tell them if she didn't know why it was happening?

Fifty

"Give me the bag," Bathezine said, hopping off the driver's seat. He took the sack from Bet's hand with a jerk and emptied it on the driver's bench.

Bet looked at the bag's contents. "What are you going to do with a wad of bandages?" She wondered if the fabric was wadding for old muskets, like she had read about. She hadn't seen any guns since she had come to the Whist and figured if they did have them, they might be the more primitive type, instead of the cartridge rifles in the Din.

Bathezine snatched up the wad and, digging his claw into the fabric, he tore them into strips. "These ain't bandages, but it might just save you. It's cheese cloth."

"Cheese cloth?" Bet said, raising an eyebrow.

"Yep," he said, handing several strips to Old Babbers. "We're cuttin' 'cross the Waste, and this'll help keep the dust out. It ain't perfect, but it'll do in a pinch." He handed Bet a strip. "Tie it 'round your head, cover your nose and mouth."

Old Babbers handed a piece to Tiny Nat, who handed it back. "We don't have a nose," he said, sounding almost proud.

Babbers shrugged and went to Alice, pulling out a long strip.

"Tie the ends to Alice's bridle. That should hold it," Bathezine said to the woman, wrapping the cloth around Jangol's elongated tusk.

Old Babbers looked over her shoulder and down her nose at the Ursian. "I guessed that much, you old bear."

Bathezine ignored the comment. He looked over the group. Errel sat on the edge of the wagon flexing his hands, Tiny Nat stood alert with the atlatl at the ready, and Old Babbers stood, hands on hips, with a glint of mayhem in her eye. "I'm guessin' you know what we're gonna do."

"We're crossing the Waste. We goin' straight for the Dead Woods, or taking a more circuitous route to draw them away?" Old Babbers said, feeling the weight of her hatchets against her hips.

"We should drive in a straight path," Errel said. "They seem to know where we're going. The ash will slow us down, and speed is everything. No point wasting time taking the long road."

"How about a diversion? I can take Alice a different direction and maybe lead them away from you," Old Babbers said, adjusting her mask.

Bet shook her head. "It won't work. I'm pretty sure the Reacher can sense where I am. Or at least where the stone is. I think it's best if we stay together."

Old Babbers nodded as she approached Bet. "Bathezine," she said, not taking her eyes from Bet. "She's with me. Alice is faster. It's our best shot."

Bathezine tugged at his mustache, looking across the Waste. Doubt crossed his face as he stood in silence. "Okay," he relented, turning to Bet. "Get Pooch-kin. We'll be right behind you. Remember, whatever Talents you have, use them. These things ain't gonna hesitate to kill us."

Bet nodded. "Okay," she said through a scratchy throat. "I'll do whatever it takes."

Bathezine seemed to frown beneath his mask. "We'll be close behind. I ain't gonna let nothin' happen to ya."

"I know," Bet said, giving his arm a squeeze. She grabbed Pooch-kin. "C'mon, my friend. Looks like we're in for more excitement."

"I could do with a little less of that," Pooch-kin said.

"I'm with you on that. This can't last forever," she said, putting the Chook-chook in his pouch.

"How deep in the woods is this tree?" Errel asked. "And how will we know if we're in the right place? The Dead Woods stretch for several miles along the edge of the Waste."

"It's not too far in. And I think it's about directly in the center. There's a big tree that looks like it was cut in half standing on the edge. Her-Gad-Ishu can scout it and keep us on track."

The crow circling above cawed its acknowledgement.

"Errel, you're with me," Bathezine said. The Andolan switched wagons without protest. "Get your mask on, hamster. I mean, Mandi-lyn."

Mandi-lyn raised her head. "Flursh descended from burrowers. Dust is not problematic, only lack of sleep." She tucked her head into her chest.

"Get it while you can," Bathezine said. "Let's move."

Bet climbed in the wagon, making sure Pooch-kin was secure.

"You're up here with me," Old Babbers said from the driver's seat, scooting over to make room. She looked sideways at Bet, her eyes squinting from a smile. "Here's where the real fun begins."

Fifty-One

Bet sat staring at the horizon, occasionally glancing behind her to check on Bathezine barely visible in the clouds of churned-up ash. Her mind continued to fall on the dream or vision, or whatever it was she'd experienced the night before. Did she really travel to the Din? And if so, did she really save Pooch-kin and take him to the gateway? But her friend had arrived in the Whist before she'd had the vision. Her mind struggled to grasp onto something solid in the confusion.

She forced herself to think about something else. There were plenty of things to think about other than some weird time-traveling dream. Like the Crickshaw. Bet hoped the tree still had enough rings left to be of some help. She thought about the tree and how it had saved her from the Floragads. For the first time since her last experience in the Dead Woods, the thought of the fungal aberrations didn't fill her with fear or just plain creep her out. Bet looked at Old Babbers and knew why. She wouldn't be alone this time.

Old Babbers caught Bet staring at her. "What's on your mind?"

"A lot, actually, but also nothing," Bet said, letting her gaze drift in the direction of the river. The wagon rolled smoothly and mostly quietly. "I expected the ride to be a little more rough."

Babbers shrugged. "Whatever Fealist-Marsh did here pretty much cut everything in a smooth line all around. Not even the clouds gather over the Waste. It's like she cut out a hole all the way to the sky. The only thing that lives here is the occasional dirt eel. Even then, they're pretty rare, from what I hear."

"That's good. I ran into some the last time I was here. I didn't really care for them."

Old Babbers laughed. "I'd have more harsh words to say if I came across them. Especially alone."

"Her-Gad-Ishu ate them, so that's two less to worry about."

The woman laughed again. "That crow can prove useful."

"I didn't think so at the time."

"Everything's useful…one way or another."

Bet watched the mountains without asking what Old Babbers meant. They had been traveling for nearly an hour and the mountains didn't seem to be any closer. "How far across is the Waste?"

Babbers shook her head. "Don't really know for sure. I've never been here. I hear it's oval-shaped. I guess it depends on where you start."

"Everything depends on where you start…one way or another," Bet said playfully, earning a wry look from Babbers.

The woman continued to stare at Bet until the young woman shifted uncertainly. "How do you feel about learning all of your Talents? It's gotta be kinda surprising, especially since ya didn't know nothin' about 'em for so long."

Bet took a breath in a half-shrug. "I don't know. It's surprising, shocking at times, but it feels natural. Like it's supposed to be. If that makes any sense. I didn't know my parents, so I never had any clue except for talking to animals. Even then, I thought it was some kinda weird gift."

"Do you know who your parents were?"

"Harrelle, the old man who lived at the farm in the Din, said they were like me and were executed. He said their names were Saul and Edna Clarenhart. Apparently I was taken away and put in the orphanage before the Dalverians could find me. Aside from that, I don't know."

"Saul and Edna Clarenhart, huh?" Old Babbers said. "Are you sure the old man was telling you the truth?"

"I don't know why he'd lie. He risked his life to help me. I don't think lying would do him any good. He even admitted to being on the tribunal that convicted them. Why do you ask?"

Babbers rolled her shoulders. "I don't know. Pops knew some people by those names during the war. He never mentioned their last name, though. But they died before the war ended, about twenty years ago, so they couldn't have been the same people."

"Hmm. Just a coincidence, I guess," Bet said. A tickle of doubt in the old man's story crawled in her mind. "If I knew I had these Talents then, I could've known for sure."

"From what I remember, Pops was friends with them. They were resistance fighters in the capital. They were killed by the inquisitors. Burned alive in their home, I think." Old Babbers hesitated. "Don't put much stake in it. I'm sure there's lotsa people with those names out there. I even know a Karatoid who goes by the name Saul."

"I guess so. He did say my house was burned down, though. Are you sure you got the years right? If you're off by a few years…who knows, maybe they were my parents."

"Actually, I think they were brother and sister, and you don't look like the product of something like that," Babbers said with a chuckle.

"Yeah, I guess you're right. Maybe Edna was pregnant by somebody else and Harrelle mistook them as a couple because of the same last name." Bet felt the doubt in the old man's story grow. Something didn't feel right about it, now that she gave it more thought. What were the odds that the very man who sentenced her parents to death would end up at the same place she would eventually be? She tried to puzzle it out, but like the travel dream, it seemed lost in a haze of confusion. Bet looked back to Babbers, finding her staring at her. "What?"

"Whatever you're thinking doesn't matter now. We gotta stay focused on what's ahead. And you, little sister, need to enhance your Talents."

Bet laughed. "You make it sound easy. How am I supposed to do that?"

Old Babbers' smile showed beneath the mask. "The hard part is discovery. Becoming stronger is easy."

Fifty-Two

Her-Gad-Ishu swooped in from the north and dove down, flying alongside Old Babbers. "Veer to your right slightly and stay on that course," Her said.

Old Babbers corrected her course. "What about the Mastives? Did you see them?"

"They have broken through the forest," said Gad. "At your current pace, you will meet them just before the Dead Woods."

"Go faster," Ishu added unnecessarily.

Babbers swore under her breath. "Go tell Bathezine. They've fallen behind." She looked backwards at Tiny Nat. "You ready back there?"

Tiny Nat secured his throwing knives and prepped his atlatl. "We are ready."

Bet leaned over to check on Pooch-kin. "Things might get rough ahead. Stay down and be ready. When we get close enough, I'm gonna make a break for the forest, and you're coming with me."

"You said there were mushrooms that tried to kill you in the Dead Woods. I won't let them," Pooch-kin said. His red-orange head crest changed to black.

Bet straightened. "I've never seen you do that before. Are you transforming into warrior mode or something?" she said through a nervous laugh.

Pooch-kin shook, and the rest of his hairy feathers transformed to black and yellow, giving him the appearance of a very large bee. "I've found that most creatures are averse to these colors. I think I'll have a smaller chance of being stepped on when the fighting begins," he said, not making eye contact.

"Okay. Just stay with me and be careful. I don't think an enraged Mastive cares about getting stung while it's rampaging." She reached out to give him a scratch.

He pulled back, avoiding her touch. "This is a difficult color to maintain until it becomes fixed. Ruffling my feathers might disrupt it."

"All right," Bet said, pulling her hand back with uncertainty. "I trust whatever it is you're doing will help keep you safe."

"Not just me," Pooch-kin said, nestling down on top of his bag.

"Remember what we talked about, Bet," Old Babbers said, drawing the young woman's attention away from the Chook-chook. "Only your inhibitions can keep your Talents from achieving their full potential."

"Right. I know. I'll do my best. But it's not easy focusing while keeping your emotions in check. Especially when something's trying to kill you."

"Just worry about hatred. Don't give into it, even if one of us falls. Giving in to it will cause you to abandon control. If we ever get a break, I'll teach you some combat techniques that enhance your Talents. But for now, I need you to reach out and see if you can get a sense of where those things are. I have a feeling you've already figured out how to expand that Talent." Old Babbers gave Bet's shoulder a reassuring squeeze.

Bet nodded, closed her eyes and let her senses expand. She had indeed learned how to expand her Talents, even into the Din. But Travelling was different. She had to be in a sleep-like state to achieve it; even then, she wasn't sure she could duplicate what she had done.

She opened her eyes and was surprised to find herself amidst a horde of Mastives charging across the Waste. Clouds of upturned ash filled the air, but she couldn't feel the effects. She twisted through the stampeding legs until they passed. Then she saw the Creedans. More than a hundred of the hill folk running at speed, exhausted, but uncaring of their condition, and all carried the same single-minded purpose of catching her to take the facet. The shock of what she witnessed nearly caused her to pull away.

After the mass of Creedans passed, she felt another presence. She looked to the distant trees skirting the Waste and saw a Mastive. This one was different. Standing twice the size of the others, with shocks of black hair covering parts of gray skin, the beast lurched forward from the woods, pushing mature trees aside like saplings. Bet considered trying to touch its mind to see if she could convince it to stop, but knew she couldn't. There was a darkness about it, which could only mean the Reacher had control.

The enormous Mastive rushed straight toward her, but Bet held her ground. There was no way the creature could harm her physically when her body was miles away. The massive beast charged ahead and, when it was nearly upon her, it stopped, looking directly at her, even though it couldn't see her. Or could it?

Bet touched the creature's mind. Surprise, almost to the point of fear, pushed her out, nearly causing her to fall. She recovered, and it was her turn to be surprised. The fear she had felt wasn't her own, nor was it the Mastive's. It belonged to the one who controlled it.

The Mastive's body seemed to ripple like a desert mirage. It stood absolutely still, frozen in place. Bet took a step back. She watched as tendrils of black, almost fluid-like smoke extended from the Mastive's eyes. The substance poured out, spiraling on the ground in front of her. She wanted to leave and rejoin her corporeal body, but couldn't. She wouldn't allow herself to give in to fear. She had to see what came next.

The blackness twisted out of the Mastive's body until it completely separated, forming a mass of undulating darkness in front of her. Bet watched and waited.

The dark, formless cloud hovered closer. Swirls of gray appeared near the top of the specter, changing into bright white eyes. Bet knew the eyes. They were same eyes as Fealist-Marsh's. Confusion roiled through her mind. Hot and cold washed over her as the form neared. What was she seeing? She had to go. She didn't want to see what would come if she lingered. But a voice stopped her.

"What are you?" the blackness said. "You are not her. How can you be here?"

Bet didn't answer. She couldn't. Fear paralyzed her. The Mastive stood, frozen in time, eyes blank and unseeing. She watched the white eyes of the form. Wisps of black fog flowed from the shapeless being, dissipating in the air. This was the Reacher. Whoever or whatever it was, it could see her and knew her Talents. A vision of the old tree entered her mind and she quickly suppressed it.

The white eyes narrowed. "Whoever you are, I will have you and take the Facet of the Din. And I will find her, and kill you both."

Hearing the words snapped Bet from her stupor. Her fear turned to anger and determination. "Not today," she said and disappeared.

Bet jerked in her seat beside Babbers, her body trembling. The woman looked at her. "What? What'd ya see?"

Bet looked at her with haunted eyes. "Go. We need to get to the woods as fast as we can."

Old Babbers shook the reins. "Go, Alice. Faster!" She turned to Bet. "What is it?"

"It's the Reacher. He's here. I need to get to the Crickshaw." Bet crawled into the back of the wagon and began filling her pouches with bearings, pebbles and whatever else she could find. She looked down at Pooch-kin, who was watching her curiously. "Listen, my friend, no matter what happens, know that you are my best friend and my brother. I don't know if we're gonna get out of this one. If something happens to me, I want you to go. Hide and get to safety. You got that?"

"Bet, I am here because I want to be. I won't abandon you, not even in final death. Your fate will be mine. I swear to that," Pooch-kin said.

Bet shook her head. "I won't let you. I don't want you to die because of me."

"My oath cannot be broken." Pooch-kin looked away. "There's so much you don't know."

Her-Gad-Ishu's caw pulled her away before she could ask him what he meant.

"They're moving faster," Her said.

"They'll be here in no time," said Gad.

"Hurry," Ishu added.

Bet looked ahead and spotted the line of trees in the distance. "Almost there," she said. Looking to the east, she saw a cloud of dust. "So are the Mastives."

"Tiny," Babbers said. "Open the crate under the bench."

Tiny Nat did as instructed. "Bombs? We didn't know you had these."

"Saving them for a special occasion." Old Babbers looked at Bet. "Gotta be prepared for all eventualities."

Tiny Nat took a petrol filled egg. "We think we know what you have in mind. Catch," he said, tossing the explosive in the air.

Her-Gad-Ishu snagged the bomb from the air and immediately flew in the direction of the Mastives, knowing what to do.

Bet looked back at Bathezine, his wagon growing smaller in the distance. "C'mon, bear. We need you."

"Don't you worry 'bout him," Old Babbers said. "He knows what he's doing."

Bet nodded and climbed back on the driver's seat. "I wish I did."

"I think you do," Old Babbers said, then urged Alice forward.

Fifty-Three

A ball of fire erupted in the distance, twice the size of the explosions caused by the Thorn Eagles' bombs the day before.

"Those things pack quite a punch," Bet said.

"Special mixture of my own. I'll tell you my recipe someday," Old Babbers said with a dry smile.

Bet watched the fireball mushroom fifty feet high. "I'm not sure when I'll need that kind of power."

"Well, today's a good example of why ya might need it," Babbers said, looking at the tree line growing closer. She pointed ahead. "Is that your half tree?"

"That's it. Just get me close." She secured her bags and grabbed Pooch-kin's pouch. "Let's go. I'll need your help."

Pooch-kin hopped in without complaint.

"Remember, the Reacher's presence is in the big one to the rear. Either concentrate on that one or avoid it completely. I don't know what's best." Bet turned to Tiny Nat. "Any sign of the rest of you?"

"We are delayed by Creedans near Illguard." He put his atlatl aside and grabbed a bomb. "We will do our best to delay the attackers."

Bet put her hand on his. "Thank you, my friend."

Tiny Nat looked at her. "There are few who consider Vivicons friends. We will protect you at all costs."

"Let's hope it doesn't come to that."

The first Mastive became visible through the dust kicked up by the explosion. Catching sight of their quarry, the leader let out a bellowing roar.

"Get back up here, Bet," Old Babbers said. When Bet returned to her seat, the woman pointed to a steel pin on Alice's rigging. "When I say, I want you to pull that pin. Get ready, Tiny."

Three Mastives, no more than a hundred yards away, charged forward. "Now! Pull it," Babbers yelled.

Bet pulled the pin and the rigging dropped to the wayside, freeing Alice of her burden. The wagon continued at speed, headed straight for the woods.

Tiny Nat reared back and threw the bomb in a straight line toward the attackers. He immediately drew a knife, paused a heartbeat, then threw it as well. A fraction of second later the bomb exploded in mid-flight sending a blast directly into the front line of Mastives.

"Almost there," Bet said, preparing for her dash to the trees. The wagon began to slow. "We're not going to make."

"Yes, we are," Babbers said, followed by a whistle.

A moment later a thud from the back of the wagon jolted the occupants, followed by a sudden burst of speed. Bet looked back to find Alice giving the ride a final push.

Old Babbers whistled again and Alice veered away. "You did good, girl. Now get to the trees and rest. I'll call you when I need you." The Fleet Ox continued on a separate path, doing as told.

The Mastives continued to rush forward, trampling over their dead comrades with no regard.

"You ready?" Babbers said. When they were no more than thirty yards away, she pulled the hand brake and the wagon lurched to a stop. "Now!"

Bet leapt from vehicle, landing at a run. She poured her energy into her legs and ran. She dashed across the open space, focusing only on speed. She moved at a pace she never thought possible, reaching the edge of the woods in a flash. Once there, she slowed her pace, stealing a quick glance back at her friends. She saw Babbers leap from the wagon and Tiny Nat jump and flitter away on small wings, high. A second later a Mastive crashed into the wagon and disappeared in an enormous blast.

The concussive wave knocked Bet from her feet, sending her flat on her back. She shook her head clear and stood. She looked back, searching for her friends, but couldn't find them in the cloud of dust and smoke. She couldn't waste time searching for their presence. The blast and smoke cloud had bought her a few moments.

"Let's get to the tree," she said, patting Pooch-kin's bag. She turned to run, her foot caught, and she fell face-forward. Bet rolled back to see the offending root that had tripped her. There was no root. A pale pink and white tendril had wrapped her leg. The Floragads had her.

Fifty-Four

Bathezine shielded his eyes from the flying debris. "What in never-ending hell did she do?" He urged Jangol through the haze, listening for the Mastives. He could hear the growling beasts in the distance, but those that had arrived first were silent.

Errel leaned next to Bathezine from the wagon bed. "Do you have the sensing Talent?"

"Nah. How 'bout you, Mandi-lyn?" He looked back when the Flursh didn't respond. "Give her a shake and wake her up."

Errel gave her a nudge with his foot. "Wake up." When she didn't stir, he put a little more behind the next nudge.

Mandi-lyn untucked her head, looking around. "What? Why is it foggy?"

"It's not foggy. It's dust. Old Babbers' wagon just exploded," Errel said.

The Flursh sat up quickly. "Where's Bet?"

"In the Dead Woods," Bathezine said. "We're lookin' for Babbers and Tiny. Do you have sensing?"

"Not in the traditional manner. I can feel their vibrations."

"Vibrations?" Errel asked.

"My whiskers aren't here just to make me pretty," she said. "Stop and

I'll look for them."

Jangol stopped without being told, and Mandi-lyn slung her scrolls. She scurried down and put her face close to the ground.

"You can leave your stuff in the wagon. No sense in carryin' it," Bathezine said.

Mandi-lyn stood, raising her head. "There's a crate of bombs in our wagon, too. I'd rather them not be destroyed."

"Wait. What?" Bathezine looked in back, finding the crate. "Thought she had 'em. Curse that woman for not sayin' I had these."

"Old Babbers is just ahead, and Tiny Nat is near the woods. There are five dead Mastives, but several more will be here in moments."

"Ya got all that through your whiskers?" Bathezine said.

Mandi-lyn didn't respond. Instead, she lowered her face back to the ashy ground. She leapt up and crawled back in the wagon in a quick burst of energy. "Get to the woods. Bet is in trouble."

The Ursian growled. "Go, Jangol!"

Bathezine spotted Old Babbers through the haze. "C'mon, Bet's in trouble." The woman ran alongside, caught hold of the wagon and swung in the back without Bathezine slowing.

"Where is she? Is it the Mastives?" Old Babbers asked as she crouched down, ready for action.

"No," said Mandi-lyn. "Floragads."

Bathezine swore through a growl, continuing to urge Jangol through the haze. "It'd have been easier if you hadn't got your wagon blown up."

"It wasn't really part of my plan, ya know," Old Babbers snapped. "But it did take out three of them."

A maelstrom of dust and animalistic rage swirled in their path, causing Jangol to jerk to the side and come to a sudden halt. Bathezine braced his legs against the footboard and threw his arm in front of Babbers to keep her from flying forward, while Errel and Mandi-lyn simultaneously slid into his back. He looked up in time to the twisting hulk of a Mastive trip as it groped, trying to pull spears from each eye. "Tiny's been working," he said, watching it fall, creating another wave of dust.

Jangol pulled the wagon around the writhing beast and headed to the woods. When they reached the copse, Bathezine leapt off and unhitched the Rhinodon. "Go wait with Alice," he said, patting him on the tusk. Instead of doing as told, Jangol charged into the woods.

"He's got a mind of his own," Old Babbers said, following close behind.

Her-Gad-Ishu flew in low. "The Mastives are still coming, you know," Ishu said, speaking before the others.

"You've only slowed them down," Her said.

"And only a little," said Gad.

Bathezine grabbed his weapons. "Bet's in trouble," he barked and rushed off.

Errel started to follow, but stopped. He pulled a bomb from the crate and tossed it to Her-Gad-Ishu. "Slow them down a little more." He turned to go but was confronted by Tiny Nat.

"Stay here and help us fight. We need to keep them away from her," Tiny Nat said, before launching another spear.

Errel hesitated. He took a breath and nodded. "Okay. What do you want me to do? My weapons were in Babbers' wagon."

"We spear them, you burn them. You'll have to get close."

The dust began to clear, and the next wave of beasts rushing toward them didn't leave any time for discussion. The blast of another bomb followed by the bellowing wail of a Mastive as it charged forward, completely engulfed in flames, made Errel rethink the plan. "Um, I don't think my heat Talent will do much good. I have a better idea."

Tiny Nat speared the nearest Mastive in the throat and loaded another projectile into his atlatl, looking at Errel. "What is your new plan?"

"Lure them to the woods. We only need to delay them, and they'll have to deal with the Floragads too."

"As will we," Mandi-lyn said as she climbed down and followed the others.

"But we can climb trees. They can't," Errel said, following the Flursh.

Tiny Nat flung another spear. "As long as they don't tear down the trees." He grabbed another bomb, tossing it to Her-Gad-Ishu, and ran to catch up.

Fifty-Five

Bet struggled to pull her legs free, but the Floragad tendrils were unyielding. The soil all around her began to churn, and she knew what that meant. Giving up on pulling away, she grabbed the white appendage holding her with both hands and tore it in two. She rolled over and stood ready to run. Another tendril sprung from the soft dirt wrapping her waist. She fought to break loose, but yet another vine took her arm. She gave a hard yank, intending to rip the rope-like filament from its owner's body. Instead, the tug unearthed the Floragad it was attached to. "Not good."

The Floragad used the grip it had Bet in to pull itself closer. More tendrils sprang from the earth, ensnaring her legs, pulling her back to the ground.

Pooch-kin crawled from the bag and studied the situation. "We'll get out of this," he said.

Bet pulled the pick hammer with her free hand and hacked into the nearest fungal arm, severing it. "Get out of here, Pooch-kin. Get to safety." She chopped at another, breaking free of that as well. But as she broke free of one, more replaced them, tightening their grip.

"I'll get to safety when you do," her Chook-chook friend said. He leapt in the air, fluttering his tiny wings. With his black and yellow feathers, he looked everything like an angry bee on the attack.

Bet watched him a second longer before turning her attention back to hacking at the mushroom arms.

Pooch-kin flitted in a circle, finally coming down beside a tendril. He bit down on it with his stubby beak, neatly slicing it apart. A string of filament reached for him, but he fluttered away before it could grab him. He landed closer to Bet and repeated the action, freeing one of her legs.

Bet tried to hack at the tendril holding her outstretched arm, but couldn't get the angle without cutting into her own arm. The ground roiled. She knew she had to get free before the mushroom body reached her or she would end up as compost. Bet swung at the one holding her waist, bisecting it cleanly. But she still couldn't stand. More tendrils sprung up, pinning her down. She hoped her friends would come, but distant explosions told her they had problems of their own to deal with.

Pooch-kin dealt with the tendrils as best he could, but they came faster than he could handle.

Bet sliced and chopped in ever increasing desperation. It couldn't end like this. She tried to focus as Old Babbers had told her, but the sheer number of groping filaments distracted her. She cut at another lacy arm and was finally able to roll to her side. She spotted Pooch-kin neatly dodging every reaching tendril while jumping in to attack. He was doing all he could, but Bet knew he wouldn't be able to do enough to save her. She put all of her focus into her strength, trying to push herself from the ground. She rose to her knees. Almost there. She pushed harder. She closed her eyes, increasing her concentration, when something wrapped her neck, jerking her back down.

Gasping for air beneath the Floragads grip, she searched for some sign of rescue. Bet looked deeper in the forest and saw a large red-capped Floragad. "Focus," she said through a rasp. She stared at her impending death, dragging itself closer on milky white arms.

Pooch-kin leapt in, biting at the rope wrapping Bet's neck. A tendril reached out and snagged the Chook-chook. He fought and bit, before another arm grabbed him.

Bet's eyes widened in horror. The ground vibrated with thumping footfalls. Were the Mastives here, too? She spotted the red-cap. "Not like this," she whispered, not taking her eye from the approaching Floragad. "I hate them."

Bet's body tensed and shook. Her vision went gray through a cloud of hatred. All of her focus poured into her anger. She felt her body heat rise, almost unbearable. Letting out a primordial scream, she stretched her arms, breaking free of the tendrils that held her. She kicked, freeing herself of their grip. She grabbed the tendril wrapped around her neck. "You wanna come closer? Then come closer!" She yanked it with all her strength, unearthing the Floragad body, pulling it through the air. Bet leaned back and swung the tendril like a lariat, dashing the mushroom against the nearest tree. She watched it break apart with satisfaction.

Seeing Pooch-kin still struggling with his captors, Bet took hold of the threads holding him and squeezed. The tendrils disintegrated beneath her grip.

Pooch-kin shuffled back, looking at her. "Bet? What are you doing?"

Bet's eyes narrowed in confusion. *I'm saving him. Why would he ask that?* Another tendril shot from the ground behind, rising to waist level in an attempt to catch its prey. She reached back without looking, sensing its direction. She caught it and gave a mighty tug, tearing the body from the earth, sending the Floragad to a similar fate as the other.

The thumping footfalls she had heard before drew closer, and she spun to meet the new danger. She reached for an iron ball only to realize it was Jangol. The Rhinodon continued past her, ramming a Floragad emerging from the ground, sending the mushroom cap flying from the stem.

Bet saw Old Babbers and Bathezine rushing up behind Jangol and sensed their worry for her. She turned away, and spotting another Floragad, she threw her bearing. The iron ball hummed through air. She watched the mushroom's stem explode into pieces and the cap fall to the ground.

"Remember, cut off the caps and they're as good as dead," Old Babbers said. She stopped and looked at the young woman and took a step back, a mix of fear and concern crossing her face. "Bet?"

Bathezine arrived in a huff behind her, and his expression immediately matched Old Babbers' when he saw Bet.

"What?" Bet asked, her voice sounding raspy with a barely controlled violence.

Bathezine's expression softened. "Bet, I need you to take a deep breath and calm down."

Bet noticed the trace of fear in Bathezine's voice. Knowing something could scare him roused the fear in her. "They were going to kill us," she said, taking quick, shallow breaths.

"I know, but we have it handled now." Bathezine put his hand out, hesitantly resting it on her shoulder and giving her a soft squeeze.

Errel and Mandi-lyn arrived, both giving Bet the same concerned look. Errel took Babbers aside. "The Mastives are coming; we need to fight them from the trees." The sound of cracking branches in the distance emphasized his point.

Old Babbers continued to look back at Bet. "She needs to get to the Crickshaw."

"I realize that. But we need to slow them down. We don't know how long she'll need to talk to it, or if it will even accept her after whatever happened," Errel said.

"Her eyes are white. I don't even know what that means. Is it some kind of Talent we haven't heard of?"

"I have no idea. Fealist-Marsh had, or has, white eyes. Maybe she's an Omia Temporian." Errel turned his head to the sound of cracking tree limbs and enraged growling. "Regardless, she needs to go."

The two trotted back to Bet. A Floragad tendril had the audacity to try to ensnare Errel. He calmly grabbed the offending arm and set it on fire.

Tiny Nat landed near the group. "You're not in the trees," he said, drawing no response. His eyes rested on Bet for a moment then looked to the others, seemingly unconcerned.

Bet slowed her breathing. She looked at her friends beneath the haze of her vision. Her heart rate slowed and her sight returned to normal. The world seemed to spin, and she fell into Bathezine's arms.

"Hey there, little one. Are you all right?" he asked, taking her by the arms, helping her stand.

Bet's eyes glassed over, staring at her friend. She shook her head, squeezing her eyes tight. Firming her resolve, she reopened them, meeting Bathezine's stern but caring look. "I need to get to that tree. Keep them away." She turned and stumbled away.

"Wait, Bet," Bathezine said, then turned to Tiny Nat. "How much can you carry and still fly?"

Tiny Nat appraised Bet. "We can't fly with her, but we should be able to leap to avoid the Floragads."

"That'll do. Take care of her." Bathezine spun around, pulling his mace. "I ain't much of a climber, but I can handle myself in the woods. Let's give 'em hell."

Old Babbers picked up Bet's hat, rolled it, and stuffed it in her back pocket. "Let's do it," she said. A look of giddy anticipation crossed her face.

Fifty-Six

Tiny Nat paced Bet's run, with Pooch-kin following close behind. When the Floragad tendrils groped for their prey, he took Bet and fluttered several yards to safety.

They reached the tree in no time, and Bet approached the old fallen Crickshaw, hoping he hadn't succumbed to the beetles and still had his memory intact. "Hey there, old friend. Do you remember me?" She rubbed her hand along the bark, waiting for a sign.

A minute passed with nothing. She scanned the length of the trunk, finding the rotted section she had taken refuge in. "Hello? Are you still with us?"

The bark split open slightly, revealing the smooth surface beneath. "Little monkey. You've come back. You've only been gone a minute. Or was it a year?"

Bet sniffed a laugh. "A few days, actually. I need your help."

The Crickshaw said nothing.

"I haven't much time. Mastives are after us and aim to kill me to get what they want. I know you are one of the Ancients, and I really need your help and guidance."

"Your Talents have grown much, but I cannot convey what you need to know through words. The insects have devoured much of my ability."

Bet turned to Tiny Nat. "I think we wasted our time. We should go."

"But you are a Traveller; time is irrelevant. A rare Talent, indeed. The rarest. Climb inside and listen." The Crickshaw's eye closed.

Bet picked up Pooch-kin. "I'm not going in there with you. What if he decides you're plant food?"

"It's perfectly safe," Bet said. "Besides, you're not going inside, you're waiting on top, out of the Floragads' reach." She gave him a toss, and he flitted to a safe landing.

"This is preferable," the Chook-chook said.

Bet reached for the edge and peered inside, not enthusiastic about sharing the space with and squashing countless beetles. "I'm sorry, Tiny. There are a lot of bugs in here. I hope it doesn't upset you if a few get squished."

Tiny Nat stepped close and looked inside. "It would not upset us. But there is no need to take life unnecessarily." His body vibrated, increasing to a barely audible hum. Moments later a variety of beetles, spiders, and moths exited the hole. The tree seemed to tremble in relief, temporarily free of the insects eating him alive.

Bet stepped back, watching the swarm scurry away. "You could make a good living back in the Din with that ability. People usually poison them to get them out of their houses."

"The Din sounds barbaric." He turned to the sound of Mastive battle calls from the edge of the woods. He hefted Bet into the hole, then prepped his atlatl.

Bet looked in the same direction, getting a sense of her friends. They were holding their own from the trees, but could use Tiny's help. "Go. They need you. I'll be fine here for the time being."

Tiny Nat dashed away without saying another word, passing Mandi-lyn and her bundle of scrolls.

"What are you doing?" the Charge of Danthbrook asked, seeing Bet disappear inside. She climbed on top of the trunk, joining Pooch-kin.

"The tree can't communicate through words. She has to do her sensing thing from inside," Pooch-kin answered when Bet failed to.

"Disappointing," Mandi-lyn said. She lowered her face to the bark, whiskers bouncing. "Perhaps I can get the gist of what's happening from here."

Pooch-kin gave a Chook-chook shrug and kept a wary eye on the darkness of the woods.

Bet huddled inside the tree, trying to get comfortable.

"Lay back. Close your monkey eyes. Feel my thoughts. Travel with me and you will learn all that I knew."

Bet did as instructed. Her mouth crooked into a slight smile at still being called a monkey. She really liked this tree. In a weird way, he was the grandfather she'd never had. Old, wise, and with a touch of humor only age can bring. His slow and patient ways gave her a sense of security.

She relaxed and stretched her mind, reaching for the tree's consciousness. She felt it, and the immenseness of it nearly caused her to withdraw. Her body felt weightless, as it had during her previous encounter with Fealist-Marsh. She entered the Crickshaw's mind, and in return, it entered her thoughts. At first the sensation was disconcerting. But it soon felt almost natural, as if it was the purest form of communication.

"You seek Fealist-Marsh," the tree said without words.

"Yes. She said I was the only one who could free her. I don't know why." Images flashed in Bet's mind, resting on a grassy plain she didn't recognize. She studied her surroundings, noticing the mountains to the north. She was in the Waste, but it hadn't become the Waste yet. "Are we really here, or are these images from your memory?"

"Yes to both. And you are both places at once."

"Can I affect the events of the past?"

"Only so much. Interfering with the past can have consequences, either good or bad. Or at times, they merely speed up the event which was bound to happen. Your friend, the Chook-chook, would have come to the Whist one way or another."

Bet stood in the knee-high grass. Bugs fluttered and zipped by, birds chirped, and a multitude of creatures scurried across the plain. Life existed free and abundant. The scene changed in an instant and a small town appeared on the plains near the river.

The next moment, the town was on fire. Multiple beings fled on a variety of creatures, or in wagons or other vehicles. A large procession of men marched forward, countless numbers, firing weapons at the escapees, killing them without remorse. Bet studied the raiders, confused by what she saw. They appeared out of focus, almost liquid, like she was looking at them through a mirage. "Why are they blurry? Because it's the past?"

"They waver because they are in the Whist. Even before what you are about to see took place, the realms were separate, each holding unique properties."

"I don't understand. I thought the destruction of the staffs created the separation."

"No. It only created the barrier."

Bet continued to watch the events unfold. The men gathered outside the smoldering town, preparing for their next attack. Something to the west caught her eye. A woman. She knew at once it was Fealist-Marsh. The woman strode forward, confident in her posture. She stood, holding the Staff of the Din and the Staff of the Whist, each at least five feet long, made of the quartz-like stone Bet carried in her pocket. The men spotted her and immediately began firing their weapons. Rifle and cannon alike fired repeatedly. But as their projectiles approached, they fell to the ground harmless and impotent.

Fealist-Marsh raised the staffs overhead, her violet skin seeming to radiate. She brought the staffs together with such speed, Bet couldn't see the movement. A flash of white light blinded Bet from what came next. There were no sounds, no explosions or cries of pain from the men. When her sight returned, everything on the grassy plain was gone. The town, the grass, the life, even the low hills had simply vanished, leaving the stark gray landscape Bet was familiar with. Everything had disappeared except for the woman.

She watched as Fealist-Marsh raised her empty hands. She looked in Bet's direction, hesitating momentarily. "She saw me," Bet said, panicked at being spotted.

"Perhaps," the Crickshaw said, not easing her fears.

Bet felt like she should leave. She didn't want to alter events, for good or bad. But she stayed, unable to pull her eyes away. All around Fealist-Marsh the fragments of the staffs rose in the air, each seeming to glow in every color of a prism. She flicked her wrists and pieces shot away, leaving brief contrails of light, like meteorites rising instead of falling. "So that's how the facet ended up in the creek. It was completely random."

"Nothing and everything is random. Watch."

The sky shimmered, and a great dome of prismatic color filled the sky and disappeared. Fealist-Marsh turned and began to walk away. She walked no more than a few steps before falling face forward in the ash. "What's she doing? Did she die? That can't be. I've talked to her."

"Watch."

Fealist-Marsh rose in the air, legs and arms outstretched. Her body curled in a ball, twisting and spinning. Her body continued to spin until something unexpected happened. The spinning ball began to gyrate, wobbling uncontrollably, transforming to a black and white mass, becoming gray with speed. Fealist-Marsh became motionless. Her body had become as white as anything Bet had seen. But she was no longer alone. Beside her was a dark figure as pure black as Fealist-Marsh was pure white. The two figures faced one another, and in the next instant, both were gone.

Bet stood dumbfounded by what she'd witnessed. "What happened?" she asked, even though her gut told her she already knew.

"An unexpected consequence of the destruction of the staffs. Your suspicions are correct. An Omia Temporian is given charge of the staffs as directed before my time. When she destroyed them, her essence split. She is both Fealist-Marsh and the one you call the Reacher."

"Is the Reacher also an Omia Temporian? If so, what hope do we have to stop him?"

"The Reacher is not. He is the void, a zero, yet encompassing everything and nothing. If he takes what you carry, he will become corporeal. And matters will be worse."

"Can he be stopped if he does?" Bet asked, knowing now that the Reacher will stop at nothing to gain what he desires.

"Only by reconstructing the Staff of the Whist."

"Where is Fealist-Marsh now? How can I save her?"

The Crickshaw remained silent for a moment. "I do not have the answers. I can show you where she is, but I don't know the location."

In a flash, Bet found herself hovering over a crystalline tower of quartz-like rock, hugging the shore of an azure sea. The next moment she was back in the tree. "You don't know where that is?"

"No. You will have to seek out Moth. It will give you more answers."

Bet lay still. She was aware of being in the tree, but held to the connection. "What do I do now?"

"These are all of the memories that remain. You have Talents that have yet to be realized. Unknown Talents. Rely on your friends. Stay true."

"I'm doing my best."

"You have allies in the forest. Call on them and they will help you win the day."

"Allies? I don't know anybody else."

"You are an Oragoth. You know who."

Bet thought on the statement for a moment. An Oragoth? "The Fangors?"

"Bet, my knowledge will be yours when we separate. We can't allow the Reacher to obtain that knowledge. If he finds me, it will be his as well."

"How do I prevent that? He's close." Even as she said the words, she knew what had to be done. Her heart ached. She wouldn't allow it, she couldn't. "I can't."

"Errel Handover has the Talent. You must. Now go. Your friends need you."

"But..." The Crickshaw severed their connection and Bet found herself sitting inside the tree.

"Go, little monkey. Even a Traveller can run out of time."

Bet climbed out, hopping to the ground. She ran her hand along the rough bark. "You are my friend. I'll never forget you."

The tree almost seemed to sag. "Goodbye, little monkey. Be safe."

Bet stood for a moment longer. The cries of the Mastives made her pull away. "C'mon, you two. We have to help."

Mandi-lyn hurried alongside Bet. "What did you learn?"

Bet looked down at the Flursh. "I learned enough."

Mandi-lyn stared after Bet as she hurried with Pooch-kin to join the others. "That tells me nothing."

Fifty-Seven

Bathezine dodged the swipe of a Mastive. He ducked behind a tree, came around the other side and gave it a debilitating bash on its knee with his mace. The creature roared and tried to pursue the Ursian, but even its rage couldn't overcome its shattered bone, and it collapsed.

The Ursian continued to the next in line, brought up his blow pipe and neatly deposited a dart in the beast's eye. The Mastive howled and charged at Bathezine. Waiting until the last possible moment, he leapt aside when the creature attempted to punch him. A rain of spears and buckshot pebbles from the branches above brought the Mastive down.

The first of the Creedans entered the fracas, and Bathezine showed a toothy grin. Two were immediately dispatched by his mace, and a third was met by his fist, knocking it unconscious before it hit the ground. Several more came at him, and all met a similar fate. Over a dozen more rushed toward him, and he decided on a different tactic and ran the opposite way.

Bathezine ran several yards, ducking under low branches and dancing past groping Floragad tendrils attracted by the movement. Losing a couple of his pursuers to the killer mushrooms, he holstered the mace and pulled the bolas off his back, whirled them twice, and spun back, sending them flying into the Creedans. Four dropped, brained by the bola, while the remaining still came toward him, screaming and waving their stone axes overhead.

"I ain't got time for this," Bathezine said after spotting another Mastive breaking through the Floragad limbs, heading directly at him. He decided against using his mace, and balled his fist. Taking a step forward, he squared his body and punched the first in the chest, feeling its sternum crack beneath the blow. He met each attacker with a flurry of flying fists and elbows. One Creedan remained. Facing the powerful Ursian alone, it hesitated. Bathezine looked at the charging Mastives, grabbed the Creedan by the arm, spun and threw it directly at the beasts. The lead Mastive knocked the hapless Creedan from the air, never breaking its stride. Bathezine retrieved his bola and resumed running.

He doubled back, running past the Mastives before they could react. He needed to stay under Tiny Nat and Old Babbers' cover from above or face the entire onslaught on his own. The choice was easy.

Bathezine rushed to get below their perches and found a Mastive violently shaking the tree Errel had taken refuge in. The Andolan dropped flaming pine cones on the assailant to no effect. Both Tiny Nat and Old Babbers had their hands full with their own attackers. He considered his options. With the beast's back to him, the bola would be useless, as the vulnerable eyes and throat were against the trunk. He pulled the mace. "I guess I have to do this the hard way."

He took a step and saw gouts of blood spray from the Mastive's head. It crumpled to the ground without as much as a whimper. Floragad tendrils sprang up and engulfed the dead creature's body. Confused, Bathezine scanned the woods to figure out what had killed the hulk. He spotted Bet jogging toward him from one direction, and the two Mastives he had juked coming from another. "Watch out! Two more."

Bathezine readied his blow pipe, but saw what looked like a large bee flutter in the air at the Mastives. The massive beasts stopped their charge and began flailing their arms wildly. After several seconds of Pooch-kin harrying them, they turned and ran deeper into the woods. He snorted a laugh at seeing the gray bulks run in fear from the Chook-chook.

Bet approached Bathezine with Mandi-lyn in tow. "I didn't know the bird had it in him," the Ursian said.

"Instinct wins out over mind control," Mandi-lyn said. "Mastives are deathly afraid of bees."

"I need Errel," Bet said before Bathezine could remark.

Bathezine pointed to the tree. "Get down here. Bet needs you." He turned to Bet. "Did ya find out what ya needed?"

"Some. We need to go to the Caves of Moth." She waited on Errel, watching him clumsily descend the tree. He jumped from the lowest branch, landing far more gracefully than his climb down.

"Andolans are not arboreal," he said with a hint of mirth. "What do you need, Bet?"

A tendril wrapped Bet's leg and she quickly tore the offending vine in two. "Come with me," she said, and began trotting off in the direction she had come.

"What's your plan, girl?" Bathezine called after her.

"A pyre for my friend," she shouted back.

Bathezine jerked at hearing her words. "I guess she knows what she's doing." He looked back and saw a Creedan attempting to scale Old Babbers' tree, avoiding her shots beneath the cover of branches. He rushed over, jerked the climber by its leg, and dragged him screaming to the writhing Floragad tendrils that had engulfed the dead Mastive. He tossed the Creedan on top, watching long enough to ensure the fungus took it. Satisfied, he called to Jangol and rejoined the fray.

Fifty-Eight

Bet led Errel Handover back to the Crickshaw at a full sprint. She stopped running short of the tree and walked the remaining distance. Putting her hand on the trunk, she looked back at Errel, fighting the tears threatening to spill over.

"What do you need me to do?" Errel asked, though he seemed to already know.

"The Reacher can't know what the Crickshaw knows. He asked for you to do this."

"Me specifically?" Errel said, sounding doubtful.

"Yes. He knows what I know and he has been giving me his knowledge. The Reacher is approaching. Please, Errel. We don't have much time." Bet wiped a tear away and picked up Pooch-kin, helping him into the shoulder bag. "C'mon, little friend. You need a break. You did good."

Pooch-kin warbled a relieved-sounding noise. "I don't disagree."

Bet ran her hand along the weathered bark. "Goodbye, friend. Thank you."

"My knowledge resides within you, little monkey. It's not goodbye."

Bet smiled and walked away, stopping beside Errel. "Do it," she said, giving him a reassuring smile. She jogged away toward the others.

Errel watched Bet go and turned to the tree. He lifted his hands. "I don't enjoy taking life."

"You are not taking my life, Errel Handover, Andolan prince. I am giving what remains of it," the old Crickshaw said. "Remember to tell Bet's story."

Errel nodded, put his hands close, and closed his eyes. His arms became rigid, and blue fire erupted from his palms. He kept his hands in the flames as long as he could, sending a continuous fountain of fire into the tree to ensure the job was done as quickly as possible. He stepped back and waved his arms, directing the fire the length of the massive trunk. "Go peacefully to the next realm."

Taking a few more steps backward, Errel saw several Floragads pop up from the dirt, trying to escape the heat. "You're next, mushrooms." He spun on his heels and ran back to the chaos.

~~~~~

Bet found Bathezine using Old Babbers and Tiny Nat's covering fire for shelter from a Mastive as he prepped his blow pipe. The beast raised its bulky arm for protection and moved closer to her friend. She reached for an iron ball to relieve him of the threat. The weight of the bearing felt good in her hand. The idea of using her Talent to turn the otherwise harmless object into a deadly projectile sent an electric excitement through her body. She opened her hand and looked at the ball resting on her palm. Harmless to deadly, she thought. Not unlike herself. She reared back to throw, but paused. Harmless to deadly. The phrase went through her mind again. She never thought she would become what she was turning into: an agent of death, doling out judgement on a whim, taking life as if it were hers to take. She lowered her arm.

Bathezine ducked under a swinging arm and shot an ineffectual dart into the Mastive's midsection. Bet watched. She wouldn't let any harm come to him, but there had to be another way. She extended her mind, touching the furious creature's thoughts. The elusive guiding hand of the Reacher was there, prodding it, tormenting the creature's mind. She felt the presence on the surface of the Mastive's consciousness. She delved deeper, touching the beast on the subconscious level. She projected her thoughts on Bathezine's attacker, no words, but subconscious ideals, images of the Reacher controlling it, and thoughts of freedom and peace.

She opened her eyes, keeping contact, pouring serenity into the beast. The Mastive stopped its assault, lowered its arms, shaking its head in confusion. Bet felt anger rise in the creature, but not its own. It was the Reacher, frustrated at losing control. In the Reacher's vexation she found his weakness. Bet's serenity split the cords of chaos controlling the creature, and her enemy's hold severed.

The Mastive's shoulders slumped. It turned from Bathezine and simply walked away, breathing heavily from exhaustion, with no will left to fight. Bet smiled at Bathezine, who returned a curious look. She walked forward to meet the next attacker, and a voice not her own echoed in the back of her mind. *You are learning, little monkey.* Bet's smile broadened.

Fifty-Nine

One by one, Bet relieved the Mastives of their tormenter, though some, owing to their aggressive nature, continued to fight, meeting untimely ends beneath the onslaught of her companions. But most left the battle and began a slow trudge across the Waste.

Mandi-lyn joined Bet. "What did the Ancient One teach you?" She asked, sounding excited for a hint of the Crickshaw's knowledge.

Bet looked at her eager eyes, partially hidden by the tricorn hat. "It's not what he taught me, but what he gave me." She walked ahead, leaving Mandi-lyn to puzzle out her meaning.

The others gathered around Bet. Bathezine rested his meaty paw on her shoulder, without saying a word. The others looked at her with a mix of concern and curiosity.

Tiny Nat broke the silence. "The Creedans are regrouping on the Waste."

Bet nodded. "The Creedans are fighting of their own volition. I thought they were being controlled like the Mastives. I was wrong. Only their energy is buoyed by the Reacher, not their will."

"The fire is spreading this way," Errel said. "We're going to have to face them."

"I know. But not alone." Bet raised her head and made a loud howling noise, using her strength Talent to amplify the sound beyond what was natural to her. She looked at her friends. "We have to get to the Caves of Moth. But the Reacher is out there. His form is within the big Mastive, waiting for us on the Waste. I can't sever his control like I did with the others."

"Then we're gonna have to take it down," Bathezine said, sounding less than enthusiastic at the prospect of facing such a foe.

"Here," Bet said, looking at Babbers. She dug through her satchel, and handed the woman the healing elixir.

Old Babbers lifted her arm. "It's only a scratch," she said, rubbing off flakes of dried blood from her skin.

"Not for you," Bet said. "When I encountered the Reacher earlier, he left the Mastive body, and it stood there, motionless. There's nothing left of the creature's mind. It's like he's a parasite and the Mastive is the host. Sorta like the Troojian wasp."

"Okay… what good is a healing elixir gonna do for it?" Babbers asked.

"I'm getting to that. Tiny Nat, take a bomb and go with her. You two are the fastest and most agile. Babbers, make a cut in the Mastive and get away. Tiny, put the bomb inside" She nodded at Old Babbers. "And you come back and heal the wound. Get clear, and I'll take care of the rest."

"What about the Creedans?" Bathezine said. "Them two ain't gonna get so close to it with all of them runnin' round."

"They'll have their hands full. Just get Jangol hooked up to the wagon," Bet said, her face carrying a look of concern.

"What, girl? What are ya plannin'?"

"I'm planning a clean getaway to the caves. Errel, take Pooch-kin," she said, handing the bag to him.

Pooch-kin poked his head out in a burst. "Wait, Bet. I'm with you. Remember? My vow can't be broken."

"I know," she said, scratching his ear. "But I need to do this alone. I can't let him use anything to distract me. That includes him trying to harm you. He'll use my love for you as a weapon."

"I don't like it. I can handle myself," Pooch-kin added.

"I know you can. But you're gonna have to trust me. Okay?"

Pooch-kin hesitated, then sank back. "Just be safe. I don't want to have to take on the Reacher by myself."

"I will be." She scratched his ear once more. "Mandi-lyn, go with Errel and Bathezine."

The Charge of Danthbrook didn't argue.

"You ready?" Bet asked Tiny Nat and Old Babbers.

"Yup," Old Babbers said with an upturned smile. She stared at Bet for a moment, her face turning serious. "Ya know, I still have a few things to teach you. But judging by what you did back there, I think you can teach me a few things, too." She pulled Bet's rolled-up hat from her back pocket and put it on the younger woman's head.

Bet sniffed a laugh. "I'll teach you when I understand it."

Old Babbers slapped her on the back. "Sometimes you gotta accept things without understanding them. Now let's go take care of this."

Sixty

The group gathered around the wagon near the edge of the Dead Woods watching the Creedans form ranks. The white-skinned hill folk hopped and pounded their chests, calling out in high-pitched whoops, preparing for an all-out assault.

Jangol returned from whatever adventures he had in the woods. Bathezine patted him and began prepping the harnesses. "What're you waiting on?"

Bet stared blank-eyed across the Waste without answering. A moment later a howl came from the border of the Dead Woods and the Waste. She smiled and looked at Bathezine, then pointed. "Them."

Bathezine followed her finger to a large pack of Fangors running between the trees, led by one with a shock of auburn fur atop of its head. He stepped back putting the Rhinodon between him and the Fangors.

"It's okay. She's my friend," Bet said, squatting to meet the Fangor. "Hello, Tuft."

Tuft approached, cautiously eyeing Bathezine and the others, who returned a wary posture. Mandi-lyn gave the Fangors an indifferent glance from the back of the wagon and returned to reading her scrolls.

"The woods are on fire," Tuft said, sniffing the air. "Is this why you called us? We'll be little help in that regard."

Bet shook her head. "No. It's the byproduct of a friend's pyre, but it should serve to rid the area of Floragads."

Tuft's ears perked up. "Then we will have the old hunting grounds returned to us in a few seasons."

"I need your help with them." She pointed beyond the trees to the gathering Creedans.

The Fangor barked to a large male. The male approached, lowering his snout in submission to Tuft. They exchanged guttural growls, after which Tuft fixed her eyes on Bet. "You have returned these woods to us. We are indebted. What will you have us do?"

Bet didn't consider it a debt, but she had to wonder if the Crickshaw had known what the end result would be. She searched her feelings and decided he had. "There's a big Mastive out there. It wants something I hold. I have to confront it."

Tuft sniffed. "It smells unnatural. Living, but dead."

"That's actually pretty spot-on," Bet said, shrugging. She motioned to Old Babbers and Tiny Nat. "The three of us need to get past the Creedans. I would like for you to occupy their attention."

"The Creedans, as you call them, have hunted us for many generations. It would be good to be rid of some of them."

"Yeah, and maybe ya can take a few back and feed 'em to your litters," Bathezine said with a snort in reply to Bet's words.

"Their flesh is tainted by the Foul. We would sooner eat mud," Tuft growled, glaring at the Ursian.

Bathezine raised his hands, not understanding Tufts words, but getting the gist of the growl. "Sorry. No offense meant." He turned his attention back to Jangol.

"Thank you, Tuft." Bet reached out her hand. Tuft sniffed it and gave Bet her paw. "You are my friend, now and always."

Tuft pulled her paw back, looking at Bet sideways. "You are indeed a different sort of human. When shall we begin?"

A loud caw from above caught everyone's attention. They looked up and watched as Her-Gad-Ishu swept in, took a Creedan by the head and flew high. A moment later the three-headed crow dropped the wildly flailing creature. They watched it fall to the ground, dead on impact.

"Looks like we start now," Bet said.

Tuft called out three quick yips and ran into the Waste followed by fifty or more Fangors. The Creedans answered the call and rushed to meet them, whooping loudly, brandishing their stone and wood weapons.

Bet led Old Babbers and Tiny Nat farther along the edge of the woods, waiting for the Creedans to focus their attention on the Fangors.

Her-Gad-Ishu continued to harry the Creedans from the air, lifting three at a time in their respective beaks, biting and dropping, removing them from the battlefield with great expedience.

"It's our turn," Bet said. "Babbers, you're first."

Old Babbers cinched her hat, smiled, and sprinted toward the Reacher-controlled Mastive.

Bet watched her go and turned to Tiny Nat. "Are you ready?"

"We are." He held the explosive in his right hand and watched Babbers as she approached the Mastive.

Old Babbers ran in a direct path at the Mastive. The beast raised its arm, ready to swipe the woman away. Babbers juked left and ducked under the powerful swing, somersaulting and landing on her feet. She brought her hatchet back, and delivered a clean, but deep slash in the creature's midsection.

The Mastive had no reaction to the wound. The Reacher's host appeared to be impervious to the gash that would've dropped any other of its kind. Instead, it spun and took another swing at Babbers, just missing her trailing foot. Old Babbers kept running, putting distance between her and the beast. She stopped and turned to face it. She twirled the hatchet in her hand and pulled the elixir from her pocket, waiting for her next turn.

Tiny Nat dashed across the Waste, bomb in one hand and a knife in the other. Long, quick strides carried him to his target in no time. The Reacher either heard or sensed the Vivicon's oncoming attack and turned to meet him. It lunged out, bringing its hands together, attempting to squash the insectoid in a clap. Tiny sprang up, fluttered his wings and came down against the gray skinned beast's body. He dug his knife into its flesh, dragging it sideways while stuffing the bomb into the gaping wound Babbers had made with his other hand.

The Mastive howled a ground-shaking roar. Tiny Nat jumped away and extended his wings mid-leap to fly away. Before he reached a safe distance, the strong grip of the creature caught him by the wing, pulling him back.

Old Babbers swore at seeing Tiny Nat snagged mid-flight, bit the cap off the elixir and rushed to save her friend.

The Vivicon flailed wildly in the Mastive's grip, but couldn't break free. With no other recourse, he extended his stinger, reached backward, finding the creature's flesh, and drove it deep, pumping in as much venom as he could while he still had life. The Mastive may have been impervious to pain, but the paralyzing properties of the venom still had the desired effect. The Reacher shook his host's hand, ripping Tiny Nat's wing away, sending his body tumbling through the air.

Bet saw her friend's body roll to a stop near the fray between Fangor and Creedan. "Bathezine! Tiny Nat's down," she yelled and pointed.

Bathezine lifted his head from his work and looked. "I got him," he said and started to move.

Errel put his hand out. "Finish here. I'll get him," he said, placing Pooch-kin in the wagon.

Bathezine was about to protest, but relented, nodding his head. "Okay. Make it quick. I don't want two to rescue."

"You always underestimate Andolans," Errel said and ran to get their companion.

Old Babbers rolled to a stop near the Mastive too late to rescue Tiny Nat, but not too late to finish her task. She darted in close, stuffed the bomb working itself loose deeper into the wound, and dumped the elixir on the gash. The skinned closed up immediately, sealing the bomb inside. "Now ya just gotta go boom," she said.

The Mastive took a swing at her, which she deftly avoided. She made a move to go, but saw the creature's other arm hanging uselessly at its side, paralyzed by Tiny Nat's venom. She couldn't help herself but to inflict another grievous injury on the Reacher. Old Babbers brought back the hatchet and chopped into the Mastive's knee. "That'll slow you down."

She looked up in time to see the creature's good arm swing back with a doubled fist and strike her full force. Old Babbers' limp body twisted and tumbled through the air, landing in a puff of dusty ash over twenty yards away.

"No!" Bet screamed. She clinched her fist and stepped into the clearing.

Sixty-One

Tuft dragged a Creedan by the neck, shaking it violently, with her huge canines buried deep in the hapless creature's flesh. A half dozen Creedans came at her, waving stone axes and shooting darts. She dropped her victim, tucked her tail, and ran at half-speed until other pack members pounced on her pursuers. The Fangor doubled-back and aided in the carnage.

After dispatching a particularly determined Creedan, Tuft caught sight of Errel Handover rushing to help Tiny Nat, and several attackers headed the same direction. She barked to her pack and raced ahead to cut off the Creedan advance.

Errel slid beside Tiny Nat and lifted his head, checking for signs of life. Noticing the charging hill folk, he took a knife from the Vivicon's bandolier and prepared to fight. Blue flame sprouted from his other hand.

Tuft charged in, her green eyes glowing wildly in the fury of the hunt. Taking the lead Creedan's head in her jaw, she killed it before it had a chance to react. Claws and fangs rained down on the group of Creedans. The din of growls and gnashing teeth combined with the wails of their prey and swirls of ashy dust, created chaos around Errel.

He lifted Tiny Nat's head again. "Hey. Are you still with us? Don't go dying now. We don't have time for that."

A moment later Tiny Nat's body vibrated and his mandibles wriggled. "We are still with you. Though we are somewhat worse for the wear."

Errel couldn't help but to laugh. "Come on. We have to get to safety." He lifted Tiny's tall frame.

Tiny Nat took in the surrounding melee. "It appears safety is in short supply."

"Are you joking with me?" Errel said through a coughed laugh. "I'm pretty sure that was a joke."

"If reality is a joke, perhaps it was."

Errel shook his head. "Lean on me. I'll get you to the wagon, and the Flursh can look at you."

"We can walk," Tiny Nat said. He took a step and his legs gave out, falling against Errel. "We will take your help."

Tuft trotted alongside the pair and sniffed Tiny Nat.

"Thank you," Errel said to the Fangor.

Tuft lowered her head to show she understood the gesture.

"If you can keep them off us until we reach the trees, I'll owe you another thanks." Errel began moving faster, half-carrying the Vivicon.

Tuft barked her acknowledgement.

The three had nearly reached Bathezine when they heard Bet cry out.

Bathezine stepped into the clearing, looking for the cause of Bet's alarm. He spotted Errel returning with Tiny Nat. "Move over. We have wounded," he barked at Mandi-lyn.

The Flursh quickly rolled her scrolls and prepared to care for Tiny Nat.

Bathezine took Errel's burden, lifting Tiny Nat into the back of the wagon with ease. He rushed back to the edge of the Waste and spotted Bet. He looked around, but couldn't see Old Babbers. He growled and rushed to find her.

Sixty-Two

Bet strode with purpose into the ankle-deep ash. She saw the Ursian running toward the Mastive. "Bathezine! Stop. I'll handle this."

Bathezine stopped and looked at her. "I ain't gonna let her die alone out there," he yelled back.

"If you go, you'll get us all killed," Bet said sternly, continuing her march toward the Mastive. She looked to the sky, spotting the crow carry off another Creedan. "Her-Gad-Ishu. Get Babbers." She pointed to where she'd seen Old Babbers land.

Her-Gad-Ishu dropped their victim and flew to get her.

Bathezine seemed to get the hint, and reluctantly turned around. A single Creedan broke through the picket of Fangors and rushed at him. The large and angry Ursian met his assailant with a powerful swing of his chain mace, sending the unwise Creedan's head flying from its body like hitting a ball off a tee. He stood watching Bet for a second longer, then jogged back to the others.

Bet grabbed an iron bearing, and continued toward the Reacher.

The Mastive's eyes followed Her-Gad-Ishu, and it limped to where the crow had landed.

"Hey!" Bet yelled, seeing what the Reacher intended to do. She stretched her senses and found Babbers. She was alive, but in bad condition. She yelled again when the Mastive didn't stop. "It's me you want. I have what you desire."

The Mastive halted and slowly turned toward her. Bet stopped and pulled the facet from her pocket with her left hand while rolling the iron ball with her fingers in her right. She had to keep him distracted until Her-Gad-Ishu got Old Babbers in the air. "Is this what you want? Is this what all of this destruction is about?"

"Give it to me and your friends will live," the Reacher said. The voice entered Bet's mind, causing her to stagger back.

Bet strained, fighting to push the Reacher out of her head. "You lie," she said.

"I do not lie. I am above your ideas of deceit. Give it to me and your friends will live."

The voice swirled through Bet's mind and she fought harder to push him away. But he had spoken the truth. There was no deception in his words. However, he hadn't said she would live. Bet closed her eyes, pushing against the other's influence and her own anger, finally finding the serenity she had used to free the Mastives. She found it buried in her own subconscious, as if waiting patiently for her to remember. She extended the sensation outward, opening it wider like an umbrella sheltering her from the Reacher's thoughts. She sensed his shock at being pushed away. Bet opened her eyes, seeing Her-Gad-Ishu fly away with Babbers firmly in their grip from the corner of her vision. "Run," she said, putting the thought into Tuft's mind.

In a burst of movement, the Mastive host charged forward, oblivious to its injuries. Bet let the serenity envelope her. She let her mind touch the body of the Mastive, finding the bomb within. With all calmness, she gripped the ball loosely, as Old Babbers had taught her, and putting all of her energy into her arm, stepped and threw. The ball sped through the air, striking the beast in the wound given to it by Old Babbers.

The Mastive stopped and looked down at its stomach. In a blink, the bomb detonated.

The blast knocked Bet off her feet. She landed hard on her back, nearly winded, and covered her face as bits of Mastive began to rain down. Bet lay there for several moments, until she found her breath and was able to stand. Opening her clutched hand, she stared at the Facet of the Din. "So much trouble for a piece of stone."

Smoke from the burning woods behind her and dust kicked up by the explosion blinded her to her surroundings. She stretched out her senses and found her friends. They were safe. She extended farther and found the Fangors running at speed, already a quarter mile away. She found the Creedans, only a few remaining, clinging to life from blast or bite and claw wounds. There was one presence she couldn't sense. She searched deeper, finding no trace of the Reacher.

Bet didn't allow herself the hope that the Reacher was dead. She strained to see through the haze. A cough nearby caught her attention. It was Errel. Soon, indistinguishable shadows appeared. Her friends were looking for her. She couldn't go to them yet. Her adversary was out there. She couldn't see him or feel his presence, but intuition told her he was there. Taking several steps farther into the Waste, she put her hand in her pouch of bearings, but pulled away. A crude weapon would have no effect on such a being.

Calls from her friends went unanswered. She continued across the Waste, waiting for the Reacher to make his appearance. Wind, pushed by the heat of the burning woods, began to clear the dust. Every one of Bet's senses was on edge and exaggerated. She could hear the crackling of burning Floragads, smell the blood of dying Creedans, and feel the touch of each sprinkle of dust as they fell against her.

Bathezine called out to her once more as the group emerged from the tree line, escaping the approaching flames. Bet didn't bother to look back. She raised her hand, warning him to stay away instead. She knew they had seen her warning.

The powdery ash hugged the ground, giving the illusion of a low hanging fog. Bet approached the crater where the Mastive had once been. What remained of the creature lay in muddy clumps of flesh. She avoided stepping in pools of blood mixed with dust, looking like a ghastly pudding spilled across the ground. The Reacher was nowhere.

She turned back, ready to give up on her game of hide and seek in the vast nothingness when a whisper seemed to caress the back of her neck.

"I see you are not above the practice of deceit," the Reacher's voice hissed.

She spun around finding nothing. "I'm not the one hiding."

A sickly laugh brushed past her ear. "I am in plain sight for those who can see."

Bet expanded her senses, finding nothing. "My sight is just fine."

The voice came from behind again, causing her to jerk. "Eyes can deceive those who use them. You are weak. And I thought I had an adversary worthy of my time."

"If I'm so weak, why do you hide?" Bet said. The longer she kept him talking the longer she had to work out a solution to her conundrum. If she couldn't sense him or see him, how could she find him?

"Hiding? Only your pathetic lack of understanding keeps you from seeing."

Frustration began to mount. How could she find nothing in the nothingness of the Waste? A word crept in the back of her mind. Nothingness. The Crickshaw's description of the Reacher echoed in her thoughts. He was the void. Everything yet nothing. The tree's knowledge was within her, but she would have to discover it on her own.

A wisp of movement touched her. "You are too ignorant to be a worthy opponent. You are beginning to bore me. Give me what you hold and I will let you live. Seeing you imprisoned by your own stupidity is much more entertaining that watching you die."

Bet searched her memories, pairing them with the knowledge buried within her. She inhaled sharply, remembering the Vapid. She'd found him by sensing the reaction of those around it. But there was no life in the waste. Even the dirt eels were gone now. "I don't think I'll give it to you. I found it. It belongs to me."

A devilish laugh swirled around her. "Stubbornness will only kill you.

And it will kill your friends. The Ursian will die, as will the bug, the Andolan, and so will the woman. Though to her credit, she should have died when I struck her. Perhaps I'll let the Charge of Danthbrook live. She could prove useful. But your little bird friend. He will suffer, and you will watch as I slowly dismantle him before your dying eyes. You can avoid this if you would only give me what I want."

Bet fought the anger simmering within, letting calm wash over her body, desperately trying to keep her thoughts from being muddled by her building hatred. If he's as powerful as he claims, then why not just take it? A warm breeze blew past her, rolling across the empty landscape. A thought occurred to her. She stretched out her feelings once again, only this time she didn't search for life or a reaction from life, she tapped the elements. Her mind became caught up in the wind, searching for the void.

When the wind offered no results, she used the dirt, her thoughts stretched out, like the roots of a tree, searching for an indication of nothingness where there should be something. Having no better luck with the soil, she tried to think of another way. There was no water to be found. Even the moisture in the air was absent in the Waste. Fire was out of the question. There was nothing to burn. Even then, she'd need a Talent like Errel's to ignite such a fire. The warm wind touched her again, heated by the burning woods and the sun's rays. Yes, a voice echoed within. The old tree had gathered energy from the sun in life, and now those particles of energy would expose the Reacher.

Letting her senses merge with the sun's heat, she became everywhere in the Waste at once. In an instant, she found a cold emptiness, a void in the warmth. She opened her eyes and, standing no more than a hundred feet away, was a darkness, a figure of wavering shadows without form. He had been there the whole time, toying with her, trying to tease out a weakness in the defenses she'd created through serene thought.

The shadow rippled. White eyes appeared in the black; narrow eyes, not unlike Fealist-Marsh's. The Reacher laughed. "Now you can see. And now you can see as I destroy you and take what is rightfully mine."

The Reacher came at her with such speed, Bet had no time to react. All she could do was brace herself and fall into the serenity that protected her. The impact of the ghostly form knocked her back. It took all of her corporeal strength to not be pushed to the ground. Bet shook off the attack, regaining her composure in time for the next pass.

The next assault came, only this time the Reacher didn't pass through her. He swirled around Bet, wisps of black shadows reaching out, trying to find purchase, groping for a hold.

Bet weathered the attack, surprised that no physical harm came to her. She realized what he was doing and why he hadn't simply killed her and taken what he wanted. He was trying to enter her mind, to force her to give up the facet. Only the strength she had found in the serenity of her mind had saved her.

The Reacher twisted around Bet, his mind extending, attempting to break the barrier and destroy her from within. "I can do this through eternity. You can't win. If you run, I will follow. Your friends will die, and you, too, will eventually join them in final death." He attacked again.

Bet pushed back, repelling each attempt to enter her thoughts. No matter how hard she tried, the barricade of peace could not be made to counter his attacks. She realized the futility of her efforts. The only hope she had to defeat the Reacher would be to find Fealist-Marsh. But she also knew that would cost her everything. He would destroy all of those she loved. He would send countless mind-controlled or cajoled assassins. They would be whittled away like a stick beneath a knife until there was nothing left. She wouldn't allow that.

"Stop!" Bet yelled. To her surprise, the willowy form withdrew, dancing around her, an apparition of hate, ready to kill to get what it wanted.

"Do you finally see the error of your ways? You cannot hope to defeat me. Your defenses are formidable, unexpectedly so, but they will eventually weaken. And you will die like all those who have defied me before." The Reacher extended a wraithlike arm. "Give it to me and save yourself the trouble."

Bet thought of her friends. She let the love she felt for them encompass her body. She would save them, she would free Fealist-Marsh from wherever she was imprisoned, and they would defeat the enemy of peace. She put her hand in her pocket, feeling the edges of the facet.

Bet pulled out the stone. Clutching it tightly, she extended her arm. She opened her hand, revealing the shimmering quartz. "I give it to you without coercion. Take it. Take it and go in peace."

The shadowy form of the Reacher became still. A flash of gray rolled over its amorphous body. A writhing tendril of darkness stretched forward, forming the rough shape of a hand. Sinewy fingers dangled above the facet. The hand hesitated, as if expecting a trap. The fingers moved closer still, slowly, waiting for the trap to be sprung. The caution was cast aside, and in a flash, the Reacher snatched the stone from Bet's hand.

Bet pulled away from the coldness of the Reacher's touch.

The shadow leaned close, white eyes meeting Bet's. "Fool. Peace is a lie." The quivering shadow coiled and twisted, creating a whirlwind of blackness. The twisting form shot into the air, expanded into a cloud of darkness and dissipated into nothingness.

Bet stood alone in the gray ash field, staring at the emptiness. Her legs trembled beneath her, and she fell to her knees. Her eyes closed and she collapsed.

Sixty-Three

Her-Gad-Ishu circled over Bet, finally landing after deciding it was safe. The great crow stood with wings outstretched, sheltering her from the midday sun.

After a minute of dreamless unconsciousness, Bet's eyes parted. Seeing the shadow caused a sudden panic; she'd thought the Reacher had returned. But Gad's soft clucking made her realize who was there and she relaxed. She got to her feet, half-heartedly brushing away the dust. "Thank you, Her-Gad-Ishu."

The crow hopped around, cawing loudly. Her leaned in close. "Now you are ready."

"Now you're ripe," said Gad.

"Not ripe, ready," Her said.

"She is seasoned," added Ishu.

Bet looked to Ishu and smiled with a nod. "I like that. Seasoned. And to be honest, Gad, ripe kind of sounds like I stink."

Ishu leaned closer, tilting his head this way and that. "Gad's word may be closer to the truth."

Bet looked at Ishu from the corner of her eye. "We'll stick with seasoned." She looked down, finding Old Babbers' hat at her feet.

The heavy footfalls of Bathezine and rattling of the wagon ended the conversation. The Ursian ran to Bet, putting his beefy hands on her shoulders. "Are you okay, little one?" he asked, looking her over.

"I'm okay," she said, smiling up at him. Her expression turned serious. "How're Babbers and Tiny?"

The pair went to the wagon with Her-Gad-Ishu hopping behind them.

Tiny Nat sat on the edge, body slumped, clutching the shoulder nearest his absent wing. "It is good to see you survived," he said, handing Bet a canteen with his free hand.

"Thank you," Bet said, taking a long drink. "How are you doing?"

"We will survive." He looked down at Old Babbers lying prone with Mandi-lyn furiously running her whiskered nose along her body while uttering indecipherable chants.

Bet looked the woman over, noticing dried blood at the corners of her mouth. "How is she?"

The Flursh ignored the question, keeping her focus on the healing. Errel came alongside Bet and handed her Pooch-kin's pouch. "She'll live. Though she took quite a beating," he said.

Old Babbers cracked one eye open. "Hey, Bet. That was some fun, huh?"

Bet laughed. "I'm worried that you thought that was fun. I didn't expect the size of that blast."

Babbers' lips parted into a smile. "Special mix of my own. I'll teach you sometime."

"Yeah. I might need it…if I ever get into the quarrying business and need to demolish a dam. Here." She tossed Babbers' hat beside her.

"You never know." Old Babbers coughed a laugh.

"Stay still," Mandi-lyn admonished the woman.

Babbers rolled her eyes at the Flursh.

Mandi-lyn tapped her pink finger on the space between Old Babbers' eyes and she fell back asleep. Mandi-lyn stole a glance at Bet. "I've stabilized her and repaired some internal injuries, but she'll need rest. We should get her to a medical ward." She went back to her work, ending the conversation.

"What happened out there? We could see you, but it was like you were fighting against nothing," Errel said. "Did you defeat the Reacher?"

Bet let out a long breath. "In a way, you're right. I fought against nothingness. I didn't defeat him. I can't. But that's not up to me alone. I only have to find the means."

"And what is that?" Errel asked.

"Fealist-Marsh," Bet said plainly, looking at Bathezine.

The Ursian tugged at his beard. "He has the stone, doesn't he?"

Bet nodded. "Yes. I gave it to him. It was the only way."

Bathezine's shoulders slumped. "Then what was this all for?"

Mandi-lyn popped her head up from her work. "It will take time for the Reacher to reconstruct the Staff of the Din. It's not like gluing together a broken lamp. It will take time and tremendous effort if he indeed has all of the fragments. She did the right thing. His attention will be elsewhere. And now I suspect we must go to the Caves of Moth."

"Yeah. That's the plan. Once I find Fealist-Marsh, we can end this." A stirring in her bag pulled her from the conversation. She opened it, and Pooch-kin's bright eyes met hers. "You're back to your original color."

"Yes. However, all of this color-changing and flying about and fighting monsters is quite exhausting." He wagged his stubby wings and settled back.

"I can't disagree with you," Bet said. She climbed on the driver's bench beside Bathezine, who gave her a reassuring pat on the knee.

Errel looked for a place to sit in the back before deciding to ride on Alice's back.

"Are ya ready?" Bathezine asked, taking the reins.

"She's ready," Her said.

"Ripe," said Gad.

"No, seasoned," added Ishu.

Bet shook her head, looking sideways at Bathezine. "Let's go."

Jangol snorted and the wagon lurched forward. A distant howl rolled across the waste. Bet answered the call with a similar noise. "I'll be seeing you around, my friend," she said. She leaned sideways, resting her head on Bathezine's shoulder, letting the rhythmic clomp of the Rhinodon's feet lull her into sleep and whatever dreams may come.

More from Rockhopper Books

Rise of the Penguins Saga

Rise of the Penguins
Book 1

The Warlord, The
Warrior, The War
Book 2

Crosscurrents
Book 3

Whispers of Shadows
Book 4

The Royal Creed
Book 5

Order of Kings
Book 6

The Great Auk War
Book 7
(coming soon)

www.ingramcontent.com/pod-product-compliance
Lightning Source LLC
Chambersburg PA
CBHW030656120726
47905CB00001B/235